# "Would you give me your counsel about the potential brides?"

Would she help him to choose his wife? Pain, like a dagger thrust, pierced her heart, leaving her breathless. Could she help him choose the woman who would bear his name and his children and possibly his love?

"You ask much of me, Geoff."

"I can only ask it of a friend, Cate. Someone whom I trust with my life." He lifted her chin so she could not escape his dark gaze. "I know it is unfair to ask you, but I ask it all the same."

"I will," she said, knowing the impossible task she set for herself. She wanted to untangle their fingers and leave quickly, but still he did not release her. As his head tilted down, she feared and prayed for the same thing. His lips touched hers with a gentleness that broke her heart again....

\* \* \*

*The Countess Bride*
**Harlequin Historical #707—June 2004**

# TERRI BRISBIN

# THE COUNTESS BRIDE

## HARLEQUIN®

TORONTO • NEW YORK • LONDON
AMSTERDAM • PARIS • SYDNEY • HAMBURG
STOCKHOLM • ATHENS • TOKYO • MILAN • MADRID
PRAGUE • WARSAW • BUDAPEST • AUCKLAND

ISBN 0-373-29307-0

THE COUNTESS BRIDE

*Available from Harlequin Historicals and*
**TERRI BRISBIN**

*The Dumont Bride* #634
*The Norman's Bride* #696
*The Countess Bride* #707

Please address questions and book requests to:
Harlequin Reader Service
U.S.: 3010 Walden Ave., P.O. Box 1325, Buffalo, NY 14269
Canadian: P.O. Box 609, Fort Erie, Ont. L2A 5X3

To my husband, Chris (because he asked me to).

# Chapter One

*Lincolnshire, England*
*August, 1198*

She knew that the blood of six young noblewomen would be on her hands. And she knew that she would sinfully enjoy strangling the very life and breath out of each one. If they continued repeating the completely inane comments of the last hour, she would be forced to kill them all.

Catherine de Severin pulled a handkerchief from her sleeve and blotted her forehead. She did not suffer the heat well and the day had turned hot after the noon meal. Trying to be discreet, she lifted her hair from her perspiring neck and attempted to cool off before her discomfort was noticed.

Too late.

"Catherine? Are you unwell?" Emalie Dumont, Countess of Harbridge and her benefactress, leaned over and whispered to her. The softness of her voice did not hide her concern.

"I am well, my lady."

Catherine heard the soft snickers that moved

through the small group of women watching the men fight in the tilt-yard. Lady Harbridge had, as well, for her expression was one of distaste. Standing, the countess motioned to those seated to follow her.

"I fear this heat is too oppressive for me today. Come, let us seek a cooler place to gather, and something cool to drink to refresh ourselves."

No one could remain sitting, or not obey the orders of the countess and the hostess of this keep. Catherine gathered her fan and handkerchief and stood. Before the small entourage could leave the yard, a loud, deep voice called out to them from across the yard.

"My lady?"

Catherine watched as the countess approached the fence and spoke quietly to her husband. The women had been watching the earl and some of his men practice their fighting skills in the yard as an amusement. But knowing that the younger Dumont was on his way here to choose one of them for a wife made the group nervous and excited. The mindless chatter had made the swordplay difficult to enjoy. Catherine turned and observed the earl and countess's exchange of words.

'Twas times like this when she could see a softness in the earl's face, an expression of love, that kept her from hating him as much as she knew he hated her. A man who loved his wife as much as the Earl of Harbridge did could not be all bad. When, in his conversation with his wife, he raised his eyes to glance over at her, the coldness filled his gaze once more and Catherine knew that Lady Harbridge had mentioned her name.

A tightening began in her stomach and grew stronger. Unease filled her as his gaze passed over her once more. She had prayed for acceptance of her fate. She had prayed for understanding. And she had prayed for the gratitude that should fill her for the earl's sponsorship. 'Twas all for naught.

Her weaknesses in character threatened to overwhelm her. Her fears and her inability to carry on conversations in the romantic style of the court forced her to the background in most situations. Her lack of standing and lack of relatives to offer the support usually given to young women of marriageable age were appallingly obvious to those here seeking that honorable state. Even drawing on her inner reserve of practiced quiet and calmness did not lessen her anxiety when faced with outsiders whom she knew not.

The urge to return to the convent, nay, to run to the convent, nearly overpowered her for a moment. Taking in a deep breath, she tried to clear her thoughts. The countess approached and held out her hand. Taking it, Catherine walked next to the woman who offered her everything she lacked, without ever making demands on her time or on her soul.

"My lord has *suggested* that I seek my chambers and rest there until our evening meal. Catherine, will you join me and bring your prayer book?" Everyone present knew the lord had ordered her to her room. Gossip would begin immediately after Lady Harbridge left their presence.

"Of course, my lady."

"I fear that this babe makes me sensitive to the heat. My lord is concerned that I not spend so much time outdoors in it.'' Her whispers were loud enough for all to hear.

Catherine knew exactly what the countess was doing, and would have kissed the hem of her gown to thank her for it. But that would undo the good being done on her behalf. By announcing the news that she once more carried a babe, another heir for her lord, she drew the attention to herself.

The group behind them fell silent, but Catherine could almost hear the questions and thoughts in their minds. This would be the countess's third child in just over three years of marriage. Catherine knew those here who sought marriage to the countess's brother-by-marriage were wondering if he would be as demanding in the physical part of marriage as his brother was. And if they would be as fruitful.

They reached the keep, where Emalie guided Catherine in one direction while the others entered the great hall. The consummate hostess, Lady Harbridge would have servants aplenty waiting to serve her guests whatever they needed.

Catherine followed the countess up the stairs in one of the towers until they reached the earl and countess's chambers. The countess did not stop yet, but led her through a doorway and up another flight of stairs until they returned the battlements. Walking along the top of the wall that surrounded the entire keep, Catherine could see the lands around Greystone Castle, almost to the sea in the east. The countess stood at her side, eyes closed, facing into the breezes that buffeted them.

''If I could spend my days here in the wind, I would, dear Catherine.''

"Aye, my lady. 'Tis much more pleasant than the heat of the bailey." Catherine remembered hearing some gossip about the amount of time the earl and his countess spent high up on these walkways, and she could feel a heated blush climb onto her cheeks. It was even rumored, if one wasted time listening to that kind of talk, that the child carried by the countess had been conceived here one stormy spring night.

"They can be cruel, Catherine. I urge you not to take their words to heart."

"Aye, my lady." What else could she say?

"Geoffrey should arrive by this evening. He will enjoy seeing you, as he always does."

"And I him, my lady."

Lady Harbridge gave her the strangest look and then patted her hand. "You may seek out whatever diversions you'd like this day, Catherine. I am truly headed for my chambers now."

"As you wish, my lady."

Catherine was still trying to figure out the meaning of her glance when Lady Harbridge added, "This babe makes me hungry and tired, and I battle between both feelings now. Could you seek out Alyce and have her send food and drink to me?" At Catherine's nod, the countess continued. "It will be an arduous task to suffer the company of these empty-headed ninnies and their mothers over this next week, so get some rest to prepare yourself."

She laughed with the countess at her words. They were her exact thoughts about this group of visitors. Catherine curtsied and turned to leave. The countess spoke once more.

"Geoffrey will be pleased to see you here."

*     *     *

*Geoffrey will be pleased to see you here.*

The words swirled around inside her head as she sat in the cool stillness of the stone chapel. This was her one place of safe haven within Greystone. Not many of its inhabitants were spiritual in nature, so most times she had the quiet church to herself. Even old Father Elwood was absent now.

Wrapping her shawl tighter around her shoulders, Catherine paced the back of the chamber. Although marriage was never part of her accepted future life, she knew that it was a must for Geoffrey. Between the two Dumont brothers, they had much land and many titles to protect, both here in England and back in Poitou and Anjou.

She knew the French king was constantly testing the borders of his lands and that of the Plantagenets, and the Dumont lands sat between. Only an established marriage and an heir would serve to settle some of the tension. The current earl had supplied both, as was appropriate, but most did not know that Geoffrey stood as heir to all the earl's Continental possessions and titles.

Catherine had discovered much about the Dumonts' unusual arrangements with King Richard while here at Greystone and back at the convent. A second son did not expect to inherit family estates and titles, but Geoffrey would. Upon marriage—a marriage that required the consent of his brother—Geoffrey would take over control of Château d'Azure and all the Dumont holdings surrounding it. And he would be invested as the Comte de Langier.

If these "empty-headed ninnies," as the countess

called them, had knowledge of his true worth, they would have been after him long ago. But the earl kept these arrangements quiet even as he'd kept Geoffrey under control. Until now. Catherine longed to speak with Geoffrey to discover what had changed to make marriage now necessary.

Geoffrey. Her best friend. And now soon to be married. She had not laid eyes on him in almost a year, although his letters kept her entertained and informed of his progress in overseeing the workings of the many Dumont estates. When she'd last seen him he'd been maturing at an alarming rate, and Catherine could only imagine how handsome and tall he would be now.

She sighed as she struggled to accept what was to come. Her heart was heavy with the knowledge that this would be the last time she saw him. For once the question of his marriage was settled, she would begin preparation to take her vows.

# Chapter Two

The small group of travelers reached the crest of the hill and Geoffrey called a halt. This was his favorite spot to stop and survey the Castle Greystone and its surrounding lands. With summer full upon England, the richness of the fields and forests was evident. Lifting off his helm, he savored the view for what promised to be the last time in many months.

"Your lands are just as rich, my lord."

Geoffrey turned to face the man who was his own steward, and noticed his self-assured expression. Was Albert now reading his thoughts, as well as managing his properties?

"*Oui,* Albert, they are that. Or shall we say they will be when they are mine?"

Albert nodded and waited on him. 'Twould be unseemly to appear grasping when his brother's generosity was without limit or question. And once the business here was finished, Geoffrey would hold the title and many properties of the Dumont family. He shook his head, still fearing to believe that a younger son could attain so much. But then, nothing in the last four years had gone according to the way things should go.

"One more task, my lord. And this one is not so onerous?"

Geoffrey smiled, torn by the one thing that stood between him and all he stood to gain. Marriage. Marriage with his brother's consent. And then all would be his.

"Not so onerous, Albert. A necessary one at that."

"I am certain that your brother will help you to choose wisely."

The subtle leering in Albert's glance belied the man's calming words. Geoffrey's somewhat colorful past with women both here and at home was well known. His brother would try to find a bride to match him in spirit, as well as titles and lands. Wouldn't he?

"Come, then. Let me meet my fate while I still have the courage to do so."

Joining him in mirth, the men spurred their mounts and followed him through the gates and up to the steps to the keep. Word of his arrival had spread, for his brother stood at the top of the stairway, waiting.

"My lord earl!" Geoff called out, as he dismounted and climbed the steps.

"Brother!" Christian answered, opening his arms to greet him.

They met in their usual bone-crushing manner, and Geoff once more knew that the affection between him and his half brother was strong as ever. They separated only when the soft but insistent voice of the countess interrupted their greetings.

"Geoff! 'Tis good to have you with us once

more,'' she said. His sister-by-marriage was becoming even shorter, but she could not be ignored. ''And you have grown taller by many inches since I saw you last.'' She wrapped her arms around him, giving no importance to titles and protocol, and his heart warmed at her enthusiasm.

''Countess. You look well.'' He returned her hug and then stood back. He knew of her pregnancy, but did not know if the news was openly shared with their people yet. He would wait for a private moment to congratulate them both on their good tidings.

''I thought that when your arrival was delayed, mayhap you'd lost the courage to face the task before you,'' Christian declared. Geoff laughed, although his brother probably did not realize how close to the truth his words were.

''And miss out on your merriment at my expense? I would not disappoint you both after your efforts on my behalf.''

''Come, then. Refresh yourself and join us for the meal. Your task can be put off that long,'' Emalie said, as she pulled him into the doorway of the keep.

Geoff took a moment to look around, wondering if the one person whose presence would be a joy to him, other than his family, was there. He glanced about the bailey and into the keep, but did not see her. Not wanting to appear inattentive, he turned and walked with Emalie and Christian into the castle.

He looked at the hall with new eyes for he had grown quite a bit since his last visit here. Geoffrey could see surprise in the expressions of many of the servants as they noticed him for the first time. Looks of approval and some of open appraisal met him as he strode toward the dais at the front of the room. He smiled with true fondness at a few people, for they had been part of his growing up here these last few years. And he was met with inviting glances from several of the women who had marked his development from boy to man. No matter how inviting those looks were, this was not a visit to indulge his passions. Not with six prospective brides within the keep…and their mothers.

Even if a wife were supposed to accommodate her husband's needs in the marriage bed and ignore his needs outside of it, he did not plan to flaunt any of his past liaisons before a bevy of possible brides. Discretion was the most important part of valor, his brother had always said.

But with every glance around the great hall, Geoffrey was disappointed. Although her letters had promised her presence here, he did not see Catherine. And nothing would give him more pleasure, especially during this time of decision making, than to talk with her. He needed Catherine's quiet wisdom and soft sense of humor to help guide him. He wondered how she had reacted to the news of his impending nuptials. Catherine was pragmatic enough to realize that their futures would take them in different directions, or at least to different places. Christian had told him of a dowry set aside for her, so he knew that she would marry. Knowing her approach to life, he did not doubt that her choice of spouse would be done efficiently and with little of the spectacle that his would involve.

He reached his seat without seeing any sign of her

among the crowd. Taking in a breath and letting it out, Geoffrey readied himself for the evening ahead. And if Emalie's uncontrolled laughter in the solar a short while ago was any indication, it would take all of his efforts to survive it.

"Are you sufficiently recovered from your journey for us to begin?" his brother asked, motioning to the servants to begin serving the food.

"With all due respect for the countess's efforts, I fear I will never be recovered enough for what is to come." Geoff smiled at Christian, but he knew from the look in his brother's eyes that Christian had read the message in his words. And he knew that underlying every action Christian took was a genuine concern for his well-being. After partaking of the food offered, Geoff wiped his fingers on the napkin next to his plate. The satisfying meal he'd just eaten began to feel unsettled in his stomach now, as he thought of what was to come.

Becoming the consummate courtier and greeting a future bride and her parents. The cream of England and France and the Plantagenet provinces sat before him, all wearing looks of great anticipation. Some simply looked hungry, and not for food....

"Emalie has some plan on how this should work, since to insult anyone's dignity and standing would be a pitiful start for your search." Christian smiled, but his eyes were full of disturbing glee.

"Most assuredly, my lord," Geoffrey answered, his voice oozing with sarcasm. "Who has the most precedence among your guests?"

Christian surveyed those in his hall and nodded. "The duke there."

"Are they enough for this evening's work, my lady?" Geoffrey looked to Emalie, whose expression was of the most serious concentration.

"Aye. We have a sennight of their attendance. One should not rush these important matters." Her frown became more evident. "Besides, I have several entertainments arranged on the morrow to demonstrate your talents and skills, brother."

Geoffrey choked on the sip of wine he had just taken, and even Christian's solid thumping on his back did not help. Surely, he and his sister-by-marriage had different skills and talents in mind?

"Dancing, my lord." Emalie looked sharply at both of them. Christian looked even guiltier than he himself. "And a hunt. Both manly activities."

"Of course, my lady. I but thought…" He began to tease her.

"I know what you thought, Geoffrey. Those other manly pursuits are of no interest to me."

"Emalie," Christian whispered, so that none but they heard his familiar use of her name. "I think those pursuits are very much of interest to you."

Geoff watched as a blush moved up her cheeks and more than words were shared between the earl and countess. She began to fan herself as though the room had become hotter, then sat back and drank from her cup. Soon she gave a subtle nod, and several musicians gathered near the dais. Ah, the demonstration would now begin.

Geoffrey stood when his brother did, and the earl offered the countess his hand. Side by side, they strode down the steps and, with Geoff following, stopped at a nearby table. An older couple rose and met them. A lovely young woman remained seated. A trembling young woman, from what he could see of her face and shoulders. Surely she did not fear him?

"My lord. My lady," Christian began. "May I make known to you my brother, Geoffrey?"

Knowing his part, Geoff bowed to both the duke and duchess and then smiled at their daughter, whose pale face turned a pasty white. Not an auspicious beginning. He held out his hand and she placed her shaking fingers in his. Lifting them to his lips, he barely touched her knuckles, as was required.

"Would you honor me by joining me in dance?" He had the distinct feeling that she was about to refuse when her father intervened.

"Melissande. Accept his invitation now."

She rose from the bench, the picture of womanly beauty. Geoffrey noticed the graceful way she stepped into the line forming for the dance, her hair flowing down her back with each movement she made. And with his blue and cream tunic and hose and her cream and blue gown, their similar hair and eye color, even their appearance seemed made to be a good match. The lovely Melissande would be a fair enough choice.

Geoffrey tried to meet Melissande's gaze through the steps of the dance, but she never raised hers from the floor. When he spoke to her to try to involve her in polite conversation, she simply looked away as though he had never said a word. Finally, he blamed her unease on this rather public first meeting and, since he knew his own level of expectation, figured the poor lass was most certainly overwhelmed.

They finished the dance and he led her back to where her parents and his brother still waited. Mayhap the rest of the introductions would go easier now that the first was done. And mayhap the other prospective brides would be more at ease, now that this first one had gone so smoothly.

He decided to be especially gracious as he ended the interval with Melissande. Geoff lifted her hand to his lips, touched it briefly and then, gaining her gaze, smiled with all the warmth and appeal that he could offer. Lady Melissande's face flushed a bright red, her eyes rolled up into her head and she fell with a thump at his feet. This was not the normal reaction of young women when faced with his masculine charms.

In the confusion that followed, with both the duke and the earl calling out commands to the servants, and with the many other maidens chattering nervously, Geoffrey wanted nothing so much as to leave; and leave quickly. As he surveyed the great hall for a way to escape, he finally saw her.

As always, Catherine made herself blend into the background. Her dress was plain and serviceable, barely a cut above those worn by his brother's servants. She stood against a wall just outside one of the doors leading to the stairs. Their eyes met for a brief moment and then she stepped back out of his view. She would not intrude on his time with his family. Geoff knew from past experience that Catherine would withdraw any time his brother required his presence. She always put his needs above her wishes.

And that was one more thing he loved about her.

The thought roared through his mind. A dizzying blindness struck him for a moment and he reeled with the strength and clarity of his thoughts. He did love Catherine.

"Are you unwell, also?" the duchess asked, tapping him on the shoulder. "Mayhap the beef was bad?"

Geoff shook himself and looked around at those standing near the still-prostrate Lady Melissande. "Nay, I am well. Just concerned about the well-being of our guest."

He heard his sister-by-marriage calling out for more room, and he stepped back with the others. Although he could be cool and clearheaded in battle, a fainting or crying woman unmanned him. Let the countess handle things. And she did so, for a moment later Emalie and Melissande were standing.

"I fear my stomach was so nervous I did not eat today," Melissande whispered in a soft voice.

"And the exertion of that particular dance was too much for Lady Melissande. Some food and rest and she will be well."

Emalie patted the girl's hand and released Melissande to her own mother's ministrations. The duchess did not look pleased that her daughter would now be removed from the center of attention.

Geoffrey tried to ease the situation, for he feared some retribution would be directed at the girl for her actions here. If the duke and duchess had come all this way, they wanted a match between Melissande and him. If the girl failed to gain his favor, she could pay for it, if her parents were of that ilk.

"My lady?" He smiled and waited for Melissande

to face him. "Would you join me to break our fast in the morn? And I promise no dancing at that hour!"

'Twas the right thing to say, for the frown on the duchess's brow lifted and Melissande offered a tremulous smile at his invitation. He could not promise her that she would be his choice, but at least she would be given a fair chance to make her case before him.

Melissande dipped into a curtsy before the group and nodded. "My lord, I would be most pleased to join you."

"Until the morn, then." Geoffrey nodded and watched as the lady, her parents and various attendants left the room. He sensed Christian and Emalie beside him and waited for their comments.

"Too frightened for my tastes," his brother whispered.

"But nice enough," Emalie added.

"Let's see what the morning brings," Geoff suggested. "Now then, my lady. Do you have another virgin to sacrifice to me before the festivities end this night?"

If she was feeling insulted, the slight tugging at the corners of her mouth that threatened to turn into a smile gave away her amusement.

"Come, Geoffrey. Let us introduce you to the lady Marguerite. Her father is a mere baron, but of sufficient standing and property as to not insult your future dignity, or your pompous brother's."

Christian let out a snort and Geoffrey fought not to join him. Emalie had complained about Christian's arrogance from the time they met, and it was obvious to him that that particular battle still wore on.

"Lead on, my lady. Let us not waste the time we have."

## Chapter Three

Moonlight streamed in through the small window high in the alcove's wall and made it seem like day. This small refuge between the back stairs and the kitchen was largely ignored by most, but Catherine favored it when she needed a few moments alone in the castle during a busy day. And this was the place where she and Geoffrey would meet and compare their adventures when they both visited Greystone— his of one kind and hers of another.

She would have to accommodate herself to the idea that they would be even more different once this week ended. She would go on to her new life, alone, and he would go to his, with a wife in tow. Catherine sighed. She wanted too many things she could not have. Too many things that she was not entitled to. A man who could never be hers.

Looking up at the rays of light and the specks of dust that danced within them, Catherine allowed herself to dream of dancing with Geoffrey, as the first two of his prospective wives had. As she'd watched from the hallway, he had led them in the steps of two dances that she knew but had never been invited to do. He had grown so much since she'd seen him— taller, his blond hair longer and his shoulders broadened by muscles not there before. Where once was the promise of attractiveness, now there was a wildly handsome, noble warrior. As if conjured by her thoughts, she turned to find him staring at her.

"Geoffrey."

"Catherine."

She stared back at him, separated by several feet of air, and marveled at the changes in him. She wasn't certain who took the first step but she suddenly found herself wrapped in his arms. Tears burned her eyes and throat, as his arms held her so close that it made taking a breath difficult. Her own arms found their way around his waist and she prayed that he would never let her go.

How long they remained in that embrace, she knew not, but the cold air of reality began to seep into her soul. Catherine understood that nothing more could be between them than this holding and she relished it for the brief lapse of judgment it was. One that would not be repeated.

Removing her hands from his back, she took in a deeper breath and let it out. He must have sensed her withdrawal, for Geoffrey released his hold on her and let her go. Now, a small distance separated them and she finally regained control of herself.

"My lord, you look well," she said with as much calm as she could manage.

"'My lord' is it now? And I thought we were friends." His voice had deepened, too. Its mellow resonance struck something within her and stirred feelings better left untouched.

"Someone needs to be aware of your titles, my lord. Who better than a friend?"

"Please," he said, taking her hand in his. "There will time enough for formality and distance. For now, for these brief moments away from all of that, can we not simply be Geoff and Cate?"

He knew. He knew that whatever they shared would be over by the end of his visit. Her heart lurched with the pain of it, but she vowed not to let him know how sad she was about it.

"Of course. Sit, Geoff, and tell me of your journey here. Was it a smooth crossing?" Catherine loosened her hand from his, stepped aside and let him sit down on the stone bench in the alcove. They would have shared the bench for their talks in the past, but now there was no room for her next to him.

"'Twas a good journey, though accomplished with some trepidation about the destination."

"You worried about coming here?"

"Well, it would be nearer the truth to say that Emalie's plans made me worry." He paused and smiled at her. "She is more devious than my brother."

"They want only the best for you, Geoff." She almost reached out to touch his shoulder, but stopped herself. They needed to rebuild the distance between them, now that it had been challenged.

"Cate, I do know that or I would have pulled up the drawbridge at Château d'Azure and never left it."

The image of him doing that, closing himself in his castle and not coming out, reminded her of the boy she'd met on her first visit to Harbridge. Or may-hap that was her on her first visit here from the convent? The worldly estate where life pulsed so fully had terrified her and she had been tempted to never return. It had been only the gentle requests of the lord's brother that had convinced her to come back.

"But, my l... Geoff, when did you ever resist a challenge?"

He moved to one side of the stone seat and beckoned her to sit. She thought to refuse, but that part of her that knew it was over between them could not. Gathering her skirts close, she slid against the wall, seeking to press against it and not him.

"Everything changes with this visit, Cate. My life, my duties. I step into the larger stage of the world when I marry and accept the titles I am destined to receive. I have no misunderstandings of the importance of the lands I will hold on the Continent," he said. He leaned his head back and let out a deep grumble of frustration. "Langier lands stand between those who would rule all of France and England, and I do not know if I am equal to the task of holding them and managing them."

He had given her his deepest secret. He showed his manly bravado and outgoing nature to the world, even to his brother, but he had gifted her with his innermost fear. She must give him something in return.

"You have listened well to your brother and his lessons of administration?"

He nodded.

"And you have surrounded yourself with wise men to counsel you?"

He nodded again.

"And you plan on using the wits and intelligence that God gave you, and not acting like a witless fool?" Those words gained a smile and eased the frown on his brow.

"Then I am certain that you will be successful in keeping the trust your brother places in you. The earl does not give it easily and would never take this step if he did not believe you were ready." Geoffrey laughed then. "'Tis amusing?"

"'Twould seem you know my brother well, for those were nearly the same words he used to me."

"I am gladdened that you have shared your fears with him and that he has tried to reassure you of your nature and your abilities." She chose her words carefully, so as to not let her true feelings for the earl show. Apparently, she did not do it as well as she hoped.

Geoffrey reached over and took her hand once more, entwining his fingers with hers this time. "I know not what is at the base of this dislike you have for him and he has for you, but I am touched that you both go to such lengths to disguise it and keep it hidden when I am here."

Catherine could not find words at that moment, for this seemed to be a time of sharing truths, and there were none that she could share with him. At least none that would not make this more difficult than it already was.

He stood, drawing her up at his side, not releasing her hand. With his other hand, he reached up and brushed away to loose wisps of hair that always seemed to be separated from her orderly braid. Her breath caught and she could feel the heat in her skin where his fingers had touched.

"You should retire, for it is late and I know that you will be kept busy with the countess tomorrow."

"Aye. She tires easily now and I am glad to give her whatever assistance I can."

"Would you give me aid, as well?"

"Anything, Geoff. But what could I do for you?"

He paused as though trying to frame his request. Was it something dishonorable? Of course it could not be! Something dangerous? He would not put her in danger.

"Would you give me your counsel about the women who are to be considered for marriage?"

Would she help him to choose his wife? Pain, like the thrust of a dagger, pierced her heart, leaving her without breath. Could she help him choose the woman who would bear his name and his children and possibly his love? The woman who would live with him and be his countess? It could never be her, but could she help him pick who it would be?

"You ask much of me, Geoff."

"I can only ask it of a friend, Cate. Someone who I trust with my life." He lifted her chin so she could not escape his dark gaze. "I know it is not fair to ask you, but I do so all the same."

"I will," she said, knowing the impossible task she set for herself.

She wanted to untangle their fingers and leave quickly, but still he did not release her. As his head tilted down, she feared and prayed for the same thing. His lips touched hers with a gentleness that broke her heart again. Their warmth had barely been shared when he pulled away.

''Promise not to leave without a farewell when this is done.''

Had he read her thoughts? Saying goodbye would tear her to pieces. She shook her head, not certain if it was in agreement or denial of his request.

''Promise me,'' he insisted.

''I promise,'' she said.

A noise in the corridor caused them to step away from each other. Was someone there? She heard nothing more, but it roused her from the confusion she felt and made her realize that their behavior was inappropriate at best.

''My lord, I bid you a good evening.'' Cate curtsied before him.

'''Till the morrow, Catherine.'' Geoff replied with a polite bow. He winked at her as he turned to leave. He was the same as always.


With the moonlight pouring over her, she'd looked like an angel. Geoff caught her unaware as she'd stood staring up in the bright moonlight. Surely she had not changed in appearance or demeanor in the months since their last visit? Ah, he realized, he was the one who had changed and now looked at this place and its people differently.

In the last year, he had fought and won his first tournament, met the nobles who ruled those lands adjoining his and had even been introduced to the royal family of France. And he had known grave disappointment as the reality of his duties to his inheritance forced the truth on him—he would not marry the woman he wanted when he inherited.

Catherine, a distant cousin of Emalie's, orphaned and with but a small dowry, might be acceptable as a bride for Geoffrey Dumont, the younger brother of the Earl of Harbridge who had no aspirations of titles or lands, but she would never be acceptable as the bride of the Comte de Langier. Without family connections, titles, wealth or lands, Catherine could never be his. And he would never ask her to lower herself in any other way, to be his without the blessing of marriage.

No matter how much he wanted her. No matter how much he loved her. And not even knowing for a certainty in his soul that she loved him.

So why did he carry out this folly and ask her to help him choose a bride? Why cause them both the pain he knew would result?

He simply could not let her go yet. He needed to share whatever time he could steal with her before he left to take his wife home to Poitou. It would be better this way. Love had little place in a modern marriage and so he would remember his first love and know not to expect more than the affection from a spouse who understood their relationship as he did. Even as he let the thoughts free, he knew them for the sham they were.

He would not lie to himself—he would keep company with Catherine when he could and would use the task she'd agreed to in order to keep her near until the last possible moment. Then they would part. If it were to be difficult in this next week, then so be it. He would be with Cate and that would make it worth the pain.

Geoff strode through the great hall and made his way to his chambers.

"They are in love."

"It has no bearing on what is to come."

Emalie sighed. How could her husband be so obstinate, even after their own trials? Turning to face him in the shadows where they stood, she thought of how best to approach this problem.

"Love means nothing to you?" Sometimes she needed to prod him out of his arrogance and into realizing the value of the intangibles that surrounded him. 'Twas ever his failing.

"Your love has meant everything to me and you know it. But as we found it after we married, so will Geoffrey. If he accepts our guidance in the matter of a wife and chooses well, love will come." Christian held out his arm to her and she placed her hand on it.

She sighed again. How could such intelligent and powerful men be such fools? She had seen this coming almost from the first time Catherine had visited from the convent and met Geoffrey. Soul mates. Two halves of the same soul that were meant to be joined together. How could her husband not see that?

"You are too quiet. That does not bode well for me, wife."

"She was a victim as well, Christian. Do you hold her accountable for his sins, too?"

"She has no family...." he said. Emalie thought to correct him, but his growing anger was apparent.

''She has no family, no wealth and no titles. She is not suitable to marry my brother.''

Emalie began to answer him, but Christian drew to a stop and pointed at her. ''Do not think to meddle or gainsay me in this, wife. I have my limits.''

She looked away and let him lead her to their chambers without further argument. She knew he thought he had won this one, but she would have the last word. Catherine had suffered much and did not deserve to be held in dishonor because of her brother's actions. Even if those actions had been against Emalie's own person.

Emalie stopped at the door to her room and blocked her husband from following her into her sleeping chamber. His puzzlement was clear and she was glad. Mayhap it would make him think about his unkind attitude and words.

''Even after three years and countless steps forward, you are still a prig.''

She slammed the door closed and forced herself not to laugh at the astonished look on his face as she did so.

# Chapter Four

Melissande.

Marguerite.

Mathilde.

Maude.

Melissande, Marguerite, Mathilde and Maude. The names did not bode well for him, for he had to always struggle to remember them. Now he was saddled with meeting strangers and trying to keep their names and faces in his memory.

Had his sister-by-marriage forgotten the lessons she'd learned about the letters of the alphabet? Even he knew that there were more letters than simply *M* and certainly women whose names did not begin so. Apparently, the only suitable women who had been invited to Greystone were those whose names began with an *M*.

"No, my lord Geoffrey, I did not limit my search for suitable wives to women whose names began thus. 'Twould only seem so."

Surprised that he'd said the words aloud, he noticed the mischievous grin that teased the corners of

Emalie's mouth. Seeing the matching glint in her eye, he was not convinced that it was unintentional. For confusion? For levity? Her reasons he knew not, but they were there somewhere.

"You mentioned six prospective wives. Two seem to be missing."

Although Emalie's lips tightened at his comment, his brother's snort of amusement was loud enough to be heard by those below table, as well as those at it.

"The ladies Petronilla and Phillippa are late risers, my lord. They tend to like the activities of the afternoon and evening far more than those in the morn."

Ah. Well, four were easier to manage than six, so Geoffrey would use this early time to meet the two who were not present at the meal and dancing last eve, before meeting the others, the *P* ladies, later in the day.

"Emalie," he whispered to her after realizing she used the title not yet known by those here. "I thought we'd decided that I was simply a knight for now?"

"'Twould seem, brother, that word of our bargain with Richard has escaped, in spite of our best efforts." Christian looked neither pleased nor displeased by this lapse.

Gazing around the tables, Geoffrey now understood why there was so much wealth and beauty on display. As much as he hunted a bride, their families hunted him.

"So, I am worthwhile now that they know I am a marquis?"

Christian snickered and leaned across Emalie to answer. "And worth far more when you inherit the title of Comte de Langier and become the sole owner of the lands that lie between Anjou, Poitou and Aquitaine.''

"Do not spare me, brother. Why are they truly here?'' Geoff gnashed his teeth at his change in status. Not now. He wanted time without the pressure of his true title being known.

Christian threw him a look that confirmed his suspicions—he was more valuable than any of the women to be considered. Their fathers wanted him for the lands and titles he would have upon his investiture, and the connections to the Plantagenet crown and the proximity to the French one.

"The hunter has become the prey, I fear, brother,'' Christian answered. "All of my hopes to accomplish this before your inheritance was known are for naught.''

"Has anyone asked outright?''

"Nay, no one yet, although many hints have been dropped in initial discussions.''

Geoffrey broke off another chunk of cheese and chewed it. Leaning back as he washed the food down with some ale, he considered his choices. He could ignore the inevitable gossip or he could have Christian make the announcement of the terms of Richard's agreement with the Dumont family. The news would be known as soon as negotiations began in earnest with the family of whomever he chose, so mayhap disclosure was best now. Subterfuge made him uncomfortable, a failing that Christian warned him about.

"My apologies, Geoff. I knew that word was out as soon as the rest of them gathered together in the hall this morn. Their visits and times of introduction were to be spread out over several days, not made into a marriage market like this.''

He nodded as his brother continued. ''But none would allow another an advantage in showing off his daughter to you unchallenged. So, here they are.''

The speculation in the gazes that met his told the story. Those assembled wanted or needed him more than they wanted to hold on to their daughter or the wealth they would need to give away in the bargain.

A marriage to Melissande of Quercy would produce a united border with the south and west of France and make the duke more valuable to Philip Augustus. Marguerite of Brittany would strengthen the Plantagenet hold on that area and stem the tide of support for the French king. The count from Navarre would gain a foothold deep in the Plantagenet provinces and secure his borders with Gascony. The marquis who held lands near Orleans and owed fealty for those lands directly to the king of France would gain esteem for capturing a favorite of King Richard's as his son-by-marriage. Marriage to either of the English heiresses would put more of England and Wales under Richard's vassals' control.

The watchful gazes and intense scrutiny made Geoff feel very much the prey here. Christian cleared his throat, gaining the attention of all in the room. He stood and spoke to them.

''On behalf of my brother, I thank you for answering our invitation. My family and I are honored by your presence and pleased that you could be here to meet with him. The countess and I have planned some entertainments for you all and I hope that your stay is comfortable and...'' Christian paused and then acknowledged the real reason for this debacle. "May it result in a marriage and a joining of families."

Geoffrey forced a smile to his face and nodded at the polite applause that greeted his brother's words. From the undisguised greed on several faces, he guessed some of the visitors were already planning ways to ensure that their daughter was chosen. The only one wearing an undecipherable mask was the Baron of Evesham, whose friendship with Prince John was known. Geoff watched as the baron's piercing gaze rested on each of the young women under consideration and then flicked back to the empty seat at his side, empty due to the absence of his daughter.

Geoffrey's observations were interrupted by his brother's announcement. "The stable master informs me that the horses are at the ready for our hunt. Come."

Geoff joined Christian and the other noblemen and made his way to the stable yard. They would hunt with dogs this day, but he knew that Emalie enjoyed using the hawks and would plan a hunt for men and women using those. Soon, amid the barking and yelling and dust and men in the yard, he lost all thoughts of a bride and faced the challenges of a hunt.

Catherine sat at the longest of the tables near the kitchen hearth, finishing a bowl of steaming porridge. With most of the men leaving for the hunt for much of the day, she would have a chance to complete some arrangements. Supplies of food and wine and ale would travel with them so they could eat in the forest rather than coming back for the noon meal.

The fruits of their labors would grace the table tonight. Catherine stood when Emalie approached.

"Nay, Catherine. Sit and finish your meal."

Emalie walked to another table and examined the foods laid out on it. Nodding, she inspected the quality and quantity of the breads and wheels of cheese. The cook arrived at her side. Now Catherine did join them, anxious to assist in any way she could.

After a short time, Emalie and the cook had agreed to the dishes that would be served at the night's feast, and arrangements had been made to retrieve any game or animals captured in the hunt. Catherine walked at her side as they left the kitchens by way of the back courtyard. She did not ask their destination, but followed along. Soon they arrived at the small graveyard where many of the Montgomerie family were buried.

But they were not there to show respect for the dead. This was also one of few places that offered any privacy in the sometimes frenzied world of Greystone Castle. And privacy was needed to discuss the startling contents of the reverend mother's latest missive regarding Catherine. They stopped near the low stone wall, and Catherine waited until Emalie had taken a seat on the bench next to the wall before sitting, as well.

"I would like you to attend the feast tonight, Catherine." Although she clearly tried to soften her tone, it was more of an order than a request.

Catherine shook her head as she answered.

"'Tis not possible, my lady. I have no place there."

"You are my ward, Catherine. You do belong there."

Catherine faced her and let the sadness she carried within show on her face. 'Twas something she had never seen before in this strength, so Emalie knew Catherine trusted her.

"I still do not understand how you can look at me at all, let alone with the generosity you do, my lady. We both know that I am the sister of your enemy, an orphan without family or connections and without wealth. I would be happier—"

"Taking the veil?" Emalie interrupted.

Catherine blushed and stammered and then just stopped and waited. Emalie could see her trying to regain control as she realized that her secret was known.

"My lady, I would have told you myself once I was sure."

"The decision is not made, then? The reverend mother misunderstood your words?"

If there was anyone less suited for the convent than Catherine, she knew her not. The vitality and curiosity that was just beginning to reappear would wither and die in religious life. This girl, denied too many years of life, needed to be among people and to enjoy life and to find love.

Catherine's eyes filled with tears and she bowed her head, not meeting Emalie's gaze. Emalie thought, and not for the first time since bringing Catherine to Greystone, that mayhap she had handled this badly. Had it been cruel, as Christian had warned, to bring her here and give her a sample of a life she could never have? But then her husband had established a small dowry for Catherine, so marriage was not out of the question for her.

Emalie shifted on the hard seat and took Catherine's hand in hers. Would the dowry so generously established now pay Catherine's entry into the convent in Lincoln? Would she never know the joys of bearing children and having a husband to care for? As if in answer to her silent question, Catherine spoke.

"The reverend mother understood me well, my lady. This is to be my last visit to Greystone. My studies are nearly done and I am ready to take my vows."

"Why, Catherine? Why enter the convent and spend your life as a Gilbertine sister?" Emalie waited for an answer. She suspected that she knew the truth of this and wondered if Catherine trusted her enough to share it with her.

"The reverend mother and sisters at the convent have been so kind to me. They cared for me during my…illness and have encouraged me since. They have taught me so much, not only from books, my lady, but in their practices and their life." A desperate undertone laced her words, as though she were trying to convince herself and not Emalie.

"Those are all reasons to give thanks and generous donations and to offer prayers to God so that the sisters may continue their good works with others. But Catherine, those are not the reasons why you should enter their life. Tell me why you should join them."

Discomfort flashed over the girl's face and Emalie felt a pang of guilt for causing it. But if this was

Catherine's choice, she would support her in this desire to join the religious life. If it was not...

"Have you not thought of marriage for yourself?"

A terrible expression of loss haunted Catherine's eyes and a soul-deep despair was now clearly written on her face. It was so obvious that Emalie's own heart hurt from it. This was not about beginning a new life as a nun. This was, as she had suspected, about losing Geoffrey.

"With no family?" Catherine asked. "With no memory of my past other than what you or the reverend mother have shared with me? How can I enter into a marriage contract under the false pretenses in which I live? What do I offer a prospective husband?"

Emalie watched as silent tears slipped down Catherine's pale cheeks. So much pain for someone who had not lived a score of years. She reached up and brushed a few strands of hair from Catherine's damp cheeks.

"You have much to offer. You are an intelligent woman with much learning. You have handled many duties of the keep while here with me, so I doubt you would have any difficulty handling the tasks of chatelaine for a husband. You are of a suitable age to marry and there are no physical impairments to keep you from bearing children. You would make any man a more than acceptable wife."

Catherine thought on the countess's words. The problem for her lay within them, for she did not want to be "suitable" or "acceptable." She did not want to be "without impairments." She wanted to be loved. She wanted to be wanted. She wanted to be pursued for her own value and not the purse or land that came with her.

What foolishness to think such things! Even she knew such thoughts were ridiculous. 'Twas simply the way of things that women were wanted for what they brought and men for their abilities to manage and protect. Marriages among the noble class were simply that—contracted arrangements. And her biggest folly was to even consider for a moment that she could be Geoffrey's wife.

Catherine removed her hand from the countess's grasp and stood. The day was early, but already the heat was building. A breeze moved the smaller branches of the tree that provided them with some shade, and Catherine walked to its trunk and leaned against it. Pulling out a linen square from her sleeve, she wiped the remaining tears from her eyes and cheeks.

These overwhelming feelings must be some last moment of weakness and unresolve within her. She was content with her decision. She had thought about all the questions that the countess had raised, and knew she had but one choice for her life. If she could not marry Geoffrey, she wanted to marry no man. And so the convent was her only option, nay, her only refuge, to avoid an unwanted marriage.

"I am content with this decision, my lady. The reverend mother will accept me and she knows my heart on this."

"Have you told Geoffrey of this? Does he know?"

Swallowing against the tightening within her throat, Catherine could only shake her head in reply. Closing her eyes, she fought for control.

"He knows that this visit is our last, for his choosing a wife will settle things for both of us." She whispered the words that declared her fate as well as his.

"And the love you share? Have you spoken of it with him?"

She gasped at the question and its implications. Others did know. As much as she tried to hide it, and thought her efforts enough, apparently 'twas not so.

In a moment, the countess was at her side. "'Tis obvious to those of us willing and able to see it." Her voice was soft and soothing. "Geoffrey has not spoken of it to you?"

Catherine realized the question at the heart of her words. Words spoken. Promises made. Betrothals were arranged on less than that.

"His honor would not permit anything to be spoken between us, my lady. He knows his duties, as do I."

The countess muttered under her breath in reply, but the words "the earl" were clear. Oh no! She did not mean that the earl knew of her feelings for his brother? No wonder he hated her. 'Twas not because he thought her a burden on his wife. He probably thought Catherine would do whatever she could to trap Geoffrey into a marriage that would be advantageous to her.

The air around her began to flicker before her eyes and Catherine felt faint. Dropping to her knees, she leaned forward and tried to breathe. She could feel the countess touching her shoulder, but then the sights and sounds around her began to fade. Just when she thought she would lose consciousness, everything began to clear and she could hear the birds in the tree above her and the noises in the yard behind her. After taking a few breaths, she felt strong enough to stand.

"My lady, I beg forgiveness if I have given any offense to the earl in this. I meant no disrespect to him or to his family and I do not claim that any promises were made between Lord Geoffrey and myself. Please tell the earl. Please—"

"Catherine, you misunderstand my words. Here—" the countess sat back down on the bench and pointed to the place next to her "—sit and let us talk about this. I would not have you mistake my meaning and my comment about the earl's knowledge in this regard."

Catherine felt the need to run growing within her. In a moment it would be irresistible, and so she excused herself from the countess's presence. Shame and guilt welled within her over her thoughts and even her dreams of happiness, a happiness she did not deserve.

"My lady? May I be excused for a short time?" Catherine walked to the gate even as she uttered the words.

"Of course, Catherine. You are not a servant here. Go now, but come to see me later."

## Chapter Five

She did not even slow down to hear the countess's reply. Instead, her feet moved quickly until she was almost running through the yard and out through the portcullis. If anyone watching thought it was strange that the countess's companion was leaving in such a hurry, no one thought to stop her. Soon she was on the road to the village, passing peasants and villagers traveling in both directions. Still, she ran on, for in truth, when these feelings came upon her, she could do nothing but walk or run from them.

When she could no longer breathe due to the painful strain in her side, and when her legs were beset with tremors, Catherine slowed to a walk and then found a spot off the path to sit down. Her hair, now loosened from its braid and coif, flowed over her shoulders. Tugging the coif free, she gathered her thigh-length hair and tossed it over her shoulders again.

That would soon change.

When she took her vows, her hair would be cut, and for the first time never be permitted to show at all. No decorative coifs or fancy braids would ever decorate her blond tresses again. A simple white habit would be her clothing for the rest of her life, and no one would ever wonder what color hair lay beneath the white wimple, coif and veil.

Catherine's breathing slowed and she sat in the shade of the tree, listening to the sounds around her. This path was one she'd taken before; it followed the course of a small stream and ended near the fields of one of the villeins. She would have privacy here. And she was safe.

There was no explanation she knew that caused these anxious feelings to build within her. So strong did they become, however, that the urge to escape grew unmanageable to her. She lost control and had to get out and walk or run until the tension left her. The reverend mother seemed to understand, as did the countess, but Catherine herself did not. Usually, she followed the impulse as soon as she became aware of it. Walking around the convent grounds and praying was acceptable behavior for the residents there so it did not draw undue attention. And here at Greystone, the countess made it clear that it was with her permission that Catherine walked where she would and when she would.

Another flaw in her character, certainly, but to find the cause she would need courage she did not have. Many times she had thought to confront Lady Harbridge or the reverend mother about the dark spaces in her memory, but a physical fear made it impossible. There was a reason she could not or would not remember from the time she came to live with her brother until she awoke one night at the convent in some sort of convalescent stay. There had to be.

Catherine climbed back onto her feet and looked toward the castle on its high mount, nearly half a league away. The walk back would give her time to collect her thoughts and ready herself for what she must face. The least she could do in return for the generosity and support of the Dumonts was to attend the banquet this evening. She would need to overcome her discomfort at being in large groups as well as being with people she did not know. She would blend into the background as she usually did, and no one but the countess need even notice she was there.

Catherine decided that she needed to face these next days and their challenges with a lighter mood. Had not the good sisters taught her that a sacrifice or good work done with a heavy heart or in regret was not worth doing? Neither the one performing the act nor the one who should benefit would, if the deed was not carried out with a pure heart.

Her love for Geoffrey would sustain her through this time of trial. She knew her place and his, and once he had chosen a bride, she herself could move on and settle in her life. Feeling her sense of calm and balance restored, Catherine decided it was time to go back to the responsibilities she had accepted in service to the countess. And to explain herself to Lady Harbridge.

Picking up her coif from where it lay on the ground, she shook it free of dust and tucked it in her sleeve. There would be plenty of time to replace it before reaching the main road to the castle, and she would enjoy the feel of the breezes lifting the hair on her shoulders and neck.

The horses were upon her almost as she set her foot on the road. Reeling back, Catherine stumbled and would have fallen, had not one of the three men vaulted from his mount and grabbed her arm at the last moment.

"Here, demoiselle. Allow me to help you," he said, as he slid his hands along her arm. Catherine knew his grip was stronger than was necessary to give her support. When his hand brushed her breast, she knew the move had been deliberate. She tugged away, trying to loosen his hold, but he was bigger and stronger than she.

His companions dismounted and approached her, and her stomach began to clench in fear. Their manner was threatening and she knew their intent without any statement of it. She was the prey.

"You have a familiar look about you, my sweet. Surely, we have met before this?" The tallest of the three stood before her and, leaning close to her, lifted a few of her curls and wrapped them around his fingers. "Although I should remember someone so beautiful and with such charms." She shivered as his gaze moved over her from head to hips and then back.

The third man, of shorter and bulkier build, moved in from behind, closing off the one avenue of escape. His fetid breath on her neck caused her stomach to heave, and she feared she might lose the food she had eaten a short time before.

"So, tell us, demoiselle, are you truly out here alone?" The first man pulled her closer and almost whispered the words in her ear. "Could it be that you were waiting for us?"

Catherine shook her head. "I am not alone," she said, hoping they were fooled. Never in all her time spent as Greystone had she feared for her safety among the villagers or the castlefolk. She had walked alone many times and never been bothered or accosted in such a manner. Her momentary surprise turned to fear as the men moved even closer.

"A sweet morsel like this for us, Garwyn? I think not. Ones like this—" the tall one now wrapped more of her hair around his fist, making it impossible for her to pull away "—are not for the likes of us unless we take them."

Catherine began to struggle in earnest and had opened her mouth to scream when a voice came from across the clearing. "The lady is under the protection of the Earl of Harbridge, who would take offense at your treatment of her." Catherine recognized Sir Luc Delacroix, Greystone's castellan and the earl's friend, and offered a quick prayer of thanks at her rescue.

"And who are you that we should not take our pleasure where we may? We are guests of the earl." All three men turned to face Sir Luc, and the two who did not hold her placed their hands on their swords in direct challenge to him.

"I am the earl's man, as are these," Sir Luc said, as a small group of men-at-arms on horseback moved closer. "From the insignia you wear 'twould seem that you are Evesham's men?"

"Aye, we are Evesham's men."

"Then release the girl and find your lord where he

hunts game in the forest on the other side of the castle.'' Sir Luc pointed off in the distance.

Catherine feared they would resist his orders, but after seeing the numbers against them, the men muttered oaths under their breath and let her go. Shaking from the terror of the averted attack, she sank to her knees as they regained their saddles and goaded their horses to a hurried pace.

''Leave the earl's people be, for I know where to find you,'' Sir Luc called out just before they moved onto the road.

The hands that touched her now were safe ones, as Sir Luc assisted her to her feet and held her up for a few minutes while her legs and breathing steadied. Then he led her to his horse. After mounting, he reached down and pulled her up behind him. Tucking her hands around his waist, he motioned to his men to ride.

''My thanks, Sir Luc.'' It was all she could force out through teeth clenching against the fear still pulsing through her.

''''Twas foolish of you to come out so far unattended, Catherine,'' he said to her over his shoulder. ''There are too many strangers among us now for it to be safe.''

''Yes, Sir Luc,'' she whispered, slumping at his rebuke. He had always been kind to her, even though his lord did not treat her that way. Now even he turned against her.

''Your pardon, for my words were too harsh, Catherine. The lady Emalie told me of your leaving and asked me to see to your safety due to just this possibility. She worries over you and I would not want to face her if you had been injured.''

Catherine did not reply immediately, but simply held on as they approached the castle gates. When the panic overtook her, she did not think of safety. She did not think at all—she reacted. She only knew that she must escape the confines that held her and did not take time to reflect on all the possibilities. She must learn to control this weakness within herself.

''I understand, Sir Luc. I do not want to trouble the countess.''

He stopped, and one of the stable boys came over to hold his horse as he first handed her down and then dismounted. Dismissing his men with a nod, he turned to her and lowered his voice.

''Did they look familiar to you, Catherine? I heard one mention that you did to him.''

''No, Sir Luc. I know them not.'' Did he think she had lured them to that spot for…for seduction?

''Worry not on this,'' he said in a softer tone. ''If you need to leave the yard or go to the village, ask one of my men to accompany you.''

''I will, Sir Luc.'' He was about to leave when she touched him on the arm to gain his attention. ''Will you report this incident to the earl?''

''I see no need for that,'' he replied. His eyes revealed the lie of his words, for he looked away for a moment even as he reassured her. ''Now, go and refresh yourself, for the countess awaits you in her chambers and bade me tell you to seek her out before attending the solar.''

He turned and left without another word, so she

sought out the room assigned to her during her stays here, and washed her hands and face, only then remembering the coif in her sleeve. Taking several minutes, she brushed her hair, gathered it in a braid and replaced the coif to cover it. Finding a light veil, she laid it over her head and placed a small cap on top to hold it in place. Now she felt more in control.

Leaving her room, she walked up to the countess's chambers and knocked. Alyce, the lady's maid, opened the door and motioned her inside. The countess sat on her bed, engrossed in conversation with her daughter, the oldest of her two children. Young Isabelle, called Bella, was a bright child of who had over three years. Her nurse stood nearby, smiling at her charge's words to the lady. After a few more moments, the child slipped off the bed, took her nurse's hand and turned to leave.

Spying Catherine at the door, Bella ran over and hugged her around the legs. "'Tis grand, Catherine. *Maman* says I can sit at table at Uncle Geoffrey's wedding!" Bella jumped up and down, still holding on to Catherine's skirts.

"Remember, Isabelle, only if you behave as a lady should." Although the countess's face was serious, a smile played at the corners of her mouth.

Bella stepped back, releasing her hold, and smoothed her gown. In a motion reminiscent of the six prospective brides, she lifted her hair, flung its red-blond length over her shoulders and shook her head so that it flowed down her back. Catherine tried not to smile at her precocious antics.

"Yes, *Maman*," Bella said as she curtsied to her mother.

Emalie nodded to the nurse, who opened the door and led the child out. The door was fully closed before the countess laughed aloud.

"She has been watching the visitors closely and learning from them. I just wish she would pick up a good trait from them and not these frivolous ones."

"I noticed she resembled Lady Melissande with her flowing hair," Catherine added, trying to lighten the moment.

"If she copies Melissande's skill with the needle and thread, I would not be unhappy. That one has talents that even I envy." The countess slipped off the bed and adjusted her own gown. "So long as Bella does not pick up her propensity to faint at the least provocation, which could prove to be a problem."

Catherine smiled, enjoying the countess's insight into the woman under consideration. Emalie had chosen with care to try to find a suitable match for Geoffrey. This was as good a time as any to broach the subject of Geoffrey's marriage and Catherine's own future.

"My lady, I beg your pardon for my behavior earlier and would speak to you about your…my lord's… the marquis…"

"Geoffrey's marriage plans?" the countess offered softly.

"Aye, my lady."

Without a word being spoken, Alyce left the room and pulled the door closed quietly behind her.

"Sit, Catherine," the countess said.

When she had also taken a seat on a chair, Lady Harbridge nodded at her to continue. Catherine took a deep breath and folded her hands on her lap. Where to begin?

"I felt some connection with Geoffrey at our first meeting nigh on two years ago, but thought it more about our nearness in age. He spoke to me as no one here did, and seemed to be interested in my thoughts and concerns. You did the same, but it was different somehow with him."

The countess looked at her and nodded once more, but said nothing.

"We would meet on the back steps at the end of our day and tell each other stories. He answered my questions and guided me in those terrifying days on my first visits here. And—" she smiled as she remembered his cajoling "—he always made me promise to return again in spite of my fears of this place and all it involved."

"Catherine, I had no idea your fears ran so deep. You never spoke of them to me."

"I feared speaking of anything, my lady. The reverend mother warned me to never speak of my past or of who I really was, and I worried that any word spoken would give away those secrets. So 'twas easier to say nothing." She looked up and saw understanding in the eyes of her benefactress.

"He was so confident and accomplished and handsome even then. He goaded and prodded and was encouraging and happy. He was the first man…" She paused as a fleeting memory of her brother crossed her mind. "He was the first man to treat me in that way. And in spite of knowing from the beginning that we could not be together, I fell in love with him."

"These Dumont men are hard to resist." The lady smiled as she spoke. "Arrogant and prideful, but honorable and irresistible at the same time."

"Aye, just so."

"Go on, Catherine."

She stood and walked to the large window in one wall and looked out as she continued.

"Ever honorable, my lady. I believe he feels love for me, although we both skirt around speaking of it openly or candidly. We have cloaked our feelings in friendship, for we both know what is expected of us." Could her pain be heard in her words? The slicing sting of denied love hurt even now. "So, no promises were made other than that we would remain friends."

"And is it the knowledge of the responsibilities he has to his brother and his king that makes it possible for you to accept that he marry another?"

"Aye, my lady." She smiled again, despite the tears burning her throat and her eyes. "If things were other than they are, I would hope for something more between us. In spite of my present circumstances, I come from an old and noble family, one with previous ties to royalty on the Continent. But without those family ties, I know I am not suitable for the titles he will hold soon."

"Catherine, these arrangements were not made to deprive you of a future marriage. Indeed, with the dowry provided to you, a good marriage could be made for you."

"I know that the earl saved my life, my lady. And, contrary to my behavior at times, I appreciate everything he and you have done for me." Catherine turned to face her again. "There is a terror inside me when I think about marrying someone other than Geoffrey. I do not understand it and I cannot explain it, I just know that it is there."

The countess's face paled a bit as though she understood more than she would say. "And so the convent is your choice?"

"Aye, my lady. I will find some measure of contentment there. I have accepted this, even though it did not appear so this morn."

"This is a big decision, Catherine, one that should be about running to something and not running from something else. Do not think you must rush into taking your vows. Speak to Father Elwood. Speak even to my husband, who can be helpful when least expected. And know that you would always have a place here at Greystone or even at one of the other Harbridge estates if you needed it."

Catherine walked to the countess, took her hand and, bowing her head, touched her forehead to it. "I am more grateful than you will ever know." Stepping back, she wiped the tears from her eyes.

"One more question before we must join the others in the solar," the countess said, as she stood and smoothed out more of the wrinkles in her gown caused by her daughter wriggling on her lap. "Geoff knows of your love, but does he know of your plans?"

"Nay, my lady. He knows not and I would prefer it that way. He has enough to consider in these next weeks."

"When you had words the other night, you did not share this with him?"

So, they had been seen. The heat of a blush crept into her cheeks. "Nay, my lady."

"Then, may I ask of what you spoke?"

"He sought my help." She was reluctant to reveal Geoff's request.

"For? Come, Catherine, you need not fear giving me the truth of this."

"He asked my advice in choosing a wife."

The words hung in the air, with nothing but the sound of the countess's huff in reply.

"Men can be so…so…"

Lady Harbridge's hands fisted and released several times and her mouth opened and closed. She seemed to be having difficulty selecting a word, so Catherine offered several. "Stubborn? Exasperating? Stupid? Transparent?"

Laughing, the countess nodded in agreement with all of them. "Transparent? So you know his real reasons, then, for his request?"

"I know it is contrived, my lady. If I accept his request, it gives him an excuse to seek me out and it gives me a reason to be present for this time. We both know this is the last time we will see each other."

The countess's own heart broke at the situation, but if Catherine could accept it with such honor, then Emalie would support her in this. She reached out and lifted Catherine's chin.

"You demonstrate such honor and sense and true love in accepting this and in helping Geoffrey. Surely it will all turn out for the best." Before they both broke out in tears, Emalie knew she must do something. "Come now, Catherine. The women await us

in the solar and I would influence the advice you plan
to give him about his choice of wife.''

"A boon, my lady?''

"If it is in my power to grant you, Catherine, I
will.''

"Before I take my vows, would you give me the
truth of these last three years? The whole of it?''

Emalie could feel the smile leave her face, and
tried to simply nod in reply. But this was something
that was owed this young woman. "When that time
comes, Catherine, if you wish me to tell you, I will.
For now, though, will you accept my counsel and not
dwell on it?''

Catherine nodded in turn, but said nothing. She
opened the door and stood back, so that Emalie could
leave first. Alyce waited outside to accompany them
about their activities. Emalie thought to ask Catherine about attending the evening banquet, but decided
not to press for much more from the girl, given the
disclosures made in these last few minutes.

Walking down the stairs that led to the solar,
Emalie was disturbed that she had no way of helping
Catherine and Geoffrey's plight. For although she
was convinced that Catherine would make a wonderful wife for Geoff, she knew well the responsibilities he bore with the titles and lands he inherited,
and the people who would count on him for protection and their living.

Her husband had warned her not to get in the middle of this and she knew she must not. So, if everything in this matter was so clear, why did she feel so
miserable about its probable but necessary outcome?

## Chapter Six

He knew he should take this selection more seriously, but after spending most of his day chasing game and being chased, 'twas a difficult thing to do. Five cups of the special wine brought from Château d'Azure also made it difficult to keep all the details he'd learned about the women clear in his mind.

Melissande was the beautiful "fainter" from Quercy. Marguerite had brown hair and was from Brittany. Mathilde with her olive complexion and black hair came from near the land of the dark-skinned Moors. Maude was the one he'd met before at her father's court in Orleans, and so he remembered her without help. And the two *P* ladies were plump.

Geoff grimaced to himself. That was not completely true, but it helped him keep their names separate from the others. Phillippa had brown hair like his mother's cousin Phillip, and Petronilla was simply the other one.

Leaning back in his chair, he could look to his left and his right and see each of them. They smiled at

him, nodded and even preened before him. He had
danced with each one tonight, spoken to each, and
yet they still remained as a group in his thoughts.
Not one of them stood out as someone to marry.
None of them. This was not an auspicious beginning
to choosing a wife.

His gaze was drawn to the tables below, where
Luc and Fatin sat. Luc was laughing at something
his wife said, and as he moved closer to her, Geoff
could see Catherine. 'Twas a surprise, for she seldom
took part in meals like this one, usually withdrawing
whenever the hall was filled with more than just the
people of Greystone. Even from here, he could see
her discomfort. He looked around and noticed that
he was the only one studying her.

"Emalie?" he whispered to his sister-by-marriage.
"What did you threaten to get Catherine to attend
tonight?"

"I but invited her to join us, Geoff."

"I do not remember the last time she willingly ate
in the hall."

"Nor do I," his brother said, leaning into their
conversation. "I, too, wondered at her appearance
here tonight. Emalie?"

"I assure you, my lord, I but invited her to eat
with us. There is nothing nefarious in her sharing a
meal, is there?"

Not wanting to be the cause of, or in the middle
of, another disagreement between his brother and
Emalie, Geoff decided to take advantage of Catherine's presence and ask her to dance. Since he had
already danced with each of his prospective brides,
another dance with one would single that one out in

a way he did not wish to do. Dancing with Catherine would help him avoid that.

Standing as the musicians began playing a lively tune, he nodded to his brother and walked from the high table, down the steps to where Catherine sat. From the corner of his eye he saw Emalie grab at Christian's arm to keep him in his seat. It did not matter. Geoff had danced with many women in this hall in the past few years and this would be no declaration to anything or anyone.

He knew the significance of it—he would share, for the first and last time, a dance with the woman he loved. Only they need know the importance of this. He caught her gaze as he approached, and for a moment he thought she would run. She did not.

He held out his hand to her and waited. It took but a moment for her to place hers in his, but in that burst of time, he prayed and hoped as he never had before that she would grant him this favor. She did. He led her to the clearing on the floor where other couples lined up in preparation for the dance. Geoff purposely joined the line in the middle so that they were neither first nor last, for those dancers drew the eyes of onlookers.

Side by side, with hands in the air, they waited. He would not speak to her until the steps began, for conversations during the dance could be hidden behind turns and steps and bows. With much laughing and noise, the dance started and they moved along with the others.

"I feared you would refuse me this dance," he whispered as one of the steps brought them face-to-face for a few moments.

"I could not refuse you, my lord." Her enigmatic smile gave him no clue to her thoughts.

"My name is…" he began.

"My lord Dumont," she finished. He realized that others were straining to listen to their words.

The dance moved faster and they parted and returned several times before he could speak to her again. Her face was aglow from the exertion of the dance, and Geoff realized how lovely she was. The others struggled to put on a pleasing appearance for him, but Catherine did nothing to enhance her beauty.

"I do not remember seeing you dance before, Catherine."

"You have it aright, my lord. I have never danced before. Not here at Greystone, that is." She turned, their hands entwined, and they slid across the floor as one.

"And yet you know this dance?" She moved effortlessly with him, never appearing to count, as he did, to keep himself in step with the other dancers.

"I have watched it many, many times, my lord."

"I am pleased that you have allowed me to share your first dance…here at Greystone."

The words blurred together as he suddenly imagined the other things he would like to share with her. They had already shared their first forbidden kiss in the alcove the other night. Their first dance tonight. Unfortunately, for all his wanting, 'twas for naught, for this would be the end of what could be between them.

He lost his step in the dance and tripped, dragging Catherine with him. She stumbled, but he caught her with his arm around her waist. He enjoyed the moment of holding her in his arms, knowing that it and all contact with her would end soon.

He gritted his teeth and clenched even tighter the arms of the chair in which he sat. His wife flinched, so he knew she was watching the debacle unfold before their eyes. And if they noticed, then the rest of those at the high table saw it, as well.

"If you would stop growling, my lord, 'twould not draw everyone's attention," Emalie whispered as she lay her hand on top of his, most likely to mask his grip on the wood.

Christian Dumont was angry. In spite of his warnings, it would seem that his wife was meddling where she should not—following his orders only when she pleased.

"He should not be dancing with her in front of our guests."

"She is our guest, my lord," Emalie said through her own clenched teeth. "Worry not, for this means nothing."

"Your words do not reassure me, lady wife, for you said yourself that they are in love."

"The reverend mother wrote to me today that Catherine desires to take her vows, my lord. Catherine confirmed her intentions to me, as well. On Geoffrey's marriage, she returns to the convent to prepare herself. This is goodbye for them, Christian. Can you not permit them this moment together?" Her voice trembled as she pleaded for his permission.

He could never resist her pleas when they were so heartfelt. She did not know the full extent of the sit-

uation with Catherine and he would keep it from her
if he could. Allowing this little time, in front of so
many, would not be harmful. A niggling feeling in
his gut told him otherwise, but he ignored it for
Emalie's sake.

"Fine, lady wife. They may have their moment
for now. However, I would strongly suggest that you
convince Catherine to return to Lincoln sooner rather
than later."

He was about to stand, when Luc approached him
from behind, leaning down to whisper near his ear.
"Evesham's men recognize her."

"You are certain?"

"Aye, Chris. They saw her today and they watch
her even now." Luc gave a small nod of his head,
which Christian followed, spotting the men Luc
spoke about.

"Bloody hell." He leaned back and looked over
the room. Fatin still sat at the table where Geoffrey
would soon return with Catherine. "Have Fatin draw
her from the hall and make certain she is safe in her
room before coming to me."

"Aye, my lord," his man answered as he left.

Emalie sat stiffly next to him. She knew something
was happening, but did not know what or how to
inquire of him.

"I was afraid of just this when she came this time.
Would you return to our chambers so we might speak
there?"

Without waiting for her agreement, he motioned
to her maid to come to her. Rising now, he helped
Emalie from her seat and gestured for Alyce to ac-

company her. But before he rejoined her he had some arrangements of his own to make.

Confirming his worst suspicions, a few minutes later one of the men identified by Luc climbed up the dais and approached Lord Evesham. As one, they watched Catherine leaving the hall with Fatin and Luc.

Bloody, bloody hell.

'Twas all Christian could do not to scream out in anger at this. He had promised on his honor to protect de Severin's sister from Prince John, and now their masquerade had been found out. He'd let down his guard for a moment, reacting to his wife with his heart and not his good sense, and now Catherine was in danger.

The safest place for her was the convent. If the worst happened and John came to claim her, Christian would not be able to refuse a royal command. The reverend mother could. She could use the power of the church and her office at the convent to prevent John's actions…at least until something else could be done. Would Richard help in this matter? The king was on his lands in Normandy now, and too busy holding together the fragmented Plantagenet kingdom and plotting against Phillip to involve himself in the affairs of some girl wanted by his brother John.

Christian stood and took his leave of his guests. Seeing the captain of his guards in the hall, he motioned to the man to meet him outside. A small contingent of men, not sizable enough to draw notice, would escort Catherine back to the Convent of Our Blessed Lady in Lincoln on the morrow. With her safely ensconced there, Christian and Geoffrey could turn their attentions back to the reason his brother was there—to make a suitable marriage.

His most difficult task was still ahead of him, for he had to convince his wife of the rightness of his actions without giving her a full accounting of his actions in the past. 'Twould be much easier to honor his vow if the dead would only stay dead.

## Chapter Seven

He was in his chambers, preparing for an afternoon of hawking with the lady Marguerite and her retinue, when the call from his brother came. Albert, his steward, and Girard, the captain of his company of men, presented themselves at his door with Christian's request to join him in the solar. Geoff pulled off the heavy leather gauntlet and left it with the page assigned to him to take to the stables.

"Why did my brother have you bring this message to me?" he asked of his steward.

"I know not, my lord. Only that we were summoned and told to come with you."

This was very strange, but they would arrive in the solar in a few minutes and he would have his answers. As they walked down the corridor, Geoff noticed a messenger sitting on a bench outside the solar. From the livery he wore—three golden lions on a red field—Geoff knew he was from the king. Visibly exhausted and covered with dirt from what must have been a grueling journey, the man stood at Geoffrey's approach and began to speak. Christian interrupted before he could do so.

"Geoffrey, come in. If you would grant me a few moments with the marquis before you speak to him?" he asked the messenger.

Geoff watched as the man nodded and sank back on the bench.

"Colby, see to his needs." Christian moved back for Geoff to enter the solar, but stopped his men with a whispered word. The door closed and Geoff turned to face his brother.

"I wanted to speak to you in private before you receive the king's messenger."

"So, 'tis from the king then?" He could feel the level of tension in Chris growing, and wondered at its source.

"Aye." Christian paused and walked over to one of the high-backed chairs near the hearth. Sitting down, he rubbed his face with his hand several times before speaking again. Although tempted to rush him, Geoff waited for the news he knew must be bad.

"I wanted you to hear this from me."

Geoff walked closer. "Go on then and tell me."

"I have sent Catherine back to the convent."

"You what?"

"I sent her back to Lincoln this morn. 'Tis for her own good that I did so, Geoff."

He felt his blood begin to heat. Did his brother not trust him to honor his word? Or did he suspect that their true feelings lay beneath the surface, ready to push through?

"Her own good? Explain this to me, Chris. How is this punishment of her for her own good?"

"She is not who you think her to be," Christian began, pouring a cup of wine from the pitcher on the table between them. Holding it out to him, he continued, "She is not who most think her to be."

"Then who is she?" Geoff took the cup and drank from it as Christian poured his own and took a swig.

"She is Catherine de Severin, sister of William."

"You told me she was Emalie's cousin, an orphan who needed sanctuary. Wait! You killed de Severin...."

"Aye. And I promised on his death that I would protect his sister from Prince John. She was the instrument of William's downfall, and I pledged to him on the field, even as I struck the death blow that took his life, that I would see to her care."

Geoffrey huffed out his breath, feeling as though Christian had punched him in the gut. He dropped the cup on the table and it wobbled precariously before settling. "That is the basis of your hatred for her? The reason why you treat her so roughly when she is here?"

"I do not hate her, Geoff. I am not happy that Emalie brings her here. I think of her brother and all of his evil when I see her, and I admit to not being able at times to separate her from him." He sat back in his chair and looked at the ceiling. "But I do not hate her."

Catherine was de Severin's sister? 'Twas difficult to accept that her goodness was connected to that villain, who had nearly succeeded in destroying everything here in Greystone Castle, including its lady. No, this did not make sense. How could Emalie befriend Catherine, indeed even create a link that did not exist, with the sister of the man who had dishonored her and tried to seize her lands and titles on Prince John's behalf? How could Catherine keep the truth from him?

"But how could Emalie accept her if she is de Severin's sister? I do not know all of it, but I know that he tried to claim Emalie and Greystone...."

Chris sighed and met his gaze. "Emalie feels a kind of bond with Catherine, since both of them were caught in John's web of deceit. She is content in her life and would see that same contentment in Catherine's, so she works with the reverend mother to encourage her and give her the opportunities that were stolen from her."

"And all of this in secret?"

"It must be so, Geoff. John is not known for accepting defeat well nor for allowing his plans to fail. He is ever questing for revenge on those who cross him. Until now, John believed that I'd had her killed on the same morning I killed her brother in battle."

"Until now?" A sick feeling grew in his stomach.

"One of Evesham's vassals was involved in her imprisonment and one of his men recognized her yesterday. Evesham saw her last night and even now sends a messenger to John. Her only safety is at the convent."

"There is another way.". Geoff knew marriage to himself could protect her as well. "I could—"

"Nay," Christian shouted. "Do not even say the words, for I will not consider them." He pushed himself up from his chair and began to pace the room. "She has no wealth. She has no family. She brings nothing to a marriage but herself and the small dowry

I have set aside for her. She is unsuitable. You must marry one of the women from the Continent in order to strengthen our claim and our position between the Plantagenets and the Capets.''

''The de Severins were a noble family. I could do worse in choosing a bride.'' Geoff could feel the emotions seething in his brother. How could he convince him of the rightness of a match with Catherine?

''The de Severins were wiped off the face of the earth three years ago by me, in order to protect what is mine and what will be yours. To admit now that she lives will be exposing my actions and my honor to disrepute, and that is something I will not do. I risked my life and saved yours to regain all that we lost because of our father's treachery against Richard. I will not stand here and see you threaten all I have worked for because you think that love is sufficient reason to bring her back from the dead.''

Christian had it right, at least in part. He had risked all to reclaim their name, their lands and their honor. If Chris was correct, the unstable situation on the Continent would continue and worsen. The pope had made his feelings about the unrest and fighting and destruction known, as had most of the various princes, dukes and counts who ruled the lands. Now, a strong alliance with one of the heiresses from one of the provinces held by Capet vassals would allow the Dumonts to keep their lands and titles no matter which king controlled the country.

But if this was at the cost of a woman's past and future, how could it be honorable? Why did Catherine have to suffer and lose all because of the battle among the royal families?

"I do love her, Chris. I know that for a certainty."

His brother stopped and stared at him from across the room.

"And it is not right nor honorable to make her to pay for the sins of her brother." Geoff glared back, his anger over Catherine's treatment growing. But he tried to offer a compromise. "If we tell no one her true identity, she will be acceptable as Emalie's relation. The de Severin girl died three years ago and can remain dead."

"I have done all that I can to keep her safe. She has been educated and thrives in her new life, Geoff. She has accepted her future, and now you as well must make your decision."

"I have made my decision, Chris. I would have her to wife. And if I must relinquish that which you hold for me now, so be it. She may not be suitable for the Comte de Langier, but she is more than acceptable for the second son of Guillaume Dumont."

"But she will not have you."

Geoff shot up from his seat and was in front of Chris in a few strides. Leaning in until they were face-to-face, Geoff clenched his hands into fists.

"She loves me."

"Emalie has assured me that you love each other, Geoff. But Catherine has accepted her life as it is and is not willing to become the weapon that tears us apart. She will take her vows when she returns to the convent."

"A nun? She becomes a nun?" Stunned by this revelation, Geoff reeled back. "She did not tell me."

"Emalie said that Catherine has talked with the

reverend mother and confirmed that this was to be her final visit to Greystone.''

''Nay,'' he whispered, finding it difficult to breathe, let alone speak. Was it his heart that pained him so?

Christian placed his hand on Geoff's shoulder. ''Come, brother. Surely you knew. Your visits here after your marriage will be few and not frequent. Hers will be fewer still.''

Geoff took in a deep breath and let it out. He had admitted to himself that his life would change after this time at Greystone. He knew it. A part of him deep inside even knew he would marry elsewhere. That painful truth, as well as the knowledge that he could not turn his back on what his brother had done for him, what he had done for their family name and honor, even what he had done for Catherine so far, made Geoff face the responsibilities he knew were his own. He finally shook his head.

''She will be safe at the convent?''

''Aye. My protection extends to it. And the reverend mother can be quite the lioness when one of hers is threatened.''

Geoff walked to one of the windows in the chamber and looked out at the courtyard below. Although the keep was busier than normal because of the number of guests, life went on as usual. His entire world had just shifted in a different direction, but everything moved on. Acknowledging that his would proceed without Catherine, he shook his head and looked at Chris.

''So long as she is safe, I will be at peace with this.''

He said the words, but the acceptance was not there yet. 'Twould take some time to adjust to this. He had not had a chance to say goodbye to Catherine and he regretted that. He would never hear her explanation for keeping secrets even from him.

''If we are done with this matter, the king's messenger awaits you.'' At his questioning look, Chris clarified, ''I have already received him and read the message for me. I know not if yours will be the same or different.'' He walked toward the door of the solar.

'''Twere not good tidings then?'' At his brother's dark look, he feared the worst. ''A call to arms?''

When Christian didn't answer, Geoff waited for the messenger to enter and present himself. Albert, Girard and Luc as well as Walter, the captain of Greystone's men-at-arms, followed the man into the chamber. Geoff stood, while Christian sat.

''My lord, King Richard bade me to bring his greetings and warmest regards to you. Here is his letter, which he entreats you to answer with as much haste as is possible.'' With a flourish and bow, the messenger held out to Geoff a folded parchment, from the bottom of which hung the king's royal seal.

''Where is the king now?''

''I left him in Normandy, my lord.'' When Geoff frowned at the man, he added, ''In Caen.''

Geoffrey inspected the seal and opened the letter. After profuse greetings and pledges of support, the real issue of the letter was made—Richard was mustering troops and wanted his loyal vassal to join him immediately in Caen. Geoff was admonished not to let the choosing of a bride interfere with his quick response. The king had written: "Bring the lady of your heart, the one who would be the new Countess de Langier, with you in all haste to present her to us. She will be accepted as your choice and you will accede to your titles if you support my actions by your presence and by that of your knights."

With everyone waiting for his reaction, Geoff was careful not to show any. Whatever the king planned, it was sufficiently important for Richard to negate that part of the agreement with the Dumonts that gave Christian control of whom Geoff was to marry, and that held off his accession until later this year, after such marriage. This was a test of Geoff's decision-making abilities, for the king manipulated better men than the fledgling count of Langier.

"Are you summoned as well?" he asked his brother.

"Either I and ten of my knights, or a necessary amount of my gold must be delivered to Richard within a month. He knows I wish not to leave Emalie now, so he gives me the choice," Christian answered. "What does he ask of you?"

"The king desires that I meet him in Caen, but that I send my knights to Château Gaillard within the month." He hedged a bit and did not give a full reply. Geoff was not certain what he would do about selecting a bride, but he liked knowing that he controlled that now.

There was silence in the chamber as each thought about the orders they'd received. Christian looked at him expectantly, as though waiting for more, but Geoff kept the rest of the missive to himself. A month did not give him much time to return to his lands, collect his knights and travel back up to Normandy to meet the king. Geoffrey knew he must leave quickly, even this day.

The others in the room waited for their lords' orders now.

"Will you transport my contribution to the king?" Christian finally asked, breaking the silence.

"Aye. When will it be ready?"

Christian looked at his men, who both nodded at his unasked question, and then back to Geoff. "I will have it here by this time on the morrow."

Geoff was about to go and make his own arrangements when his brother stopped him.

"This must be kept quiet. The allies and vassals of Phillip are all about us and I would not want the king's plans known too soon. 'Twould be wiser if I were to appear to send you on a mission to one of our other properties while I continue to negotiate with those here."

Geoffrey nodded at his wisdom, realizing it was a sound plan. "Does Emalie know of the king's summons and the cost of it going unanswered?"

"Nay, and I would not have her know of this yet." Christian met the gaze of each of the men and made his point clear. "These are the affairs of men and kings, and not for her to worry about."

They were brave words, but Geoff did not doubt for a moment that Christian would pay for them when the countess was apprised of the situation. Some things had not changed between the earl and his wife in their three years of marriage, and Geoffrey had witnessed it before. It would not be an enjoyable scene to watch unfold.

A sense of excitement grew within him as he re-alized that, although this wouldn't be his first battle, it was the first time he'd been called upon as a vassal to the king. The first time he would defend his king under his own banner. Geoff waved his hand, ges-turing for Albert and Girard to follow him. He wanted to have a private discussion with them about his arrangements, mayhap even send Albert and an-other on ahead to Château d'Azure to prepare for their arrival and the needs for their march north to Normandy.

To keep this out of the sight of those who might report the movement of vassals and knights, he would need to keep up the marriage-mart activities and his wooing of each of the women here. And since the choice of a wife was now in his own hands, he decided to take a closer look at the ladies Melis-sande, Marguerite, Maude, Mathilde, Phillippa and Petronilla.

He sent word to the lady Marguerite, apologizing for his delay, and promised to be there presently to have their afternoon of hawking. He'd broken his fast with Maude, he'd walked the gardens with Mathilde, he planned to take Phillippa on a tour of the battle-ments of the keep before supper and he would end his wooing with Melissande at supper and Petronilla at the morning meal. That would not work, he real-ized, since the *P* ladies favored not the morn. He would sit with Petronilla at supper and Melissande in the morn. Then, with a clearer idea of whom he should marry, he would leave under the king's orders and ask Christian to complete the arrangements.

With his plans made, Geoff instructed his men to

be ready to depart in the morning, and then went to the mews to meet Lady Marguerite. Mayhap the strenuous work of hawking and paying court to five other women would tire him out and help him ignore the heaviness of his heart, now that Catherine was gone from his life.

# Chapter Eight

"I will have Marguerite of Brittany to wife."

If Christian was surprised by his brother's quick decision, he did not show it. They stood in a small chamber off the great hall and made final preparations for the journey and the transport of Harbridge gold to Richard in Caen. Christian had decided to send several knights after all, so their traveling party was made larger by four. Two were knights from the Dumont estates who wished to return home, and the other two were English knights who had never traveled to the Continent and wanted this opportunity.

The gold was loaded onto several packhorses and sent ahead of Geoff's men, so as to not draw too much attention. They would catch up within a few hours and travel down the coast, then by sea to La Rochelle, and finally inland through part of Brittany to Château d'Azure. The journey would take nearly a fortnight and the march up to Normandy would take another. Even using the available rivers to shorten the journey, Geoff would reach Richard just before his deadline to do so.

"Send me word of Richard's plans and I can see to the arrangements." His brother held out his hand and Geoff grasped it tightly.

"If I have your permission, I would like to tell Emalie before I leave. Unless she is ill?" His sister-by-marriage had not been present in the hall this morn, and no mention had been made of her. He suspected other causes, but thought that childbearing might be taking its toll on her.

Chris released him and began muttering under his breath. Finally, he looked up and met his brother's gaze. "You may tell her, since she will hear nothing I say."

"She is angry over the gold?"

"No, there is no question of her compliance in that matter," he said, waving his hand and shaking his head. "She is furious at other things I've done." His brother looked more miserable than pleased, so Geoff could only wonder at what had transpired between him and Emalie.

"Is she in the solar or her chambers?"

"She has vowed not to cooperate with any of my efforts and will not leave her chambers." Chris sank into one the chairs next to a table. "You will find her there."

Geoff nodded and stepped away. Chris stood and they walked through the door together.

"Godspeed in your travels, brother, and in the coming battles."

"And to you in yours, my lord," Geoff answered. "I fear yours are no less dangerous than mine."

"'Ware your head when you open her door."

Geoff laughed, not without a full measure of sympathy for his brother, and strode through the corridor and up the stairs leading to the lady's chambers in the corner tower. He knocked on it and waited for an answer before entering. Emalie stood and rushed to him, greeting him with much enthusiasm.

"You go to do your duty with the king? You must truly be excited."

She seemed to understand his thoughts and he nodded in agreement. "'Tis an honor to be called as vassal to aid the king in his plans."

"Pah! Stupid men killing other stupid men, and for what gains?" She shouted her question, but before he could answer, she did it for him. "More land, more wealth, more power. It never changes."

"Is this argument with me, my lady, or did I enter someone else's?"

This appeared to lessen her anger and she let out a breath. "Your pardon, Geoff, for my outburst. 'Tis someone else's battle indeed."

Now he did feel sorry for his brother. Whatever the issue of this fight, 'twould not go well for Christian until he settled things with his wife. And the strange symptoms of breeding seemed to make the countess even more emotional and less willing to listen to reason.

"I will keep you in my thoughts and prayers and wish you much success in your endeavors for the king."

"My thanks, Emalie, for all of your work on my behalf. How long will you have to suffer the presence of the brides?"

"Until you and Christian make a decision or until

word of your departure and Richard's summons is known.''

''Chris wants to delay knowledge of my departure for as close to a sennight as possible. Can you endure that long?''

''I am ever the dutiful wife to my lord husband, fulfilling his every command.''

He winced at the sarcasm in her voice. Things were not good between the Earl and Countess of Harbridge. The blame for this was partly his, and Geoff wondered if the news of his decision would make things better or worse. And he feared having her anger aimed in his direction.

''Emalie, I have made a choice.''

''And does my lord husband agree with your decision? Is she suitable as a Dumont bride?''

His eye twitched at her tone again. So, 'twas not about the gold. It was about the bride choice.

''Marguerite of Brittany.''

The silence between them grew as Emalie turned and looked out the window of her chamber. Not sure what to do, he waited for her response.

''I wish you both well in this match.'' Her words were the correct ones, but there was no feeling of warmth or support for his choice.

''Emalie, how have I offended you?'' he asked as he approached where she stood. She turned to him now and met his gaze. ''What could I do differently?''

The fight left her and her shoulders slumped at his words. ''There is no offense given by you, Geoff. You do what we were both raised to do—carry out our responsibilities no matter the cost. 'Tis the way of things.''

''Are you not happy with your marriage to my brother?'' At her look, he added, ''I know that there is some difficulty between you now, but before this were you not happy? Do you not love him as he loves you?''

''Yes,'' she answered begrudgingly. ''Do you love her?''

''Marguerite? Nay, there is no love between us. Did you love Christian when you married him? I seem to remember it differently.'' Geoff had been present for part of their first year of marriage and he did not remember love between them. Sometimes there was not even civility. ''At least she will accompany me to my home and I will not have to take hers.'' The words escaped before he could stop them. Emalie's eyes glazed over for a moment, then cleared and met his.

'''Tis right you are, Geoff. I did not accept your brother nor his right to my home easily. I loathed all that he did when he took my father's place in this very hall. 'Twas not an easy way to begin.''

''Marguerite does not seem to loathe me, so mayhap we will deal well with each other in marriage. What think you?''

Emalie was in his arms, hugging him, in a moment. ''You will do well together. She is the only one of the women here with any backbone, and you Dumont men need someone able to stand up to your arrogance, yet she is compassionate at the same time. I have seen her dealings with her parents, her maids, even with children, and I think she will do well as your wife.''

Geoff was overwhelmed by her words. Feeling the lash of an insult wrapped in compliment confused him. But apparently she was pleased with his choice.

He stepped back from her embrace. ''I must go now, Emalie. Keep safe and be well.'' He walked to the door and opened it. ''And make peace with my brother, for you know you do not want this discord between you over something that can never be and something that even I have accepted.''

''Will you marry at the Château or in Vannes?''

''I have not thought on it. That is something to be worked out in the agreements, but first I must see to my king's wishes.''

''I would like… I mean, I am certain my lord husband would like to host a celebration here in honor of your marriage.''

''When all things are settled, I would like that, sister.''

She smiled then through her tears, and he took his leave. His brother and she would surely clear up their argument and they would be of one accord again. Geoff was certain of it, since he knew they did have the bond of love between them.

He took his leather gloves from his belt and pulled them on as he walked down to meet with his men and leave. He was nearing the main floor when he spied Baron Evesham entering a small alcove with a man Geoff did not know. Stepping softly, he listened to their words. Luc had told him of Evesham's camaraderie with Prince John, and this furtive meeting reeked of something not right. Geoff approached with caution and stayed a few yards from where they met.

"She is back at the convent," the other man whispered.

"Are you certain?" the baron demanded.

"Aye, milord. I saw 'er enter the gates meself."

"Did you send word to the prince as I ordered?"

"Aye, milord, just as ye said to."

"If you are wrong or lose her again, I will inform His Highness that you are the one who lost her the first time. Do you understand me?" The sounds emanating from the alcove told Geoff that Evesham was pushing or shoving the man.

"I do, I do, milord! Forgive me, milord. She were screaming terrible that day and the one, 'e cuffed 'er on 'er 'ead and she crumpled, she did. She looked dead, she did, when they carried her out. 'Ow was I to know she weren't?"

"You fool! Hear me now, for a mistake could cost both of us much. Take those three that saw her in the forest with you, and meet the prince's men at the convent. They will recognize her and not let her slip away again."

Geoffrey held his breath. They spoke of Catherine! She was not safe in the convent, for John was on his way there and would do what he had to do to get back something or someone he wanted.

None of this made sense to him, but he knew that the prince took whatever he wanted. He remembered vaguely that John's threats were at the heart of what had brought him and Christian to Greystone three years ago.

He checked to ensure no one was nearby, then left

the keep in the opposite direction from where Evesham and his man still spoke. Walking into the bright sunlight, Geoffrey saw his men near the stables and headed toward them. He thanked God that they were wearing their mail and he his, for they could leave immediately. He took the reins from the stable boy and mounted his horse in one leap.

"We ride," he called out in a loud voice, and kicked the sides of his horse to push for a gallop.

He and this group of knights had traveled and fought together before, and he knew they could sustain a hard pace for as long as their mounts held up. Familiar with the forest and the smaller roads surrounding Greystone, Geoff knew he could reach the convent on the outskirts of Lincoln before Evesham's men could.

He would wait until they were closer to their destination and then tell the men what his plan was. The only thing he could think about was that Catherine was in danger and he had to get there to protect her.

He must.

He did not know all that had happened in the past, but he could not allow Catherine to pay yet again for the weaknesses and sins of her brother. Christian Dumont had promised her protection, and Geoff would carry out that promise. No harm would come to her while he still had life or breath.

## Chapter Nine

Beads of perspiration rolled down her brow and her back as she toiled in the rear section of garden. In spite of the large trees that spread their shade over most of the plots, the heat of the day, combined with having her head covered with a sturdy kerchief and wearing long sleeves, made for a sweaty afternoon. But Catherine did the work cheerfully, allowing the peace and monotony of it to lull her into a state of calm.

After so many days of upset, so much time spent worrying, she felt wondrously good to be at peace with the decision she'd made. She and the reverend mother had spent most of the previous day in discussion and prayer, and now Catherine believed she could accept the way her life would go. Even though Mother Heloise did not completely agree that her vocation was a true one, Catherine would stay until the abbess was convinced, then take her vows. The Gilbertines allowed lay men and women to dwell among them, so not being accepted as a novice immediately posed no problem.

Catherine sat back on her heels and blotted her forehead and face with the edge of her sleeve. Looking at the expanse of unweeded garden, she knew there was plenty of work ahead of her.

*And 'twas a safe place to hide away.*

Where had that thought come from? Was she hiding? Catherine picked up the small spade near her and plunged it into the moist soil, loosening some tangled weeds. Not really hiding, she decided, but she had removed herself from the center of several battles.

Summoned by the earl, she had answered his call early yesterday morn. From the raised voices within their chamber, Catherine had known she was the cause of some deep dissension between the earl and countess. She had waited a moment or two before knocking on their door, long enough to know that her presence was inflaming many tempers. Surprisingly though, her audience with the earl was one of the calmer ones she'd had in her several years of visiting the Dumont household.

With his voice low and his tone even, the earl had explained that the danger he had sought to keep her from had come back, and that she must return to the convent until he could deal with it. He'd said that he could not tell her all of the details, but she had his word that this danger was real and impending.

Catherine had never doubted his word, and was convinced he spoke the truth. Truly though, it was the look of terror on the countess's face that had persuaded her more thoroughly than any words spoken.

Chills moved down her arms and back at the memory of the haunted gaze of Emalie Dumont. As their eyes met, Catherine had felt fear within the countess. The scariest was that Catherine had known the fear was for her and not the countess herself. She'd nearly tripped running to her side....

"My lady, you are not well," she said, kneeling beside her.

"I will be well when I know you are safe within the convent walls." Lady Harbridge reached out and touched a cold hand to her cheek. "Do as my lord husband advises, Catherine. Please."

"Can you speak of this danger, my lady? Make me understand?"

"No," the earl and countess said together, though the earl's voice was more emphatic. The lady looked to her husband, then away from both of them, allowing him to answer.

"Catherine, this is for your own good. I know you do not remember all that brought you into my care, but I promised to keep you from danger and I will honor that promise."

"My lord, tell me what I do not remember. Please!" Tears filled her eyes and made her throat burn.

"I know you think I hate you, but I do not. Indeed, when you know the truth, it is you who will hate me." His voice was the kindest it had ever been, and the urge to weep filled her. "But we have not the time to expose all our truths now. Your safety depends on your quick return to the convent. There will be time enough later to ask your questions."

The countess would not look at her or speak, and Catherine shivered in fear. She rose to her feet, looking at the earl and then his wife. Nodding, she waited on his orders.

"Sir Walter will take you back himself. He awaits you in the side courtyard. Gather only what you need for the journey, and the countess will arrange for the rest of your belongings to be delivered to you."

"Aye, my lord," she said, bowing her head before him. This might be the last time to calm the niggling doubts within her, and so she asked him directly, "My lord, is this about the love I bear for your brother?"

He strode to where she stood, and a part of her was tempted to cower. Instead she met his steely gaze and waited for his answer. The earl looked at his wife once before replying to her question and the challenge within it.

"I promised your brother that I would see to your protection, Catherine. That is what this is about—my word of honor given and kept."

Her brother? She knew that the earl had killed her brother. Gossip had revealed that fact during one of her first visits here, but she kept the knowledge to herself and did not ever ask about it. She knew no details except that there had been a challenge made and accepted, and her brother had died in the fight.

Why would Christian Dumont promise anything to the man who had caused such mayhem for his and the Montgomerie families? In truth, she did not remember much of William. He'd left when she was still a child, going off with the sons of other nobles to make his way in the world and to seek whatever diversions and challenges he could. He was a stranger to her when she went to live with him after their parents' deaths. He'd left her in the care of servants until the day he'd summoned her to... To where? She did not remember.

The earl's explanation caused more questions, but he had told her there was no time. If he had shared this truth with her, could she not share one of her own in gratitude for his efforts on her behalf?

"My lord, I would have you know that I do not wish to come between you and your brother. I have no intention of declaring my love for him or making him choose between me and the responsibilities he carries for you and your family."

She watched as a look of satisfaction passed between Lady and Lord Harbridge. Obviously, the concern that she would cause a conflict between the brothers was one they held, and hopefully one that she had calmed.

It was then, with a quick and wordless farewell to the countess, that she found herself escorted back to the convent and, after a long night, was now working the garden in the heat of the day....

Tearing loose another hardy green weed, she threw it in the pile she was gathering, and reached for yet another.

A commotion near the main building of the convent drew her attention, for it was so out of place here. Loud voices, men's voices and the sounds of weapons. Weapons? Swords? Here? Brushing the dirt from her hands, she stood and watched as the reverend mother came running toward her, followed by armor-clad knights.

Catherine could not move. Although Mother Heloise's face was anxious, she did not seem overly upset by the interruption to their daily routine of prayer and work. Holding her spade almost as a weapon, Catherine waited.

"Catherine, you need to come with me."

"But Mother," she said, as she watched the knights walk closer, "who are these men and what is happening?"

The tallest man drew nearer and lifted his helmet from his head. When he'd pushed his mail coif off his head, she blinked at the sight of Geoffrey Dumont before her. The other knight revealed himself and she recognized the captain of Geoffrey's guards, Girard. Geoffrey came closer and took her hand.

"Catherine, please accompany us into the reverend mother's chambers. We must speak." She must have given the impression of refusing or delaying, for he whispered, "Now. Quickly."

She nodded and allowed him to lead her with his hand on her arm. The tension in his body and in his manner was obvious, and she kept pace as best she could with his long strides, moving into the building that housed the main chapel, the reading rooms, the kitchens and dining halls, and the abbess's chambers. He did not pause as his man took up a position next to the door and waited for them to pass. Strangely, she noticed that he stepped in front of the doorway as Geoffrey closed it behind them.

Released from his grasp, she took the chair before Mother Heloise's table and waited for him to speak.

"Catherine, I am under orders from the king to return to him in Normandy. I want you to come with me."

She gasped. No words would come to her in response to his request. Her mouth dropped open, but she could not speak.

"We do not have much time, for you are in danger here. Mother Heloise is content with my explanation and the truth of my words. Will you come with me now?"

Stunned at his invitation, but still not understanding it, she finally forced out a reply. "Where, my lord? Why?"

He pulled a stool over and sat before her, so close that the size of him blocked everything from her view. She had never seen him so decisive, so focused, so forceful.

"King Richard has summoned me to meet him at Château Gaillard for some purpose as yet unexplained. He has granted me full use of my titles and powers as Comte de Langier and—" he paused and lowered his face nearer to hers before continuing "—my choice of wife."

"He must want something from you badly if he offers you all that," she said without thinking.

Geoffrey's expression lightened a bit and he smiled at her. "'Tis the way of kings, Catherine. They grant you all that is already yours so that they can command your obedience and cooperation."

"What must you do?"

He took her hand in his and entwined their fingers in a most inappropriate way, considering where they were and who was witness to his actions. But Catherine could not bear to let go.

"I must bring my wife to him and probably fight Phillip of France with him."

Confused, she tried to sort out her thoughts. What

was he asking her? "Do you wish me to accompany you and serve the woman you choose as wife?"

"Nay, Catherine," he whispered. Touching his roughened palm to her cheek, he lifted her face until she looked into his eyes. "I wish *you* to be my wife."

For one endless moment, she let the words go through her and imagined that all she had dreamed of would come to pass. She closed her eyes and saw them together in the sunny valley he had described to her so many times. His main estate, the Château d'Azure, named for the blue glow of the stones when the sunlight reflected off of the nearby lake and river and hit the glass-like finish, sat high on one hill facing the entrance to the valley. Rich, abundant fields surrounded the castle and several villages dotted the countryside. His castle...his lands...his wife?

Her reverie ended when he squeezed her hand, and she stared at Geoffrey. A feeling of distance grew and soon she felt as though she were watching this scene from somewhere else, that someone else was speaking.

"Nay, my lord. It cannot be," she said, pushing away from him. "Your brother surely objects to your choice."

Geoffrey stood and looked at Mother Heloise. Turning back to her, he answered her doubts. "Although the king's orders supersede even my brother's wishes, Lord Harbridge does not disagree with my choice in a wife."

She blinked at his declaration. His gaze did not falter, but she noticed his cheeks pulsing as he clenched his teeth tightly. This made no sense at all.

"I know that this must be a shock to you," Mother Heloise said from behind Geoffrey, "but we must act with all haste. The count transports valuables to the king and must be on his way. Even now his men await you outside the gates."

Catherine stood on shaking legs and looked at her mentor. "You know the earl's mind and heart on the subject of his brother's marriage, Reverend Mother. How can this be?"

Before the nun could respond, Geoffrey interrupted. "I spoke with him at length yesterday and again this morn after receiving the king's orders, Catherine. I named my bride and he did not object."

"But my lord—" she began.

"Geoffrey. You must call me Geoffrey."

"Geoffrey, surely the other women are more suitable for you. I bring nothing to you in marriage. We cannot do this."

He stepped closer and took her hand once more. "Do you love me, Cate?"

She could not speak, so she simply nodded.

"Do you promise to obey me and live with me and give me children if God grants them to us?" He pulled her closer to him until their mouths almost touched. "Do you, Catherine?"

"Geoffrey, we must not," she said, shaking her head at his impossible request. "You do not know—"

"I know that I love you, Cate. I know that I have the king's permission to take you as my wife. If you love me as I think you do, you will give me the words I need to make us one."

Her love for him overwhelmed whatever vestige

of sense and foreboding she had, and she let the words come. "I do promise, my lord…Geoffrey. If you would have me as wife, I would have you as husband." He tilted his head down until she felt the heat of his mouth on hers. His lips moved over hers in a gentle kiss.

"Are you satisfied, Mother?" he asked, turning to the nun who was observing their every move.

"Catherine, is it your free choice to join with Geoffrey Dumont in marriage?"

Unable to understand how this was coming to pass, yet unwilling to give up the hope that it was indeed happening, she nodded to the nun. "Aye, Mother," she sighed, "'tis my choice."

"Then, child, come, for we must sign the betrothal documents so that you can be on your way."

"Betrothal?" she asked, as Geoffrey opened the door and spoke an order to his man. "Now?"

"Catherine, you cannot accompany the count unless there is a formal agreement, one that offers you the protection of his name and provides for you in the event of his death. I will not permit you to leave here in his care and custody until this is settled and the count has agreed. Here, now, is the priest who will bless your betrothal, and I will stand witness to it." The nun's tone left no room for disagreement, and in a way Catherine was comforted that the reverend mother still acted to protect and care for her.

Feeling as though she moved through a dream, Catherine watched as the room filled with not one, but three priests, a clerk who took a seat at the table and began to write, the reverend mother's assistant abbess and two of Geoffrey's men. Words were spoken in Latin, and if she could have paid attention she would have understood them. Looking from person to person, she noticed every face wore a different expression, from happy to complacent to accepting to questioning to...only Geoffrey smiled as she turned to him.

"Trust me, Cate. All will be well," he whispered as the priest droned on.

"I do trust you, Geoffrey. I trust you completely." She answered him in a whisper so as to not disturb the words being spoken over them. She knew in her heart that she could trust him with her life. At her statement, his smile slipped slightly, but he squeezed the hand he held.

Soon, a quill was held out to them and Geoffrey took it, signing his name with a flourish. Catherine's hand shook when she reached for the sharpened feather pen, but he wrapped his fingers around hers and helped her. Then the reverend mother and the priests and other witnesses followed them in marking the contract. Still in a daze, she felt the touch of Geoffrey's lips once more to seal the bargain, and then they were announced as man and wife in the eyes of the church.

Another knight entered the now crowded room and waved to Geoffrey. "A quarter hour at most, my lord," he called out. At his words, everyone in the room moved, scurrying in different directions, until they were alone once more with the reverend mother.

"Catherine, would you check to see if Sister Anne has brought your belongings for the trip to your husband's home?"

Determined to enjoy this dream until the very moment she awakened from it, she nodded in agreement. She did not understand how this had come to be, but she would accept this intervention in her life as a gift.

Geoffrey released her hand and guided her to the door. As she reached to turn the knob, she realized that she had never washed her hands, and had gone through the most important moment of her life covered in dirt.

# Chapter Ten

"Do not disappoint me, my lord." The reverend mother's expression turned from warm to sternly cold as soon as Catherine left the room.

"I do not plan to, Mother," he answered. Not happy that she questioned his integrity, he continued, "I will guard her from all dangers."

"Ah, but can you guard her from yourself and the damage you can do to her?" The nun moved from her place by the hearth and approached him. "Neither of you know her past, and yet you would gamble on her future. I fear she will be caught between when the truth comes out."

Without the luxury of time, he could not engage in a long conversation, and yet he wanted to know the past that haunted Catherine. She had been a victim of the prince's machinations, he knew. What more was there?

"Then tell me quickly what I must know to protect her." He moved to the door and reached for the knob, intent on leaving at once before the prince's men could arrive and capture her.

"Will you stand up to your brother for her?"

He let out an exasperated breath and ran his hand through his hair. "I have done that."

"Nay, my lord. So far you have used subterfuge and some lies to gain her hand. When the truth is known, will you stand with her against your brother and the king?"

"I have not lied in this, Mother. You saw the documents that give me title and power and the choice of wife. The king's word—"

"What name did you give your brother this morn as the woman you would marry?" The reverend mother's words were whispered, but they carried the force of a shout.

He had not lied; he had simply omitted the truth.

"Does not the end justify the means we use to get to it if 'tis an honorable one? I will marry her. I will stand by her, no matter who or what appears in our way." A stab of fear and doubt and foreboding struck his heart as he said the words. He drew a deep breath and changed the direction of their words. "John's men are on their way here and I must get her away now."

"I allowed this to go forward because I believe your intentions are good and that your love for her is true. But my son," she said, placing her hand on his, "the powers of evil can be strong, and overwhelm even the best of intentions. In spite of all that she has seen and lived through, she comes to you pure of spirit and heart. Do not use her as the weapon others have. Do not destroy her in your quest to prove yourself against others."

A loud banging on the door interrupted whatever

else they might say. "I must go, Mother, but you have my word that she will be safe."

"Go with God, then." She made the sign of the cross in front of him and followed him out of the building into the small courtyard. Catherine already sat on a large horse, looking very fragile and yet undaunted. The nun went to her and whispered some words as Geoffrey gave his last orders to his men. He knew well the three knights who stayed with him to bring Catherine to safety.

Their route had changed now, and instead of traveling down the coast and across to La Rochelle and home, the men escorting the gold would meet them in Oakham, so that they would journey with a larger force of knights to the southeast coast of England, across the Channel to Cherbourg or Barfleur. 'Twould be on to Caen and through Rouen to his formidable Château Gaillard and the king. Since even the reverend mother knew not of the changes to their route, they should be safe from any intervention until they reached Normandy.

He mounted and took the reins from the boy holding Catherine's horse. She would need all her concentration staying on the animal she rode, since it was no lady's mount, but a knight's solid mount. Moving closer to her, Geoffrey leaned in his saddle and kissed her, wanting to remove the fear from her eyes.

"All will be well, Catherine. I swear it."

A tremulous smile was his reward, and with a nod to the reverend mother, he followed his knights into the forest, away from the convent.

They traveled toward the coast, turning eastward

and southward. Geoffrey knew that this part of England close to Nottinghamshire was filled with John's cronies, and they could not afford to be found. Dressed plainly as they were, such a small group as theirs would not draw much attention. He knew of some smaller inns where they could stay unaccosted by thieves or outlaws or princes. Once they reached the Cinque Ports, he would take his place as Comte de Langier, seek transport across the Channel from the king's men and report to Richard as ordered.

Hours passed as he pushed them along their chosen route. Finally, he saw that Catherine could hardly sit aright, and called them to a stop. Leading her horse off the road and into a clearing, he dismounted and removed his helm and coif. Then he held his arms up to her. Without hesitation she leaned into his embrace and he lifted her to the ground. Feeling her unstable legs shaking, he kept her in his embrace, even as the other knights took the horses away to rest.

A day ago, nay, even this morn, holding her so would have been unthinkable, but now she was his. The betrothal gave him all rights to her; the wedding was simply a formality that could be accomplished at some convenient time. By her word and her signature, she'd given herself to him. But doubts at his own manipulation of her plagued him.

"Come, sit you down over here and rest a bit."

"There is no feeling in my legs. Can you help me walk?" she asked instead.

He wrapped one arm around her waist and waited for her to take the first step. Catherine held on to his arm until her legs began to move on their own. Gritting her teeth, she grimaced in pain as, step by step, the muscles awakened. Searing cramps pulsed through her until the blood finally started flowing again and her legs were her own once more.

"My thanks, my lord. I can walk now," she said, letting go of his arm.

"Mayhap I do not wish to release you," he said, his voice teasing and lighter than she had heard it today.

She searched his face for some sign of his meaning. Everything between them had changed the instant he had arrived at the convent, and she did not feel as confident in knowing his meaning as she would have just days before. But when he turned her toward him and tilted his face to hers, she knew he meant to kiss her.

His lips were soft and warm on hers at first, then pressed more ardently against her. The touch of his tongue sent shivers through her, and as she gasped, he slipped it inside her mouth and touched hers. Tremors rocked her and heat built from within as he tasted her and she tasted him. Grasping his tunic, she held tightly as his kiss went on and on, touching and tasting and licking until she could not breathe. His hand slipped behind her head so that she could not move away, and she opened wider for his heated touch.

Then she could think of nothing, feel nothing but the heaviness of his hand on her head. She was trapped against his mouth and could not breathe. When she attempted to pull away, his hand held her in place and she began to panic and struggle against his hold. The enticement of his kiss had been replaced by something else, something darker she could not identify, but something she feared in some deep place within her soul.

Geoffrey must have realized his kiss was no longer welcome, for he removed his hand and released her lips. His gaze ran over her face and she knew he was confused. As was she.

"Did I hurt you?" he asked, stepping back and examining her. "I forgot that I wore my mail when I held you so tightly."

"No, my lord, you hurt me not."

"Cate, I ask too much of you in one short day." He paused as one of his knights approached and spoke only to him. "Jean has discovered a small stream not far from here, if you would like to wash?"

Between the work in the garden, the heat, the effort of riding miles as they had, and the sheer excitement of the day, Catherine knew she must appear unkempt and smell atrocious. "I would welcome that, my lord."

"Come, let us take advantage of it, for I would like to put many more miles between us and Lincoln before nightfall."

He guided her along a beaten path behind Sir Jean. Her legs felt better with each step, though part of her dreaded the thought of getting back up on that horse. They reached the rapidly flowing brook and the water looked so appealing she was tempted to walk right into it. She paused on its banks and savored the sound of the water rushing over stones and roots as it passed.

"There are some bushes there," Geoffrey began. "So that you may...take care...of your needs." His stammer, combined with the reddening of his cheeks, told her of his discomfort in discussing the subject with her. How could men be so earthy one moment and such tongue-tied mumblers the next?

She laughed and nodded, leaving without a word. Although maneuvering was difficult, she made quick work of it, for she longed to dip her hands in the cool stream and wash her face. It was as she pushed back through the shrubbery that the reality of her situation struck her.

She was betrothed to Geoffrey Dumont.

She was traveling to the Continent with her betrothed husband.

They were together.

Catherine stumbled as the truths struck her. This morning she'd been determined to enter the convent, and by nightfall she was a wife to Geoffrey. If it had not happened at the convent with Mother Heloise as witness, she might not have believed it real.

"Cate? Are you well?" he called out to her as she lurched from the trees.

"I…" She stopped, not knowing what to say. The shock of the day's event was wearing off and she felt waves of emotion coming through now. "We…" she said, but she could not finish the thought behind the words. He was at her side and holding her before she could try to walk.

"Come, love," he said, guiding her steps and giving her some of his strength. "Refresh yourself and I am certain you will feel better."

Instead of fighting his advice, she went along with it. There would be a time when she could form coherent thoughts and ask the questions ruminating within her. He knelt down and drew her to the water's edge. Holding her waist, he helped her lean forward until she could cup her hands in the water and bring it to her face. Catherine spent several minutes simply enjoying the coolness of it. Pulling a linen square from her sleeve, she dipped it into the water and wiped her neck.

"Here, let me help you."

Before she knew his intent, he lifted the heavy coil of her hair and the scarf from her neck and, taking the linen from her, wiped her skin with the cool cloth. It was a heavenly relief. Then she caught sight of their reflection in the small pool at her knees and realized the personal nature of such a touch.

Sitting back on her heels, Catherine met his gaze. "I have many questions, my lord. Questions that cannot be ignored."

He did not look away, but let her hair drop down on her shoulders. "Yes, my lady. I am certain you have many."

My lady? Had he just called her "my lady"?

"I fear there is not time or adequate privacy now to discuss the many issues we must settle between us." A smile tugged at his lips as he looked over at their escorts. "If you can continue, I promise that your questions will be answered this night."

"As you wish, my lord. But would you answer one for me now?"

One question had been burning in her thoughts. Everything had seemed to be impossible between them. The objections of his brother, her lack of status, his value in land and wealth, and many more. So how had this happened?

"Why me? Why did you choose me, and why now?"

Geoffrey aided her in standing before he answered her. He did not seem to be searching for words, or unsure of what to say. He took in a deep breath and let it out. Reaching for her hand, he lifted it to his mouth, turned it and kissed the inside of her wrist in a way that sent chills inching down her spine. She looked up and their eyes met. His love was plain to see there.

"Now...because it had to be," he said. "You... because for me there is no other."

## Chapter Eleven

Later than he would have liked, they entered the yard of a small inn. One of his knights awaited them near the gate, motioning them toward the stable. Geoffrey was disappointed to learn that in spite of his gold, only one chamber could be had for the night. Although his men grumbled a bit, sleeping in the stables or even out in the open was not unfamiliar to them while traveling.

He assisted Catherine from her horse, and once their mounts were taken by boys who identified themselves as sons of the innkeeper, his group moved inside to find food.

It took longer for her to regain her strength this time, so he knew she was exhausted. She had not said as much, but he saw the signs in her face and in the slowness of her movements. As they walked into the inn, Aymer told him of the arrangements. Taking her to a table in the common room, Geoff sat at her side while the food, plain but filling, was placed before them.

Never once did she complain, but when her eyes

closed as she spooned the thick stew into her mouth, he knew she needed sleep even more than sustenance. Without a word, he lifted her in his arms and carried her up the short flight of steps to the room that Aymer led him to. Not as spacious as his antechamber at Greystone, the chamber did appear clean and free of rodents, and he saw a pallet in one corner.

Gently, for she was already asleep in his arms, he laid her down on the rough bed. Taking a blanket from one of their sacks, he covered her with it. After confirming his plans with Aymer, Geoff closed the door, dropped the bar in the brackets and moved to where she slept. In the light of one candle, he sat and watched her.

She was his. Though it would not be without struggle or confrontation, and though he was certain his brother would not stand by his decision, she was his now.

When he had realized the meaning and the danger in the conversation between Evesham and his man, Geoff had known he must act immediately. His original plan had been to simply remove Catherine from the convent, take her with him to Poitou and keep her there until it was safe for her to return. Once he'd arrived and spoken to the abbess, his heart had discerned his course. And now, after racing away from the convent and most likely John's troops, here they were.

The flame flickered, throwing light and shadows over her, and he marveled that she was now his. Covered with dust and worn out from their travels, she still looked like an angel to him. He knew it was his right to touch her, but he hesitated to even remove the scarf that covered her head. Deciding she would sleep more easily without its constraint, he reached under her hair, untied the ends and tugged it free.

Once her golden hair was exposed, he could not help himself. Lifting the length of it from under her, he loosened the leather cord that held the ends and used his fingers to free the long tresses until it formed a pillow around her head. A tremor shook him as he ran his hand through the soft smoothness of it. The hardness in his groin was difficult to ignore.

She was his.

When they'd met and begun conversing with one and other, he had never thought of Catherine in terms of desire. From the beginning, they'd been friends, comrades who shared their hopes and dreams. She'd actually answered his questions about women, and Geoff realized, looking back, that she'd given him advice about pursuing them. When he'd finally discerned he loved her, that knowledge had come with the realization that he could never have her. Now, because of the whims of a king, and with their words of declaration and the signing of documents, he would have her, body and soul.

Not for the first time since he'd claimed her earlier this day, he let his thoughts touch on the passion he felt within her. Soon he would have her beneath him in his down-filled bed at the Château. Covered only in the silk sheets that had been a gift from Sir Luc on his return from the Crusades, Geoff would make her his in all ways.

His body clenched with desire so strong he ached to take her now. But he would not.

He could not. Not until her questions were answered and things between them were sorted out and settled. She was not some round-heeled wench to be bedded at his whim. Catherine was his betrothed wife and he would wed her and bed her in the way a lady wife should be.

He reached out and touched her cheek and was surprised as she turned to his touch. He moved closer to her and pressed his lips to hers. She sighed his name in her sleep and then turned on her side. Although he would like nothing more than to remove his mail and curl his body around hers to sleep, his duty to protect her was more important.

Placing his sword on the floor next to him, he lay down on his side and faced the door. With his hand on the hilt, he permitted himself to sleep lightly, ready for any intruder or other threat. When the candle sputtered out, the night's quiet surrounded them.

Catherine could not help the groan she uttered as she turned onto her back. The noises of morning, the wakening birds and sounds of people in the yard outside her chamber encouraged her to open her eyes. But her abused body resisted. Every part of her hurt. The sound of a clearing throat forced her awake and she turned her head to find Geoffrey next to her on a pallet.

"Good morrow to you, my lady." His smile warmed her heart.

"And to you, my lord." She returned the greeting, then, realizing their position, felt a blush creep onto her cheeks.

Geoffrey rolled away from her and stood up. She marveled at his strength, for he still wore the mail shirt. Walking around the small chamber, he rolled his shoulders and stretched his arms out, apparently loosening muscles tight from sleeping on the floor, or nigh to it, considering the thin mattress of straw they'd shared. After a few minutes, he turned and lifted his sword, replacing it in the scabbard on his belt.

''I apologize for the meanness of these accommodations, Cate, but I feared seeking hospitality from any of the noblemen in this area. I wish not to be found yet.''

''I am not unfamiliar with such plain chambers, so fear not.''

She sat up and noticed that her hair was loose from its braid. Gathering all the strands in her hand, she untangled them with her fingers. 'Twas then she noticed him watching her movements, even mimicking them unconciously with his fingers and she saw the unfamiliar but recognizable glint of desire in their blue depths. Unsure of herself for the first time with him, she stopped and let her hair drop over her shoulder and into her lap.

He strode to the door, lifted the bar and set it down, leaning it on the frame. ''I will send a servant to help you dress, Cate. Come down to break your fast when you are ready.''

She nodded, and he was gone without another word. She lifted her arms and stretched as he had, trying to work out some of the pain in her back and shoulders. She spied a chamber pot in the corner and took care of her needs before anyone arrived. Catherine was unpacking her leather satchel when the knock came.

A few minutes later, she was washed, with her hair under control and held back with a clean wimple and barbette. At least traveling would be easier with it gathered more tightly in the woven braid that the maid created. Unfortunately, Catherine had no clean kirtle or surcoat, so the woman took her dusty clothing and shook it vigorously to remove as much dirt as possible. When she was dressed and ready, the serving woman offered to take her to her husband, but Catherine decided she could no longer wait for answers. She sent the woman back down to bring Geoffrey to the room, where they would have a measure of privacy.

With no place to sit but the pallet, she stood and waited. The sound of his feet on the steps leading to the room made her hold her breath. Her palms dampened and she wiped them on her surcoat. Swallowing against the bile that surged in her stomach at the questions that must be asked and answered, she took a breath as he opened the door.

"Are you well? The servant said I should come to you."

He strode into the room and she noticed that his hair was wet. There had not been time enough for him to bathe, so he must have found some barrel or bucket and dunked his head in it.

Geoffrey took her hands in his and looked her over from head to feet. "You appear refreshed, but I vow only a bath and a night spent on a real bed will truly make you feel better."

The mention of such personal things brought the heat of a blush into her cheeks. "I would speak with you before we leave," she began.

"We have little time, Cate." He opened the door wider for her to leave.

Catherine took hold of the door, closed it and leaned against it. "We must use it well then, for I can go no farther until I learn the truth of our situation." Crossing her arms over her chest, she hoped he would realize how serious this was to her, and give her what she wanted and needed—an explanation of how they'd become betrothed and why they were fleeing from Lincoln.

"Cannot or will not?" he asked, as he too crossed his arms over his chest and waited.

She swallowed again, nervous about his reaction. Before today, as friends, they'd stood as equals, but as his betrothed wife she was now under his domination. He owed her no explanations, and she owed him everything, including obedience to his commands and demands. Their world had shifted and she worried about how he would treat her now.

Shaking her head, she thought of the countess's words to her about the Dumont men needing women who would stand up to them when they were in a mood to plow ahead, and she smiled. This was Geoffrey before her. She should not worry. Catherine decided that to offer him less than she was, for fear of something being different between them, would indeed cause the difference to happen.

"Will not," she said, standing up a bit straighter before him. Then, in an afterthought, she added, "My lord."

His smile lightened her heart. Then he laughed. "Do not change, Cate. You never took pity on me or deferred to me before, so I hope you will not begin

now. This can only work for us if we are honest.''
He held up a finger to her and then moved her from
the door. Opening it, he called out to one of his men,
who must have been standing in the stairway, and
then he offered her his arm. ''We must talk and you
must eat, so let us take our food into the yard where
my men prepare our mounts. Come, we will settle
things between us now.''

She allowed him to assist her down the steps and
out into the yard, filled now with the activities of the
day. Catherine walked at Geoff's side until they
reached a small clearing next to the stables. With the
sun barely up, the air was cool and fresh and gave
no indication that another summer's day was on its
way.

A young boy approached carrying a tray and, at
Geoffrey's order, he placed it on a tree stump and
left them. Then Jean, Aymer and Michel took what
they wanted and walked back to where their horses
stood tied to a railing. Catherine watched as they ate,
insulted each other in the way of men and continued
to prepare for their journey.

''I thought that knights needed their squires.''

''Aymer and I squired together at the keep of his
uncle and are not so far removed from it that we
forget how to do our own work. Worry not for them
and their self-respect, Cate. Once we arrive in Caen
and the rest of our men arrive from Poitou, they will
have their squires and the appropriate amount of attention due them as esteemed knights.''

She looked at the food, and the sounds emanating
from her stomach reminded her that she had not finished her dinner the night before. Geoffrey walked

into the stables and brought back a low stool for her to sit upon. Breaking the still-steaming loaf of bread left to them, he held out half of it to her. "So, ask your questions."

"Tell me the tale of what happened yesterday. The earl did not give me details when he ordered me returned to the convent." She bit into the crusty bread and chewed it as she waited on his answer.

"My brother summoned me to tell me that he had you taken back to the convent. He gave me little explanation except to say that the danger that caused you to stay in hiding these last few years was Prince John." Geoffrey paused and then looked off into the distance as he asked, "Why did you never tell me who you were?" His voice shook as he asked the question, and she thought he might be hurt that she'd kept the truth from him.

"I did not want you to hate me."

Now he turned to her and reached for her hand. "Why would I hate you, Cate?"

"You and everyone at Greystone knows that answer better than I." She looked away. "No one would tell me the whole of it and to this day I know it not. I heard only that the earl killed my brother in a challenge and that my brother was the villain and deserved to die for what he'd done to the countess and to the earl." She felt her throat tighten as it had all those months ago when she'd heard the gossip for the first time. Shame at her brother's actions, whatever they were, overwhelmed her once more.

Geoff was at her side in a moment and put his arm around her shoulders to comfort her. "I know not even the full account of the causes of that challenge.

I was a youth then and interested more in…well, the things that interest young men.'' His eyes sparkled as she looked into them.

"A youth, indeed, my lord. I have heard tales of what interested you during your early days at Greystone, and their names are Marie and—''

He placed his hand over her mouth to stop her from speaking. Then he laughed out loud, gaining the attention of his men. Taking a chunk of cheese from the tray, he continued. "Cate, until this morn I knew only what Christian and Emalie told me of you—that you were some distant relation to Emalie, orphaned and placed at the convent due to some illness. As you recovered, you were brought to Greystone for visits, and that is when we met.''

He released his hold on her shoulders and lifted her chin so that she was looking at him directly. "I fell in love with the penniless orphan and care not that she had a brother who is long dead.''

Catherine was almost willing to accept his explanation, but she feared that he knew much more than he was admitting to her.

"You must see that neither the penniless orphan nor the sister of the disgraced William de Severin is suitable as your wife.''

His face betrayed a momentary flash of guilt, and she knew that he had considered both of those reasons as obstacles to this match. "I have been told that the de Severin family has a noble history, one that would rival even the Dumonts' legacy. 'Twas not so long ago that the Dumonts were in disgrace with this king, but our fortunes changed. Mayhap the de Severins will see such a change with this marriage?''

''But my lord, I do not understand why the prince is against me. Did the earl give you any reasons why I have earned Prince John's ire?''

''Only in some vague connection with your brother. Did you know that William served as John's champion for several years?''

Her body reacted before her thoughts could. A tremor shook her entire being, causing icy shivers down her spine. Had she known that her brother was champion to John? She thought she might remember that and thought it might be the reason she'd been called to England. The same confusion and darkness that filled her whenever she tried to peer back into that time happened once more, and she shook her head. ''I am not certain.''

''Cate, we will play these Plantagenets the way they play each other and keep you safe by aligning with the king and Queen Eleanor. 'Tis how Christian gained Emalie and Harbridge.''

''Why do you believe that the king will stand by this? And the earl cannot be supportive of it, for I spoke to him the morning I left. He fully expects you to marry one of the heiresses. I assured him that I would not...'' She paused, remembering the assurances she'd given to the earl the morning before.

''*...I do not wish to come between you and your brother.... I have no intention of declaring my love for him or making him choose between me and the responsibilities he carries for you and your family.*''

''What did you tell Christian?''

"I told him I would not come between the two of you."

"Cate, you will not come between us. Once the marriage is formalized, he and I will reach an understanding over this. You forget, I am not his little brother, the second son, any longer. The king has recognized my rights and I make this decision. You are my choice."

Geoffrey stood, put the cheese back on the tray and offered her a cup of ale. She sipped it as she pondered how to broach the most disturbing of her questions, or rather, her secrets. So little of that time between her arrival in England and her awakening in the convent did she remember. Bits of memories, words and feelings were there, but most of it was a terrorizing blank to her.

"You do not look convinced of my words."

"My lord…" When he frowned at her, she began again. "Geoffrey, there is so much that you do not know about me. Much I do not know myself. Mayhap we should wait?"

"Worry not, Cate. There will be time enough for us to discover that which we know not about the other. We are joined and I will take you to the king for his formal acceptance of our marriage and my vow of fealty."

Geoff reached for the chunk of cheese again and broke it, handing her one of the pieces. Although she wanted with her heart and soul to be his wife, she feared that the truth of her missing years, whatever it might be, could tear them apart. If this marriage was solemnized, there would be no recourse for them.

"So, what are your plans?" Deciding to put off her fears for the moment, Catherine needed to know what faced her in the coming days and weeks.

He smiled at her. "I am pleased that you trust me in this, Cate. We ride as soon as we are finished here, and meet up with the rest of my men in Oakham, then on to Bedford and through London. I would wish for a quicker path, but we must make for the Cinque Ports and its ships to take us to Richard and keep out of John's sight before we reach there. 'Twill take us at least a sennight plus three days on land before taking a ship to the Continent."

"Ten days of riding?" She rubbed her back at just the thought of that much time spent on the back of a horse.

He laughed aloud again. "I would make it as comfortable for you as I could, but a cart or wagon for you would slow us down too much."

She shook her head. "I will survive this journey, my lord. I am hardy enough to face it."

"That's my girl! Come now, finish your food and we will be on our way." Geoffrey glanced over at the stables. "The horses are saddled." His men approached, leading their mounts. "If the weather and roads hold, we should make it to Oakham by dark. Are you ready?"

He held out his hand to her and she paused before accepting it. Was she ready? If she was to be his countess, she needed to demonstrate the courage he was showing her, the commitment to him and to a marriage that she'd never thought to have and the love she knew they shared. Holding her chin a bit higher, she reached out and grasped his hand.

He pulled her to him and kissed her fast and hard on the lips. Then she found herself on the back of the same horse she'd ridden the day before, heading out of the small yard in front of the inn. And they rode.

## Chapter Twelve

The winds whipped her hair free of its covering, but she stood at the highest place in the keep and let herself be buffeted by them. The force of them usually soothed her, and she waited for that relief now. 'Twas not to happen this time. She'd sought this refuge several times over the last two days and had not found the comfort she needed.

With his path illuminated by an almost-full moon, Emalie nodded as the guard passed her yet again on his rounds of the battlements and then turned back to the wall's edge. Sighing, she knew that until she spoke to her husband and told him the contents of the missive from the reverend mother, she would have no peace. Of course, once Christian discovered what had occurred, Emalie would have no peace, either.

Then he was there, as though her thoughts alone had conjured him, his face stern and his eyes dark with tension. Her husband stood without a cloak, heedless to the chill winds blowing around him. A second passed, or mayhap minutes, as they stared at each other. His eyes gave away nothing of his feelings to her, and sadness filled her at the breach to come. He would not bear the news well; the actions of his brother would hurt him deeply and he would think every word spoken by her about Geoffrey and Catherine was a betrayal.

"My lady," he said, coming closer. "You should not stay long in this chill."

"I was about to come in, my lord. You did not have to seek me out." Emalie knew she must face her husband.

"I have missed your company, Emalie. Come back to me?" The intensity in his gaze didn't lessen, but the longing in his voice was clear, his expression more vulnerable. "I cannot tolerate this discord between us."

His outstretched arms weakened her intentions to stay aloof, and she ran into them. She savored the moments of unadulterated love while he held her, knowing that the night would most likely end with them apart once more.

"Let us seek our chambers, for I must speak with you," she finally said, after several minutes in his arms.

He leaned back from her and she knew he was searching her face for some indication of what was to come, but she stepped from his embrace and led the way to her chambers. Once there, she removed her cloak and hung it on a peg, sat in the chair before her dressing table and waited for him to close the door.

"I have not seen such a look of fear on your face for a very long time, wife. What have I done to deserve it again?'' He stayed near the door as though he hesitated to enter her domain.

''My lord... Christian...'' she stuttered, trying to find a place to begin.

''I know you are angry, Emalie. I know you think me wrong in sending Catherine back and in my insistence on a wife for Geoffrey other than she. But please do not dissemble in our dealings with each other, for surely we have come further than that.''

She started to stand to face him, but he stopped her with a wave of his hand. ''Sit. Tell me, Emalie. Just tell me your news. Is it the babe?'' He nodded at her and she realized he thought her pregnancy in danger.

''Nay, Christian. I am well. The babe is well. 'Tis not that that forces me to bring you such tidings. The reverend mother has written to me...'' She paused and took the folded sheets from the purse on her belt. Unfolding them, she held them out to her husband. Mayhap reading the nun's words for himself would be better than hearing her speak them.

''I remember no messenger from the convent this day,'' he said, as he stepped close enough to take them from her. Then he moved to a lamp in a sconce on the wall. She did not bother to tell him when the letter had arrived, for it would only increase her sins against him.

She could see him react to each bit of news in the missive, for his stance became rigid, his face flushed and his grasp on the delicate parchment tightened. It was the complete look of betrayal and pain in his eyes when he raised them to her that tore her heart in two. He held the letter out before him.

"You knew? When did this letter arrive?"

"Christian, please let me explain."

He crossed the room in three steps, and she stood to meet him, resisting the urge to back away. He would never raise a hand to her, she knew. But the dark look would have scared her senseless if she had not known.

"When, Emalie? Simply tell me how long you have had this and not told me?" His breathing was labored and she could see his cheeks tighten as he clenched his teeth in anger.

"It arrived yesterday morn. I only did as Mother Heloise asked."

"You honored her request, but not mine. Is that what you say, *wife?*" He forced the words out. "Hers and not mine?"

"Please, Christian, hear me. The betrothal between them is binding. It is done. Geoffrey had the king's permission and did not need yours." His eyes flashed and she knew she had chosen the wrong tact in which to approach the matter.

"Done? I think not, wife, for until he claims her as his bride there is still time to stop it."

He turned to leave, but she put her hand on his arm to halt him. "Is that what you want, Christian? To chase them down and stop this? Do you want to bring this family squabble to the king and have all on both sides of the Channel gaping at the antics of the Dumont brothers?"

"A family squabble? Is that what you call it? 'Tis so much more than that, but a woman would not understand about a man's honor."

Slapping her with his armor-encased hand could

not have hurt her more. Gasping, she sat back down. She felt the hot tears pouring down her cheek and knew the pain in her chest was from her heart breaking.

Women not know about honor? Who did he think took care of the broken hearts and bodies and spirits left after men fought for their honor? Who bore the marks in their souls of men's battles for it? 'Twas always the women who picked up the pieces of the shattered lives left after men finished their games of honor. And always women who bore the cost in loss.

However, antagonizing him with the words she wanted to scream out would do no good. Emalie searched the dressing table for a handkerchief and blotted her eyes.

"He is a grown man. Now named count and about to be enfeoffed of the lands and people of your family. He goes to fight for his king. Christian, why can you not accept his choice and support him in this?"

"And let the de Severin family win? Let William's sister be named countess when 'twas his acts that nearly cost me my bride, my life and all that I hold dear?"

So, 'twas as she suspected—the old wounds still festered within him. She recognized the struggle that surged in his conscience and in his heart. In a while, he would reconsider his words and realize that William de Severin's acts had brought him all he held dear. For now, the anger over his younger brother's challenge to his authority as head of the family, and the hurt over Geoff's pursuing his own goals without consulting him, were too strong.

Taking a risk, she stood and approached him,

reaching up to touch his cheek. He flinched at the contact and moved back from her.

"You would take their side and keep your word to another and not to me. That is the worst of this, Emalie. I thought we were of one mind and one heart. But I was wrong."

She closed her eyes and waited for him to leave. Nothing she could say now would matter. He saw her actions as betrayal. She could only hope that his thoughts would calm and he would see that they *were* of one mind on this. They both wanted the best bride for his brother, one who would support him in caring for their lands and people and in fulfilling his duties to king and country. They only differed over who they thought that woman was.

The door closed quietly and she was alone. Giving in to the tears, she grieved for the distance between them. Mayhap she had acted incorrectly in not trusting him to do the right thing. Although his words to her said one thing, had he acted against his brother or Catherine? Had she simply not given him the chance to prove himself the man she thought he was?

Emalie chose not to call her maid for help, but climbed into her bed and tugged a blanket over her. She did not hear his movements in the adjoining chamber, and worried long into the night.

It seemed that no sooner had she closed her eyes than a knock came on her door, alerting her of her maid's attendance. If Alyce thought it strange to find her fully dressed on her bed, in the same kirtle and overgown as the day before, she said nothing of it. And after the unsettled night she'd spent listening for signs of Christian's return, Emalie did not care.

Noises alerted her to his presence in his bedchamber. Cocking her head, she heard the sounds of several people and tried to discern what was happening there. Much activity was followed by silence, and she wondered what her husband was about this morn. She did not have to wait very long to discover the truth.

Drawn to the window of her chamber, she found the courtyard bustling with activity. Carts were being filled and harnessed to horses. Knights of the various noblemen stood waiting for their mounts, or sat on them awaiting their lords. Emalie leaned closer and watched as those who had been guests prepared to leave, and leave quickly, from what she could see.

"Secrets are difficult to keep."

She turned to find Christian, dressed in his mail and carrying his helmet under his arm, standing in the doorway between their rooms. Emalie was shaking before she even realized what this meant. When she did perceive the meaning, she found it nearly impossible to breathe. Christian handed his helmet to his squire and came toward her.

"Where do you go, Christian?" she asked as he helped her to her chair.

"I had hoped to avoid answering the call of the king myself by sending my gold and some knights. But now, 'twould seem a good idea to present myself there."

Clutching at his hauberk, she whispered, "Forgive me for choosing wrongly. Please, Christian, I did not mean to hurt you by my actions. Truly," she begged.

"That you can hurt me says much about what is between us, Emalie. For now, know that I love you," he said, kissing her on her forehead. "I will return as soon as is possible."

"Who goes with you? When do you leave?"

"I take my four knights and two squires from Poitou and Luc. Walter remains here, charged with the protection of Greystone and its lady."

"What do you mean to do, Christian?" She watched as he loosened his hold on her and stepped away. He was already detaching himself from her; in spite of his words of love, she could feel the distance between them widening with each moment.

"I have always had Luc at my back in battles small and large. I want to be there for Geoffrey as he faces his first test as vassal to the king."

This was a good sign, she thought. There was no anger in his voice as he spoke this morn.

"I would come with you, husband." She stepped toward him, but he moved away.

"Nay. You will stay here. I need no more interference from you in this."

Hurt and yet enboldened by his orders, she asked what was in her thoughts. "And their betrothal? What will you do about Catherine?"

He stared away from her for a long second and then answered without looking at her. "Press me not on that issue, lady. It is too raw for me to decide at this time how to proceed."

Christian turned and walked to the door. With his back still to her, she heard his words of farewell. "Be well while I am gone."

'Twas some time later when the keep and courtyard had quieted after so much activity, that she realized what had happened. Christian had taken with him all those he had brought to Greystone three years ago. Only Montgomerie knights and vassals remained. And after praying so much for it to happen those years ago, Emalie knew now that she really did not want it, after all.

## Chapter Thirteen

The next six days of Catherine's life were a blur of traveling in daylight, sleeping in darkness and eating meals in the saddle, at tables or by the side of the road in alcoves of shade. Too tired to do anything but hold on as Geoffrey guided her strong horse along the roads heading south through London and out to the coast, she simply existed in that twilight.

She liked the mornings best, for that was when she and Geoffrey would have a chance at privacy. His men found inns along the way, where she and Geoff usually had a chamber to themselves, although once, just north of London, they shared it with his knights, too. For short periods of time, she would even ride with him, shamelessly sitting on his lap and wrapped in his arms as they galloped southward. Not much speech was possible between them, but in snatches of conversation she learned much about the Dumont family and Geoffrey's life before his father's death.

She cautiously spoke of her own childhood and the years after her parents' deaths, and they discovered even more things in common. Geoffrey's mother was a second wife, as was her own. Catherine and he each had an older brother. Both their families' histories went back many generations in the areas from whence they sprang, and both had suffered setbacks under the Plantagenet kings.

Although they commiserated over the tyranny of older brothers, they carefully skirted speaking too candidly about either Christian or William. 'Twas fine with Catherine, for she had few clear memories of William except her childhood ones. And try as she might, nothing would penetrate the numbing blackness in her memory of her days before Greystone.

She looked forward to seeing Geoffrey's home, and although the thought of being his countess scared her, she considered it with some amount of pleasurable anticipation. Geoffrey assured her that she would carry out her duties competently and he would be there to support her, as she would him.

One aspect of their upcoming marriage was not a topic for discussion between them. They had shared many hopes and dreams, but never did she broach the subject of their physical union. The truth was she only knew she dreaded it, and could not discern the reason for such feelings within her.

Certainly Geoffrey's kisses had been pleasurable. From soft touches to harder caresses, they incited heat and excitement through her body and left her hoping for and wanting more. She knew not what that might entail, but from overheard whispers during her visits to Greystone and the gossip of women in the solar, she sensed Geoffrey not only knew about it, but reveled in it.

He could exercise his conjugal rights at any time he wished now that they were betrothed. The consummation would finalize their joining and make it unbreakable in the eyes of the church. Would he take her before they arrived in Caen and before he was sworn to Richard? Before the king confirmed his choice of bride?

These strange thoughts crept into her mind at the most unexpected times, but usually when she awoke to find herself wrapped in his arms or when he held her closely as they rode together. No doubt the nearness of their bodies caused such thoughts and worries in her.

Since he never spoke of it, she believed it was not a concern for him—until the night they spent in an inn on the Canterbury road. An inn large enough to accommodate them in Geoffrey's request for a larger private chamber with a real bed and even a tub with enough hot water for a real bath. He had announced that they were making good time and could spend a few extra hours there, stopping well before nightfall and mayhap even getting a later start in the morn.

At first she greeted his words with relief, then with trepidation. As they were shown to their chamber and a maid came to assist her with her bath, Catherine realized that she would not be sleeping alone this night, or sleeping with a husband who wore a mail hauberk, on a rough pallet on the floor. The luxury of the room after so many nights in much less was inviting. Clean sheets and a thick mattress over a well strung frame promised hours of comfort. Hours sleeping next to a man who had the right to take her for his pleasure. 'Twas an unnerving thought, that her body was now not her own.

Soon she sat before a brazier and allowed the maid to towel dry her hair and then brush it with soothing strokes from her scalp to the ends. The warm chamber lulled her toward sleep, and she rested her head on her crossed arms and enjoyed the calming strokes. She did not know what made her look up, but when she did, Geoffrey was standing in the doorway, staring at her.

The maid curtsied, handed the brush to him and, at his gesture, left. Her breath held, Catherine watched as he walked behind her and lifted his hand to her hair. Then he stopped, and she waited anxiously for his next move.

"May I?"

Although she sensed he meant more than simply brushing her hair, she nodded without looking back at him. Before the touch of the brush, he wrapped her hair around his hands and leaned in to smell it. His nearness, his own clean and masculine scent, the heat of his body behind hers threatened to overwhelm her. Every nerve within tensed as she waited for his next touch. Was this the time? Would he take her now? What would happen? What must she do? She could not calm the shaking that passed through her.

Geoff felt the tension growing within her, first at his approach and now at his touch. Instead of being a pleasant anticipation of what could happen between them, he knew by the quaking in her that she was terrified. He stood and placed the brush on the small table near the bed. Then he turned and waited for her to look at him. It took a few minutes, but finally she raised her eyes and, as he'd suspected, they were filled with fear.

"I will not hurt you, Catherine. I have promised to keep you from harm's way. Yet you look at me with such terror in your eyes that I must wonder if you do not trust me as you've said."

She dropped her arms to her sides and walked a few steps toward the bed without saying a word. Then she nodded to him. "I do trust you. It is just that this part is the reason why I was content to go to the convent unmarried. I never thought to give myself to a man."

His heart warmed with the knowledge that she had shared her deepest worry with him. "Do you fear that it will hurt, that you will not enjoy it, as some women do?"

"Something from the time I do not remember has instilled a terror within me. I do not know the cause, but I do know it lies not with you." She stepped closer and stretched out her hand to him. "As I told the countess, you are the only man I would consider doing this with."

"*This?*" he asked, teasing her over her words. "What is *this?*" He took her hand and pulled her gently to him. So she had consulted Emalie about him.

"Carnal knowledge," she whispered, so softly that he almost did not hear it. Her words were muffled in the tunic he wore.

Lifting her chin so that he could see her face, he smiled. The becoming pink blush colored her cheeks and he noticed that some of the fear was gone from her eyes. But not all of it.

"I do want carnal knowledge of you, Cate. I want to know the feel, the look, the very smell and taste of every part of you." His own body already reacted to her nearness, tightening and pulsing. "And—" he took her hand and placed it on his chest "—I want you to know mine as well. I want there to be pleasure for both of us."

"I like your kisses, my lord."

"There is no place for titles here, love," he said as he leaned down to touch her lips. If she liked kissing, he would start there. "Let me kiss you, then."

He kissed her mouth and then her brows and then touched his lips to her cheeks. She sighed and he took it as agreement to go further. And so he did.

She stood before him in a plain linen chemise that tied at the neck. Tugging on the string, he loosened the garment and let it slide down to settle on her shoulders. Nuzzling and licking his way, he followed the gentle curves of her neck and kissed her shoulders. She was soft and enticing, and the scent of something floral wafted up from her freshly washed hair as she turned restlessly under his attentions.

With his hands at her waist, he could feel her short excited breaths and the movement of her chest and stomach. He slid his thumbs up to touch the edges of her breasts. She arched nearer to him and he thought he would explode. Her innocent passion aroused him and he wanted more, so much more. He moved his mouth down to the rising slopes of her breasts and then took one tightened nipple into his mouth. She gasped and grabbed for his shoulders as she leaned her head back and let him have his way.

His mouth left a wet spot on the linen, which was now transparent to his sight. The enticing bud under it was still erect from his suckling. Without pausing, he took the other one and teased it in the same way. Catherine said no words, but her body told him that she was enjoying his touches and his kisses. He wanted more and he wanted her now.

Geoffrey released her breast and took a step back. Her passion-filled eyes and swollen lips caused his own body to react, and the urge to fill her with himself and his seed grew stronger and stronger within him. Her lack of fear encouraged him and so he took the next step.

"Let me see you," he said, in a voice so gruff with desire that he nearly did not recognize it. Foreplay was not new to him. He had played these games with women from the time he was a squire, but never had he wanted someone this much. And he wanted her to enjoy it as much as he was.

She nodded to him once again and he reached out and lifted the chemise over her head. She turned away in a maidenly display of modesty that inflamed him even more. The sight of her hair flowing down her back and outlining a shapely bottom and legs made him harder. As she turned to face him, he knew he was about to see heaven.

Long tresses hung over her shoulders, but did not keep her body hidden from him. The aroused tips of her breasts peeked through the blond hair cascading over the feminine curves, and he could clearly see the enticing triangle of darker blond at the top of her thighs. Now his mouth watered and his hands itched to touch her. Just as he gave up fighting the need to grasp her, she spoke.

"May I see you as well, my l... Geoffrey?"

He could not have been more pleased with her request. He pulled at the ties of his tunic and swept it off, never looking away from her gaze. She had seen him shirtless before, but he worried that the sight of his erection would scare her once more. He leaned down and tugged off his boots and then undid the straps holding up the hose. Rolling them down his legs, he slipped them off and stood before her. All that was left was the short breechcloth he wore for riding, under his mail, then she would see the proof of his desire for her. Opening his arms to her, he invited her closer, and the heat of her body against his nearly melted his control completely.

He guided them back until he stopped by the edge of the bed. Sitting down, he looked up at her. "Let me touch you."

"I would rather have you kiss me again," she said.

Taking it as a sign of her naivete and inexperience, he realized that he could touch with his lips and tongue, and so he began where he knew she meant— her mouth. Tasting her over and over, he plundered her lips until they were both breathless. Then he moved down to her breasts and suckled the tight buds again. She stirred against his mouth as he did so, and Geoff recognized that her breasts were sensitive places.

Her palms roamed over his shoulders and back, and he liked the feel of them on his skin. He lifted his hands and held her hips so that she would not back away from what he planned. Leading with his tongue, he licked and tasted the soft curves of her stomach, moving closer to the curls at the apex of her thighs. Her legs shook at his approach, and he knew he wanted her on the bed.

"Let me taste you." Catherine's frown told him that she did not know the treasure he sought. Smiling, he reassured her. "Let me taste you, Cate. Wherever I want."

Her tremulous smile gave him the permission he sought. He had not pushed her beyond her boundaries yet. Geoff lifted her and turned, placing her on the bed next to him. Sliding down to kneel between her legs, he looked into her questioning eyes.

"Let me taste you," he repeated as he placed his mouth there in the most sensitive of place on a woman's body and teased her with tongue and even teeth. And he marveled at the ease with which she fell into it with him.

Catherine leaned up on her elbows and watched him, gasping at his touch and arching her body against his lips even in her confusion. Chills filled her and heat poured from her with his every touch...with his every taste of her. How could he do that? She had never touched where his mouth now did, had never known the kinds of pleasure that existed there, or that kissing and caressing could cause such a chaos of feelings within her.

A pressure built inside her, tightening and tightening until she thought she would scream. He increased the speed of his movements against that place and then he pushed deeper with his tongue, finding a spot that did indeed make her scream. Instead of stopping, he drew what he had found into his mouth, as he had her breast, and suckled it, even using his teeth. How could this be? Now her body worked on its own, pushing against him, demanding more with its spasms, and he answered its call.

All thoughts fled as he directed so much attention there on the aching flesh that her body did explode, in waves and waves of pleasure and throbbing. He followed the signs her body gave him and continued until there was no more tension left within her. Exhausted by the pulsing and release, she fell back and tried to regain her breath.

But he was not done. Stripping off the cloth he wore, he climbed onto the bed and knelt between her legs. He leaned forward and entwined their hands and then stretched himself over her, touching chest to chest, stomach to stomach, thighs to thighs. Catherine felt his manhood against her and knew that this would be the claiming. Her body still pulsed with the arousal he had caused, and she opened her legs to him.

Before he could enter, he paused and asked his question again. "Let me have you, Cate. All of you." He had placed the decision with her, and part of her was ready, open and accepting of his possession. But something else in her soul was not.

This action would fulfill their betrothal. There would be no turning back, no denial or release from the promises once he pierced her maidenhead with his flesh. Geoffrey's options—to compromise with his brother, or to make another selection—would be severely limited and costly to change if he claimed her in this way. And she would rather risk angering him over it now than facing his disappointment later when she *did* come between him and his brother, or between him and his duty.

"No, Geoffrey. We must wait." She tried to slide from under him, but his weight and position made it impossible. "If you change your mind later after speaking to your brother or to the king, this will make it difficult for you."

Her words both startled and angered him, for his eyes grew dark and intense. He never lost control, though, for his body stayed perched at the opening to hers and never ventured in. He stared at her, searching her face, and he took in deep breaths. After a moment or two, he pushed his hardened flesh beneath her bottom and, with a groan, spent himself without entering her.

A deep sadness filled her as she realized that he had honored her denial. She lay, covered in sweat and his body, and waited. After a minute or two, he lifted himself off her and stood by the bed. Pushing the hair from his face, he walked to the now-cold tub of water and dipped a cloth in it. His movements and his expression were rigid now, as she watched him wipe off his manhood and then rinse the cloth and bring it to her.

Without a word, he turned her on her side and, when she would have objected, wiped her bottom and lower back clean of any remnants of his release. Then Geoff released his hold on her, tugged on his hose and tunic and boots and left the room without another word to her. She had ruined this as surely as she had ruined his life.

## Chapter Fourteen

Slamming himself down at a corner table in the inn's public room, Geoff cursed himself for the fool he was. And for things done and left undone. A serving wench brought over a cup of ale, waiting for him to drink so she could refill it at once from a pitcher. He must have that look about him that told of a need that must be met. Finally, at his wave and with an added penny for her troubles, she left the pitcher for his use, and tugged her blouse down to expose her ample bosom and her willingness to satisfy another type of need.

When he closed his eyes, he could feel the suppleness and heat of Catherine's flesh against his. He could hear her moaning as he kissed and licked his way down her body to the place where he would plant his seed. He had been so close, so very close, to making certain no one could challenge this betrothal when she'd called a halt for the same reasons. He knew she had her doubts, but his were something new to him. And that he stopped was the biggest surprise of all.

Drinking the cup dry and then filling it once more, he considered his actions with her. They had been moving toward this consummation for all the days since he took her from the convent, and they both knew it. She had not resisted him—well, not after she became accustomed to his touch and his kiss. She'd accepted all he gave, and with her actions asked for more.

Another cup of ale was gone and the pitcher nigh to empty before he realized why her questions were so troubling. For days he'd told her that nothing would come between them, that she was his choice, both Christian and the king would accept her, and this was meant to be. And for days he had believed it. Indeed, he had pushed aside any lingering doubts and decided that this night would be the one when they were joined in all ways. His instructions to his man who made their arrangements—that he wanted a place big enough for a private chamber—had made his intentions clear to one and all.

Even Catherine in her naivete had known what would happen this night. And she'd welcomed him until that last moment. He rubbed his eyes with the heel of his hand and leaned back against the wall. Nay, she would have welcomed his possession of her if he had not prevaricated at that special moment. In giving pause, he had given voice to his own doubts. And she would not let him take that step if he doubted the rightness of it.

Damn him! He lifted the cup to his mouth again and swallowed deeply from it. He did have doubts; he did fear what Christian would say and do at their next meeting, and he did wonder whether he had acted in defiance of his brother's edict rather than for his love of Catherine. He had managed to keep all of those uncertainties out of his way when he thought her to be in danger. Now, when it was time for him to claim her, those qualms raised themselves.

If he had just taken her and not stopped. If he had simply pushed through her maidenhead and claimed her as wife in all ways. If he had just... He raised his cup again, but his arm was stopped before he could drink.

"Is aught amiss, my lord?" His man Aymer sat down next to him. "I did not expect to see you until morn or later."

He and Aymer had been friends for these last two years, finishing out their service as squires in his uncle's household before both being knighted in a tournament several months ago. They had fought together, practiced together, even drank and wenched together. When this plan had begun short days ago, and they had ridden off to protect Catherine, Aymer had given his full support. Aymer, another second son who would inherit nothing, was his man and planned to swear fealty to Geoffrey when they arrived at Château d'Azure.

"'Tis well. I just came down for something to drink."

Aymer lifted the pitcher to fill his own cup and found it empty. Geoffrey looked at him and knew that his friend guessed things had not gone as expected. "'Twould appear that you have indeed had something to drink."

When Geoff waved to the serving maid for more

ale, Aymer stopped him. "I have not had enough yet, Aymer. Summon that wench back here."

"My lord… Geoff," he said, placing his hand on Geoff's arm, "you have had enough. I suggest that you go back to your chamber and close whatever breach has opened between you and your lady."

"You are right, friend. But I know not how to do it without compounding my mistakes with more of them."

"Do you want her to wife?"

Geoff felt the haze of drink sneaking up on him. Of course he wanted her. He had taken all these measures to insure her safety and to keep her at his side. Of course she would be his wife. He nodded at Aymer's question.

"Do you want her in spite of your brother's objections or to spite your brother?"

And there it was. The bald truth. The deepest fear. Now put into words by his closest friend, he could ignore it no longer.

Had this been about him and Chris, and not about Catherine at all? Was Geoff so full of his own esteem that he had tumbled recklessly into this misadventure and dragged Cate in with him?

He truly needed another cup of ale.

He did not answer, for he knew not what the answer was. Although he hoped his actions had been for the best of reasons, part of him, the part that was grateful to Cate for saying no to him, saw the challenge of a younger brother to an older one in it. The need to prove himself a man to one who had always been the man of the family.

Merde.

His head hit the wall behind him and he hoped the pain would clear his thoughts. It did not. Closing his eyes, he thought about Catherine.

He loved her. He did. Without doubt or reservation, he wanted her to wife even though she was not his brother's choice for him. He had loved her even when there seemed to be no way for them to be together. He had simply taken advantage of the opportunities and made it happen.

"Doubts would be expected, Geoff. Neither you nor I were raised to inherit such as you have. Now that you have, I think a bit of uncertainty will dog your steps for a while. Lose not sight of what is important to you, and I think things will turn out for the best."

His head and thoughts began to clear as some of the fear of these revelations seeped away. What was important to him? Upholding his duty to the king. Upholding the restored honor of the Dumonts. Most important was upholding his word, his pledge to the woman who lay in the chamber overhead. His doubts were not completely gone, but he felt as though they were manageable now.

"My thanks, Aymer. Are you settled for the night?"

Aymer laughed and nodded across the room at a lovely young woman who sat watching them. "Aye, my lord. Have no worries on my behalf."

Standing, Geoff gained his balance and then watched as Aymer was welcomed into the willing arms of the buxom lass. Without delaying further, Geoff strode to the stairs that would lead him to

Catherine and the reckoning he had brought on himself.

He pushed on the door and peered into the room before entering. Several candles still flickered, throwing shadows around the chamber. Quietly, he opened the door wider and stepped inside. Trying to move without noise, he placed the bar in the bracket to secure the door for the night.

Her sigh caught his attention and he turned to face her. She slept on, curled in a tight ball in the middle of the bed he had so carefully requested for them to share. He walked closer and watched her for a few minutes.

Guilt tore through him as her breath hitched several times, telling him clearly that she had cried herself to sleep on his account. The path of her tears tracked down her cheeks and he reached out to touch them. Once more, she'd shamed him with the honesty of her feelings. And the dishonesty of his own.

With only a thin blanket over her, she would not last the night without taking a chill. The stone walls kept the chamber cool in most weather, even the heat of summer. Spying her chemise on the floor where he'd thrown it, he picked it up and shook the dust from it. Then, when there was no alternative left to him, he touched her shoulder to wake her so she could put it on and get under another layer or two of bedcovers.

"Cate. Wake up, love," he said softly, not wanting to startle her. Her swollen eyes opened slowly, not seeing him at first, but then she pushed away from him, dragging the thin coverlet with her. He watched as the confusion of sleep left her and she took in her surroundings, then looked back at him. Her expression was blank and he could not think of how to begin. She did it for him, in the worst possible way.

"My lord, I beg forgiveness. I did not mean to refuse you. I am ready now if you want to…if you want…" Her words trailed off and he felt like the biggest villain. Tears spilled from her lovely blue eyes once more and her hair was a tangled mess. And somehow, through his stupidity, he'd made her believe this was her fault.

"Catherine, please listen to me," he began, handing her the crumpled gown. "There is some fresh water in the pitcher. Come," he said, gathering the gown together and placing it over her head. "Wash up and then we can talk." He helped her from the bed and guided her to the basin.

It took a few minutes, but soon she was back in the bed, under the covers, looking far better than when he'd found her. Once she was settled on the side away from the door, he sat with his back against the headboard and took her hand.

"I think I liked this better when we were Cate and Geoff."

"So you think this was a mistake, after all?"

"Nay, Cate, not that. 'Tis just that things are so different between us now and I do not know how to proceed in these more delicate matters we've never had to face before."

"I have failed you then? I feared as much when you left as you did." She sat up next to him. "I did not know what you wanted, my lord. I promise to acquiesce to your…needs the next time. If you tell me how to change what I did wrong, I will do as you ask.''

She would be the death of him yet. "Cate, you did nothing wrong.'' Her doubtful expression told him that she did not believe it to be so. "You were the only one showing any sense tonight," he said, turning to face her. "You were right to stop me from taking that step in the heat of passion, without thinking of all the consequences.''

"You do not want this marriage then?" She held her breath, no doubt waiting for his repudiation.

"No, 'tis not that. You seemed to read my doubts as easily as you read Latin, Cate. I do not like things between Christian and me to be unsettled. I do want the king's acceptance of you and his confirmation of my titles and lands. I want to do nothing that will threaten this union, and if waiting to consummate our betrothal, waiting until the king pronounces me holder of the Dumont estates, is necessary, then that is what we will do.''

"Until Caen?"

"Until Caen. I want nothing to undermine our marriage.''

"Nor I," she said in a whisper.

"Let me hold you." He nearly bit his tongue when he realized how close to a sexual request his words were. If she noticed or objected, she did not say, and did not hesitate to come into his embrace. Smoothing her hair away from her face, he waited for her to relax against him.

Although she seemed accepting of his actions, he knew she did not understand what had happened between them. Her body had reacted to his touch, but he was certain that Cate's mind did not grasp the whole of it. Geoff wanted to reassure her that she was in no way lacking, nor had she acted inappropriately in the physical matters between them.

"I would speak to you about tonight, Cate. You need to know that what happened between us and the arousal you felt was something I hope is always there for you."

"But I screamed. Surely 'tis not acceptable between husband and wife?"

"It makes a man feel powerful indeed to draw that sound from a woman. Your sounds increased my own pleasure, Cate. Do not hesitate to give them to me when we finally complete the passion that has started between us."

The memory of that noise, the keening sound that had started in her throat and moved through her and out as his mouth brought her to climax, was as intoxicating as the best wine from his vineyards. Nay, the sound of it and the look of wonderment on her face and the smell and taste of her essence as it poured forth had been more invigorating and exciting than anything he could think of.

The part of him that wanted to bury itself in her made it known that these thoughts and words were as arousing now as she had been earlier. Shifting on the bed so that it was not so evident, Geoff knew he must speak of it no more.

Cate had other ideas. "Would you tell me what else is to happen between us? The reverend mother did not have much guidance for me in this matter, due to the rushed ceremony, no doubt."

Nothing could squash a man's desire so quickly as

thoughts of the reverend mother counseling Catherine on matters of the flesh. He shivered at the connection, one that should simply not be thought of in the same breath. Nuns. Sex. Nay, not together. More comfortable now that his manhood had relaxed, he tried to speak nonchalantly about the final step they would take.

"When we reach that part of passion again—after you scream for me once more..." he said, enjoying the blush the crept up her neck onto her delicate cheeks. "After that, I will put myself inside you and release my seed there."

She gazed at him and he saw the look of enlightenment as she remembered his release beneath her earlier. "Will that hurt? I have heard women speak of the pain."

"I confess to not having bedded any virgins in my sordid past, Cate. I, too, have heard that there will be some small measure of pain and a bit of blood to mark the taking of your maidenhead."

He could not ever remember having spoken words of such candor with anyone before. Men did not speak of this, not with each other, not with women. But her questions, asked so forthrightly, deserved answers.

"A virgin's blood," she whispered.

"Aye. 'Tis the proof of your virginity. But I swear I will try to make the pain a slight one, one that you will not remember for the pleasure. Be not afraid of that moment, for it will pass quickly between us."

She moved closer to him and smiled. "I am not afraid."

"Can you forgive me my blunders tonight?"

"Only if you forgive mine."

"Then we are at peace?" he asked, wanting to be
certain that no worries would mar the rest of their
journey.

"We are at peace."


*"Give me your scream again," he ordered
through the darkness that always surrounded her.*

*He thought she screamed in pain, but hers was one
of pure fury. She had fought the fear and confusion
for so long, but this outraged her to the depths of
her soul. Although she hated him to think that she
submitted to his wishes, she did scream again. Her
body shook with it, her throat burned from it and her
soul felt the defeat that it meant.*

*She had lost everything that she held dear. Her
family, her home, her name—all gone now. The only
thing of value left to her had just been stolen from
her. And he laughed at her pain and her anger.*

*"Give it to me now and I will stop this." She knew
he lied, as he had each time. "Scream and then tell
me your secret. 'Twill be over then."*

*He reveled in her loss, and she could hear the
pleasure he gained from it. As she felt the wet touch
of his fingers on her breast and her cheek, and
smelled the metallic odor of spilled blood, she knew
that he marked her with her own. As on a hunt when
those on their first kill are marked with the blood of
their prey, he smeared her with her own.*

*"You will give it to me. Never doubt that you will.
No one can save you—there is no one left for you.
And without your maidenhead, you have value to no
one. You will always be mine."*

*The darkness pulled her in and she screamed no more.*

Struggling awake, Catherine sat up and fought to breathe. Her screams and the voice still echoed in her head, and she looked around the room for its source. A few beams of moonlight came in through the shuttered window. Enough for her to see that the room was empty but for her and Geoffrey. And he slept next to her, snoring lightly even as she shifted and moved.

It must be the excitement of the journey and her exhaustion that caused such strange wakenings. Gathering her hair over one shoulder, she lay back next to Geoffrey and allowed his warmth to soothe her frayed nerves. She turned on her side and he followed her, curving around her and holding her close. She felt no fear as he held her, so she knew it must be some bad dream. Soon, she felt the pull of sleep once more and let it come. As it did, she also remembered something from those dark times.

She was not a virgin.

When Geoffrey finally claimed her, he would find no virgin's blood, no proof of her virginity, for she had lost it already. She could not bleed again, even for him.

Would he forgive her if she could not remember it?

## Chapter Fifteen

The winds of autumn would come soon and bring coolness to the land. September would begin, and with it would come harvest time in England. From the sight of so many knights and fighting men amassed in Dover, she knew it would bring war to Normandy and France. Word was out that King Richard was mustering troops for some action on the Continent, and the hunger for war and its rewards spread even before their arrival in the northernmost of the Cinque Ports.

Their journey through Sandwich had been slowed by the presence of so many fighting men and their followers. The overflow of people camped along the road, for the inns and rooms of Sandwich were filled. Geoffrey had sent his man ahead to speak directly to the constable of Dover Castle.

As a nobleman on the king's business, Geoffrey told her they would have suitable accommodations before their voyage and a prompt delivery over the Channel in one of the ships reserved for the king's use. If Geoff worried over the numbers of travelers on the roads or in the town, he said nothing to her. By the time they reached the gates of Dover, Michel was there with directions to their lodgings and an invitation to dine with the constable, Lord Reginald, at the castle that very evening.

Her only worry was her lack of clothing, but Geoffrey would not let her dwell on that. And with the sea in front of her and the saltiness of the fresh air reviving her spirits and her travel-worn body, she looked forward to the rest of this trip with some anticipation.

When they arrived at their rooms, Geoffrey surprised her with a new chemise, a kirtle of blue with a matching surcoat trimmed in gold and blue, his colors, and veils for her head. How he had managed this while on the roads, she knew not, but she appreciated his thoughtfulness and care. Now she could attend the dinner at the castle without worrying that she would shame him with her appearance.

Finally, with the help of a maid and the escort of Geoffrey and his men, she arrived at Dover Castle. The edifice sat on the plateau at the top of the cliffs and commanded an impressive view of the Channel below. Entering through the gate, they proceeded to the keep and its main hall, where the meal would be served. With so many traveling through Dover, the event promised to be a loud and raucous one.

The surprising thing about it was the appearance of the dowager queen, Eleanor of Aquitaine. All activity halted at her entrance, and Catherine watched in awe as this legend among all of England—nay, the world—walked unaided up to the high table and took the seat of honor at the right hand of the constable. Nigh to four score years she had lived, and even in her dotage she was a woman of strength and, as gossip would have it, unflagging determination to hold together the Plantagenet kingdom and provinces. Once the queen was seated, Geoffrey tugged on Catherine's hand.

"Come, love. We must take our seats and not delay the queen's meal." He pulled her along the edge of the hall toward the front.

"Wait, my lord. You cannot mean for us to sit...there?" She nodded to the table on the dais, at which the highest ranking of those present sat. Then she noticed the spaces to the right of the queen. "Surely you jest."

She had never met Eleanor, neither here in England nor in Anjou as a child. And she was not certain that she would ever be prepared to meet her. What did one say to the wealthiest and most influential woman in the world? Someone who had defied kings and popes, who had gone on Crusade and who had married two of the most powerful kings of England and France?

"Cate, our place is there." Geoff looked at her and must have seen her fears, for he stopped and whispered to her. "You are Catherine of Blaye, the betrothed wife of the Comte de Langier, and must be seated as such. Come."

The pounding in her head increased with every step forward. Her palms were growing wet and she felt beads of perspiration gather and roll down her back. She would not be able to do this. Even for Geoffrey.

But he did not slow his pace or stop. She gathered

her gown in her hands and walked up the steps and then at his side as they approached the table. Instead of stopping at the empty chairs, he escorted her to Eleanor, as was appropriate. He bowed, and Catherine dipped into a deep curtsy as Geoffrey introduced her.

"Your Grace. May I present my betrothed to you? This is Catherine of Blaye, though lately of Lincoln." He turned to her and began to introduce Eleanor by her titles.

"Catherine, Her Grace, Eleanor, Duchess of Aquitaine, Countess of Poitou—"

"Geoffrey! The girl has eyes in her head. She knows who I am and needs not hear all of those acclamations. Here, girl, let me see you."

Catherine stood and moved closer to the queen. Eleanor reached out and, with a heavily bejeweled finger under her chin, lifted Catherine's face to hers. She dared to meet the gaze of the queen. Eleanor smiled at her boldness.

"A beauty, my lord. Although she is not known to me." The queen turned Catherine's head to one side and then the other, examining her closely for any signs of familiarity. "Her parents?"

"Her parents are dead, Your Grace. They were distant cousins of Lady Emalie of Harbridge, and so Catherine has been ward to the earl and countess these last few years."

"I hope not too closely related?" Catherine understood the reference to the concerns of consanguinity and affinity raised in both of Eleanor's own marriages. The glint in the queen's eyes as she asked told Catherine she was jesting.

"No, Your Grace. Just far enough apart," Geoffrey added.

"Come to the solar on the morrow, lady. I would speak with you. You may accompany her, my lord."

Eleanor turned back to Lord Reginald, and Catherine realized her presentation was over. Offering another curtsy before backing away, she breathed a deep sigh of relief that this first introduction was done. And what an extraordinary first introduction— to the queen herself! Geoffrey led her back to the seats assigned them and she sat down, barely noticing any of the food before her. She had met Eleanor of Aquitaine.

"Are you well, my lady?" he asked as he held out his cup to the serving boy. "You look pale to me now."

"I have never met the queen, my lord. I admit to being somewhat overwhelmed." She sipped at the cup he offered her. The wine, of excellent quality, moistened her dry mouth and throat.

"You did extremely well, for she invited you for a personal audience."

Now Catherine did quiver, for what would she say to the queen? What could she say without revealing too much or the wrong thing?

Geoffrey grasped her hand and brought it to his lips. "Nay, Cate, worry not on this matter. I will be with you and all will be well for us."

"Aye, my lord," she agreed, but she was not convinced of it.

She realized, as Geoffrey offered her pieces of venison and pork, that these introductions must be done if she expected to be his wife. This would be her practice, her training for meeting the king and the other nobles in Caen. Once she'd made the decision to face this challenge straight on, the rest of the meal and even the night spent wrapped in Geoffrey's arms raced by with great speed.

With immense delight, she discovered another gift of clothing waiting for her in the morning. This gown was a pale shade of green, trimmed with a darker one. Geoffrey was making such an effort that she be arrayed properly before the queen and other nobles that it touched her heart. An hour prior to noon, as directed by one of Eleanor's ladies-in-waiting, they arrived and were directed to the solar.

Although not usually a place for men to gather with the women, the crowd in the solar this morn was a mixture of gender and class and origins. Catherine heard various dialects of the French tongue being spoken as she followed the servant. Latin, Greek, Italian, even some of the harsher guttural tones of those living in the Holy Roman Empire's northernmost provinces. Eleanor drew them all to her for her wisdom, her power and, most important, her influence on her son, King Richard.

Catherine peered back and saw that Geoffrey was indeed following her, but the call of many others slowed his progress. She paused to wait for him, but Eleanor's servant urged her forward. Not wanting to disobey, she continued through the long narrow chamber until she stood before the queen. Catherine sank before her in a curtsy, waiting until her name was spoken to rise and greet Eleanor.

"Your Grace," she said, bowing her head.

"My dear Catherine, welcome to my gathering. Come, sit by me and help me to sort my threads."

The lady nearest the queen handed Eleanor a large wooden box, which she passed on to Catherine. Surprised that the queen would perform such mundane duties, Catherine nevertheless took the seat designated and began to separate the skeins of threads by color. Handing them to Eleanor as she called for them, she soon lost some of her nervousness at this meeting.

"My lord Dumont is very different from his brother, is he not?"

"Aye, Your Grace, in many ways he is." Her fingers sorted through the lengths of embroidery threads as she spoke.

"'Tis most likely due to having different mothers."

"Just so, Your Grace." So long as the conversation stayed on these informal matters, she would be fine.

"Is he ready to take his place as vassal to the king in his own right?" Eleanor's voice never changed as she shifted the questions to those of a much more personal matter.

"I believe he is, Your Grace. He has learned much from his brother the earl and from his tutors and other mentors. Especially in these last years, since the king's agreement to give him the Dumont lands, enfeoffed to him alone."

There was a pause and Catherine did not look up from her work to see if the queen was looking at her. Had she said too much?

"You have much confidence in your betrothed,

Catherine. How long have you been acquainted with the younger brother?''

''I was taken as ward to the earl and countess nigh on three years ago, Your Grace. I live mostly at the Convent of Our Blessed Lady in Lincoln, but have visited Greystone and the other Harbridge estates often.''

Although the queen's voice was soft and her manner one of friendly interest, Catherine understood the nature of this conversation. The queen was gathering facts for later use. Geoffrey had warned her of such methods on their travels to the castle, and had urged Catherine to tell the truth as much as possible.

''Your education, my dear. What did you learn from the sisters there?''

''I can read and write Latin and English fairly well, Your Grace. My skill with numbers is passing fair and I can play the flute with some modicum of talent.'' She paused before going on, and lifted her hands before her. ''And my work with the needle and threads is, as Mother Heloise and the Countess of Harbridge say, acceptable.''

''Are you fluent in the languages of the Continent? Langue d'oïl, for example?'' the queen asked in that tongue.

''I can speak that, Your Grace,'' she answered in the formal language of the Ile de France. ''As well as the one you favor in your lands, the land of my birth,'' she said, continuing in the langue d'oc that was so prevalent in Eleanor's southern provinces. Her first lie.

''And in my son's duchy? What will you speak there?'' Eleanor probed more.

Although she was growing wary of the questions, Catherine answered as expected, in the dialect of Normandy. This was her native tongue, the language of her childhood and of her family and of her ancestors. The words flowed smoothly in answer to the queen's question.

The queen's scrutiny intensified and Catherine finished speaking quickly, then changed back to the bland version of court French spoken among the ruling and noble classes. Just as it seemed that the queen would ask another question, Geoffrey approached through the crowd and bowed.

"Your Grace," he said, rising. "What think you of my lady?"

"She is charming, my lord. 'Tis no wonder you chose her to have to wife."

The words hid more than they said, and Catherine shivered. The queen noticed.

"Catherine, I have monopolized much of your time. Before you go, would you fetch me the coverlet from my bed? I grow chilled from the sea air."

Catherine placed the skeins of thread back in the box and stood.

"My sleeping chamber is through that door." Eleanor smiled and nodded her head to one side of the wall behind where they now sat.

She had been dismissed. Catherine walked toward the chamber, knowing she'd not only been dismissed, but also removed from the room. Without insulting her, Eleanor had gotten rid of her so that she herself could interrogate Geoffrey. Would their answers to her questions be the same? Had she said something to raise the queen's suspicions?

Catherine entered the chamber as directed and gathered the coverlet from the bed. When the servant closed the door behind her, she knew she was to wait before returning to the solar. Taking advantage of the privacy, she prayed that it would all work out for them.

What would Geoffrey say?

He watched as she walked away from them, convinced that Catherine knew the real reason for Eleanor's request. With dozens of servants and retainers strewn around the room, she did not need Catherine to carry out this errand. But who could refuse a request from Eleanor of Aquitaine?

"She is lovely, my lord," Eleanor offered.

"Aye, Your Grace."

"And intelligent."

"Aye, Your Grace," he agreed once more. The less said the better.

"And," she said, turning to face him where he stood, "she is not from Blaye. Your Catherine is from Anjou."

Geoff did not reply. He waited to see how far Eleanor would push their deception.

"I suspect that she is not your brother's choice for your wife." She laughed softly. "From your expression I see I am closer to the truth than you would like me to be."

He could feel the blood drain from his face as she taunted him quietly. To the others in the chamber, they were engaged in polite conversation. Only they knew the seriousness of it.

"How did you come to be betrothed to her? She

is without wealth, I assume?'' He nodded, trying to put words together to tell their story. ''I expect that the Earl of Harbridge is not happy that you let an heiress such as Melissande of Quercy slip away.''

He had heard tales of Eleanor's abilities to discern not only the facts in a situation, but also the subtleties and nuances. Now at the end of seven decades of life, she was sharper in judgment than anyone else he knew.

''Worry not, my lord. I would hear it from you before I judge. Why are you betrothed to her?''

Geoffrey decided that 'twas best to simply tell her the truth as far as he could. Eleanor had proven a worthy ally to his brother in the past, even saving their lives by calling upon Christian to aid her. If she suspected that he was lying to her, she could prove herself a formidable enemy.

''To protect her honor and her life,'' he said without hesitation. Then he looked at the queen and gave the real reason. ''And because I love her.''

He was not certain how she would react to his words, so he looked away and waited.

''Ah, my lord. You aspire to the courtly ideals that I preached in those long-ago days of my youth. Those ideals are strained now against the true nature and mores of the world in which we live.'' Eleanor looked toward her bedchamber. ''What did you say to overcome your brother's objections? He has the right to approve your marriage until you attain your titles, I believe.''

The queen knew entirely too much of his situation. How could she have such facts within her grasp?

''The king's orders changed everything, Your

Grace. The reward for coming at his call is the immediate investiture of my titles and confirmation of my choice of wife.''

The queen sat back against her chair and did not respond to his words. This must be something unknown to her. She tapped her fingers on the arm of the chair and stared off into the distance as she digested what he had told her. Eleanor nodded to her lady-in-waiting and the door to her chamber was opened for Catherine. The questioning was at an end, but would she support or oppose this marriage?

He read the nervousness on Catherine's face; the slight furrowing of her delicate brow and the paleness of her cheeks told him that she worried at the outcome of this interview. As she brought the requested coverlet to the queen, she curtsied and held it out for the queen's servants to place on their mistress. Eleanor's eyes widened as she looked closely at Catherine, but then the expression of surprise faded from her face.

''I am to Caen and the king on my way to Fontrevault. Since I go first to Richard, you must travel with me there so that I may lend my support to this worthy cause.''

''But Your Grace, I travel with seven knights. I would not impose our party on your generosity. Lord Reginald assures me that we will have passage by week's end.''

''My lord Dumont,'' she said as she stood. Everyone in the room quieted to hear her words. ''God willing, I leave on the morning tide and you will leave with me. Lord Reginald will make it so.''

Her voice carried through the chamber and all

heard it. No one could refuse an offer such as this from the queen. Geoffrey took Catherine by the hand, and she lowered herself in a curtsy even as he leaned forward in a bow.

"Your gracious offer cannot be refused. We would be honored to accompany you on your voyage and journey to Caen."

Before he could back away, the queen brought him closer with a wave of her hand. Geoffrey leaned down so that he could hear her words.

"Arrange the witnesses for the bedding and claim her before you reach the king. You would do well to heed my words on this matter."

Taken aback by her advice, he stumbled a few steps to where Catherine stood waiting. Never would he have expected those words from the queen. In her wisdom, she obviously thought there was some valid reason to finalize their marriage prior to presenting Catherine to the king.

If he had given her his word and assurances that they would not consummate their betrothal until Caen, how could he go back on that now? So it was with a sick feeling in the pit of his stomach that he did not heed the queen's words.

# *Chapter Sixteen*

With their horses stowed safely below deck and their few belongings stored in the small cabin assigned them for the voyage, Geoffrey took Catherine on the main deck to watch as they left England behind and headed for their life together. Although being on the queen's ship lent a certain measure of security to their travel, his knights still guarded the gold they carried for his brother's scutage payment to the king.

As God had apparently willed it and the queen had ordered it, the weather had come up clear and the winds favorable for their departure, so within a hour or so of dawn, the ship left the port of Dover on its way to the northern coast of Normandy.

If all went as expected, the rest of his knights would meet them at the Château Gaillard on the Seine within another sennight. Geoffrey had left the decision of their route and method of travel up to Girard. His man knew time was short and timing was important to the king's plans, so Geoff did not doubt that the men of Langier would arrive as needed.

They did not see or talk to Eleanor while boarding the ship, and while he'd thought they might be summoned to a meal, they were not. Word spread that the queen was not traveling well and would be in her chambers through the voyage. 'Twas the first sign of weakness that he ever remembered hearing of the indefatigable queen.

But Catherine glowed on the sea. The air and motion as their ship crossed the waves seemed to strengthen her and make her more beautiful than before. Whatever exhaustion and physical problems the difficult travel on horseback had wrought, the sea released them. She stood at his side as the winds took them farther into the Channel, and he gave in to the temptation she offered in being so near and so alive.

He conspired to see her as he fantasized—with her hair freed of its confining snood and being blown wild by the winds. Just before they sought their cabin for the night, he took her in his arms and kissed her breathless. Then, tugging the confounded accoutrement loose, he shook her tresses free and enjoyed the sight of them. Although she tried to recapture her locks into a braid, he grasped her hands and prevented her from doing so. Catherine laughed at his antics and promised that her hair would always be loosened in their chambers.

Although he did not arrange for the formal bedding as the queen had suggested, he did share Catherine's bed and he pleasured her with his mouth and hands and body until she moaned for him. There was no reticence at all in her reaction to him, and he managed to hold his own desires in check with difficulty. He waited only for the night he claimed her, and then she would know the depth of his feelings for her.

And just longer than a day after they'd set sail from Dover, the queen's ship approached the port on the coast of Normandy closest to the king's city of Caen. Arrangements for landing, unloading their horses and getting provisions for the ride to the castle were made by the constable's men on board as part of their duties to the king.

Eleanor's retainer gave Geoffrey and Catherine leave of her, so that they could travel at their own speed to Caen, and by late morn they were on the path that would lead them to his titles, their marriage and his duties to the king.

Only one day remained before coming into the presence of the king. Geoffrey thought on Eleanor's words, but decided that waiting until all objections were answered was the better way to handle this. His precipitous removal of Catherine from the convent precluded them from going back, so he would meet with his brother on their return, and make peace with him. Mayhap, as Emalie had suggested, they could celebrate their marriage at Greystone.

They passed many people on the road to the castle, and Geoffrey's stomach tightened in anticipation of receiving his lands from the king the next day. Geoffrey had been presented to Richard long ago, in good circumstances and bad, but he had not seen the king in several months and knew nothing of his plans or why this call was so important that it made Richard grant concessions in return for Geoffrey's participation.

Soon they were on the road leading to the Exchequer's Castle, as it was now called, and he leaned over and grasped Catherine's hand. The smile she offered did not say much of pleasant expectations.

"Soon, Catherine, soon," he said, lifting her hand to his lips and kissing it. A smile filled her face. He kissed her hand again and then let it go so that she could maintain control of her mount. No longer the sturdy mount she'd ridden across half of England, this one was made jittery by the crowds on the roads.

Their group approached the castle from the north, along the wide avenue that led over a drawbridge and moat, through the outer wall and on to the Vieux Palais. William the Conqueror's original donjon now stood before them, while Richard's father had built the Vieux Palais and the Hall of the Exchequer to house all of the king's officials and services. His treasury was overseen there, as well as official documents and the administrative details of the Plantagenet kingdom here and in England.

Aymer led them to a place where they could dismount and prepare for their entrance into the palace.

"The king awaits you, my lord," he said, helping Catherine to the ground. "And you, as well, my lady."

The four knights sworn to Harbridge unloaded the satchels of gold from the packhorses, and each carried two. They would present them to the king, but then take them to his exchequer, who would verify the amount and keep an accounting of their use. Aymer led the way, with Michel and Jean following them and the knights with the gold at the back.

Up two stairways and down a corridor they went, passing many knights and lords and ladies who were all awaiting the king's attention. Geoff greeted several he knew as they passed, but did not delay their progress. There would be time enough later to speak to his acquaintances. At last he could see the high table on the raised dais and hear the voice of Richard, Coeur de Lion, over the others. Geoff paused and took a deep breath. Then, with Catherine at his side, he moved forward.

He stood at the bottom of the dais and waited for the king to pause in his discussions. When they were noticed, he bowed deeply, still holding Catherine's hand as she dipped almost to the floor, as was expected before the king. Holding their positions, they waited for the king's greeting.

"Dumont!" the king shouted. "'Twould seem you spared no time in answering my call. Come and greet your king."

Richard stood on the dais, hands outstretched to him, so Geoffrey climbed to the top step. There he knelt before the king and bowed his head. Richard touched the top of it and then placed his hands on Geoff's shoulders, pulling him to his feet. 'Twas not the formal pledge, but a sign nonetheless that Geoffrey Dumont and the estates and wealth of Langier were sworn to the king.

"Your men?" he asked, peering around Geoff to look over the group.

"The Langier knights travel directly to Gaillard, Your Grace. They should arrive by week's end."

"Excellent!" the king called out. "And they will be led by their count, who will take his oath of fealty to me this very night."

The first part of their bargain would be fulfilled by night's end. Did Richard remember the rest of it?

"Who stands with you? Bring them forward." The king stepped back and crossed his arms over his chest. Although there was a chair near him, he chose to stand.

"These are my men, Sir Aymer, Michel and Jean. And the Harbridge knights carry my brother's payment in lieu of his attendance here before you."

He waved the knights forward and they knelt before the king. Intent on introducing Catherine next, Geoff did not see the entourage approaching from the side.

"Only half of the gold pays my scutage, Your Grace. The other half is a gift in gratitude to our liege lord on the occasion of my brother's investiture as Comte de Langier."

"Christian? Why are you here?" Shocked over his brother's sudden appearance, Geoffrey could not even begin to contemplate all the implications of this. It did not bode well, though.

"His Grace summoned me, as you well know, brother, and I chose to bring half the knights requested by him." Christian walked up the steps and stood at his side. "And I would not miss witnessing your oath to the king on behalf of the Dumont family."

So, his brother had known or discovered the contents of Geoff's summons to the king and the rewards offered. Most likely the reverend mother would have informed him of the actions taken at the convent. Still, regardless of how he'd found out the truth, part of Geoffrey was pleased to have his brother at his side. Except...

"We will continue business this evening, but there is one who you have not introduced to me. Bring her forward."

Would Christian voice his objections now? To the king? Geoff hesitated for a moment and then turned to help Catherine up the steps. She was standing off to one side, nearer the onlookers than to his men or Christian's, as though she was trying to hide. Did she fear repudiation now?

Once more she did not fail him, for as he raised his hand to her, she moved forward and took it, allowing him to escort her up to meet the king. She did surprise him in one thing. Before kneeling before the king, she gifted his brother with a nod of deference, not ignoring him as she probably wanted to.

"Your Grace, may I present my betrothed wife, Catherine, to you?"

The silence around them grew as the king inspected Catherine and as Geoff waited for his brother's voice to speak out against her. Then Richard spoke.

"Since you have already impressed my mother, I have no doubt that you will do the same to the rest of our court, Lady Catherine. Rise now and be welcomed here."

Geoff heard Christian's indrawn breath, but did not meet his gaze. Instead he reached down to assist Catherine to her feet and then waited for the king's dismissal.

"Tonight then, I will accept your oath before all of my nobles. Your first duty to me will be your attendance at the meeting of my councillors in the morn.'' Richard brought a man to him with a wave. ''My steward will see to your needs. Harbridge, send your gold to the exchequer in the hall.''

A flurry of activity followed, with everyone hurrying to carry out the king's orders. Soon only Christian, Catherine and Geoffrey were left standing before the dais. Another servant came forward and informed them that Catherine was being housed within the queen's apartments. With a look of much trepidation, she walked off behind the woman to go to her chambers to prepare for the night and the important festivities ahead.

That left him there to face his brother for the first time since he'd ridden off to the convent. Without telling him of his plans. Without telling him of the king's grant.

When he would have spoken, Christian stopped him. ''Let us seek out our chamber and some measure of privacy before opening wounds.''

They followed another servant through the Vieux Palais and out through the courtyard to another building. This one was a barracks made to house many knights and fighting men. As due their station, they were given one of the few private chambers for their use. When the servant left, pulling the door shut behind him, it was time for the reckoning that Geoffrey knew would come.

''Why, Geoff?''

''Why what? Why did I take Catherine from the convent? Why did I not tell you of my plans? Which of those do you wish to know?'' Anger built within him. He was tired of needing his brother's approval and permission. Tonight he became his own man and things would be different.

"What have I done to lose your trust?" Christian sat down on one of the cots in the chamber and put his head in his hands. "Why did you not trust me in this?" he repeated.

"'Tis not about trust, Chris. 'Tis about claiming my inheritance, my rights."

"Inheritance? You have no inheritance, Geoff. Remember your place—you are the second son and by our laws and practices nothing comes to you that I do not grant." Christian looked at him with bleak eyes before continuing. "And despite the deals I have struck with the king to regain the lands that should be mine, and give them to you, you did not trust me enough to tell me your true intentions."

Guilt burned Geoffrey's gut and bile churned as he heard the accusations. He was the second son of the long-dead Guillaume Dumont who had paid for his sins of betrayal with his lands, his titles, his life and nearly the lives of his sons. If his father had lived and kept faith with King Richard, all would have gone on his death directly to Christian as his heir. Geoffrey would have received some small amount of gold or a small gift of property and been expected to marry a woman whose dower lands he would protect and pass on to their son.

'Twas the way of it.

And now that he was instead receiving the rich portion of the bargain worked out by his brother, he should have looked for a bride to form alliances, one who would bring more wealth and lands that his son would inherit. Instead, he was going to marry the woman he loved. A woman who brought nothing to their union but herself.

He loved Catherine, and he would stand by his pledge to her. But he finally understood some of his brother's reasons for being angry over his choice.

"I would have told you. When I heard Evesham plotting to kidnap her, I knew I must act."

"Pah," Christian yelled. "That was simply an excuse on your part to ignore my objections, my valid objections, to your considering her for marriage." He stood now and paced the cramped length of the chamber. "My men and those of the sheriff of Lincolnshire could have protected the convent from any attack. If you had told me of the threat, I would have acted immediately to bring her to safety." He stopped and turned to face his brother. "But you saw this for the opportunity it was—you could take her from the convent on the pretext of the coming danger and, knowing the reverend mother would not allow her to leave with you under any other circumstances, you used the king's orders and that nun to secure the betrothal to an unacceptable bride."

"I told you I wanted her to wife. I told you I love her. You forced my hand in this." The words and accusation sounded false even as Geoff spoke the words, but at least he'd said them.

"You wanted her? You love her? If that is true, you would never have brought her into this. She is not suitable for many reasons, only some of which you know, some you cannot even begin to guess at. For those of us of noble blood and standing, love and want are not reasons to marry. Honor and duty and security are. And you have turned your back on all who have gone before you by pledging yourself to her.''

Geoff watched as his brother leaned against a wall and closed his eyes. Instead of anger, Geoff saw only exhaustion and pain in his stance.

''I am protecting her honor now. I have made my pledge to her, and to break it would dishonor her before all.''

''Have you slept with her?'' his brother asked.

Clenching his teeth, he did not answer at first.

''Come, Geoff, have you consummated this betrothal or not?''

''No,'' he said quietly.

''Why not? You had the right. You had the time and surely the opportunity, if you've been traveling together for the last eleven nights. Why did you not take her and seal the bargain made?''

The words of explanation were right there waiting to be said, but his brother's questions raised the same doubts that had plagued Geoff since London. Why had he not? What was he waiting for? What held him from acting on the betrothal?

''You see, somewhere inside of you, in the place where you think and do not act on feelings, you know this is wrong. You know you have moved hastily or else you would have sealed this contract with her blood on the sheets.''

''This is not wrong, Christian. Do not misunderstand my hesitation. It was for Catherine that I delayed.''

''You delayed for her then? Mayhap she is showing the kind of levelheadedness that Emalie claims she possesses. Or mayhap it was simply maidenly fears? Did she ask for more time to accommodate herself to this? To you?'' His brother became distant, as though hearing another conversation or seeing another place in his mind. Then he looked at Geoff and waited for an answer.

''She knew you would have objections and did not want to make it impossible for us… She did not want to make things difficult between you and me.''

Christian pushed away from the wall and pointed at him. ''She did not want to make this betrothal irrevocable. Catherine was giving you a way out of this, giving both of you a way out, with your honor intact.''

Geoff could not argue, for those were Catherine's reasons exactly. Although he did not want to disavow their betrothal, she had given him the chance to do so if necessary.

''I do not want a way out of our betrothal, Christian. I will marry her.''

''All I ask is that you consider my words and consider if you are taking this path only to prove yourself in control of your life. Tonight, you become Langier. Will you bring honor to its long history or will you bring disgrace upon it? That is the question you must answer for yourself.''

Christian moved past him to the door of the chamber. ''If there is nothing else to say between us, I need some water and to find out where my clothing is.''

''There is one thing I want to say.'' Geoff stopped him with a hand on his arm. ''I admit to having much to consider, and to having considered much during these last few weeks, but I have something for you to contemplate, brother. How many of the objections you raise about Catherine are truly about you and not at all about her? About your regrets at choices made? About the anger you feel at being challenged by your younger brother? About your discomfort with possibly being wrong in this?''

His brother opened the door, and there was Luc Delacroix, followed by a line of servants carrying trays of food and drink, washing cloths and basins, as well as their bags. Christian nodded to his man and the room was filled with everything needed to make them comfortable and ready for the festivities of the night.

''I will give you some privacy now and go to see if Catherine is settled in her room,'' Geoff said.

''Did that go as well as it seemed, my lord?''

''Leave it be,'' Christian mumbled as he dipped his hands in the basin of water and splashed it on his face. After days in the saddle and in his mail, he was anxious to get it off. Reaching for a towel, he wiped his face and glared at his friend. ''You know that it did not, so why do you torment me with your questions?''

''I had hopes that you two could settle this between you and not make it of interest to the Plantagenets. Things have a way of getting out of control when it moves into their line of sight.''

Luc moved around the chamber, rearranging the meager furnishings and pushing the pallets into three areas. They would share this room, while their men were in the one of the common areas. At least until they left for Château Gaillard and whatever the king planned there.

"I fear that is too late now. From Richard's comment and the arrangements here, I surmise Catherine has already been presented to the queen and made a favorable impression."

Luc picked up a cup and filled it from a jug of wine. Passing it to him, he asked, "And you are certain that would be a bad thing?"

"I cannot believe that you ask that of me! You know who she is, you and I both know—"

"Suspect."

"We know what most likely happened to her during that year in John's control. No matter what he may have promised her brother about her safekeeping, we know what he is capable of."

"What will you do now? Will you object when the time comes?"

"Luc, I swear I do not know." Christian walked to the small window high in one wall and peered through it. "I know that this is not about blaming the girl. Truly, 'tis not. He could have so much more than what she brings him."

"More? How so, Christian? More lands, more titles, more wealth? Certainly. But have you watched them together? Do you see what she truly brings to him?"

"And what will happen when he learns the truth of her illness? Of her missing years? Of what happened to her? How will he feel about their love when he learns he was not the first? That another man or men knew her flesh before he did?"

His friend's face became thunderously dark and

Christian knew the wrong words had been spoken. Once more he had reminded Luc of his wife Fatin's life as a harem slave before they had married, a reminder better left unspoken. Suddenly, he could not breathe. Luc grabbed his tunic with such force that it closed the cloth and the mail under it around his throat. When he was about to lose consciousness, the grasp was loosened and he fell to the floor, gasping for breath.

"He was right. This is more about you and your anger than about whether or not he should marry Catherine. We have traveled down this path before, my lord, and I thought you had learned the lesson along it. Do not head this way. Let the past go." Luc whispered the words in a harsh voice, one filled with emotion.

"That is why I seek to make him understand. I struggle with this still. At least you have no proof of past indiscretions in front of you every day when you wake."

At his words, Luc hissed with an indrawn breath, but a glance told him that his friend understood the pain within him.

There. He had voiced his deepest weakness. He would never know if the daughter he raised as his own had been fathered by the man he'd killed or by the Plantagenet puppet master behind it all. For even though William de Severin had said only he bedded the countess, doubt still lingered within Christian's mind about the extent of Prince John's role in Emalie's downfall.

"I would save him this pain, this uncertainty," Christian added bleakly.

Luc approached him and put a hand on his shoulder. "'Tis far too late for that, I fear. If you wish to save him from pain you must arm him with the truth before another disarms him with falsehoods. Make him understand."

"And if he still wants to marry her?"

"He is his own man now, Christian. He would not deserve your respect if he let you make this decision for him. He would not respect himself."

"I will think on this. He has been like my son and I struggle to think him a man on his own."

"And do not fathers and sons struggle to find an accommodation of each other? Now, I do not wish to be maudlin with you, so let this go for now. Here," he said, holding out some cold meat to him. "Eat something while I go learn the lay of this land."

A moment later Luc left, off to do what he did best—search out the facts and the situation and prepare Christian for whatever came his way. Luc's attentiveness to details had saved him many missteps, aggravation and even harm in their years together. His friend's perspective had saved Dumont many nights sleep, and even his marriage to Emalie. Out of respect for all that, and the pain in his heart over his separation from his wife, both in distance and in discord, Christian realized he must find peace with all these issues before he lost everything he held dear.

## Chapter Seventeen

After the austere conditions of the convent in Lincoln and despite her recent visit to Greystone, Catherine was not prepared for the ostentatious displays in Richard's court. War might be in the offing—indeed, just over the next horizon—but that did not stop his nobles and knights from feasting and drinking and celebrating any event that needed merriment.

No fabric or style or headpiece or jewel or ornament of any kind was missing among this gathering. Although Catherine wore clothing that Geoffrey had gifted her with, she felt very much a drab pigeon among festive peacocks.

But Eleanor had done much to soothe her fears, and now Catherine was determined to enjoy this night's festivity. She would see the man she loved ascend to his title and step out on his own, away from his brother, and become the man he was destined to be. Even if nothing else came to pass, she was thrilled to be witness to this.

As she walked to the hall with the queen's ladies-in-waiting, she could feel a nervousness inside her.

Although she hadn't visited the place of her birth for a number of years, she still worried that someone would recognize Catherine de Severin. 'Twas not likely, but still possible. The only people present who knew her real name were Geoffrey and the earl, and she knew neither would reveal it to anyone.

They arrived to much fanfare as the queen made her way to the high table. From whispered instructions, Catherine understood that she herself would sit there, with Geoffrey. Following Eleanor, she climbed the steps, circled the table and found herself seated not only next to Geoffrey, but beside the Earl of Harbridge. She lost whatever appetite she had as she took her place.

Geoffrey clasped her hand and leaned over to kiss her quickly. His honest emotions lifted her dampened spirits, and she remembered the new clothes she wore.

"I am most grateful for your generosity, my lord," she said, smiling at him. "I hope you are pleased with this gown as much as you liked the others?"

"If you are happy with them, I am pleased, Catherine."

She realized he and his brother were both arrayed in their best, even to the chains of gold that hung around their necks. She decided to make the first attempt with his brother.

"May I compliment you both—" she looked from one to the other "—on your appearance this evening? I do not remember seeing either of you so splendidly dressed before."

Geoffrey smiled widely and patted her hand. "'Tis a very special night, Cate, and I am pleased you can share it with me.'' He leaned forward, looking past her at his brother. ''What say you to my lady's compliment?''

If the truth be told, the earl appeared more prepared to vomit than to speak to her. But his years of courtly training won out over any anger on his part.

''A new tunic,'' he mumbled without any further explanation. Well, at least he had not shouted words of repudiation to those assembled. She silently thanked the Almighty for the small kindness granted.

The earl's attention was taken by the queen, who sat on his other side, and that gave Catherine a reprieve from having to converse with him. Geoffrey, however, devoted all of his attention to her through the meal—feeding her from the platters filled to overflowing and carried around by the servers, drawing attention to her empty cup so it could be refilled and even including her in the conversations around him so she would not be left out.

Soon, the subtleties and sweet wines and sugar-coated wafers and pastries were served, marking the end of the meal. Geoffrey tensed as the servants cleared away trenchers and platters. She knew the ceremony would soon begin, and she took his hand under the table to offer him her support and her love.

The king stood and walked around the table to a high-backed chair that had been placed there for his use. Charles, Bishop of Caen, followed the king and stood at his side. When all was ready, the king's herald called out to the assembly, demanding that the Count of Langier present himself and do homage to the Count of Poitou for the lands he held. When Catherine expected Geoffrey to stand, he did not. Instead, the earl stood and walked slowly over and knelt before the king.

"Christian Dumont, Comte de Langier, when your lands and titles were returned to you as a reward for services rendered to the crown, you named your brother, the younger son of Guillaume Dumont, as your heir. Do you confirm that it is still your wish to name him so?"

The earl raised his head and stared directly at Geoffrey. Catherine could not take a breath as she watched the exchange between the two brothers. Geoffrey still clutched her hand under the table, and she felt the tremors as he heard his brother's affirmations. This gifting of property and title was extraordinary among nobles, and Catherine recognized the importance of it.

"Aye, sire, it is my wish." The earl's voice carried throughout the hall, echoing to the back.

"Christian Dumont, when your lands and titles were returned to you, you declared that at the time of his majority or at a time designated by the crown, those lands and titles would be conferred on him. Is it your wish that it be done so now?"

Her heart pounded in her chest as she observed the royal drama before her. There were hundreds of persons present, and yet no sound marred the silence and the majesty of the moment. Christian raised his lowered head and once more stared across the table at Geoffrey. His confidence in his brother was obvious, and tears clogged her throat as any misgivings about his motives fled.

"Aye, sire," he said loudly. "It is my wish."

"What sign do you give that this is done of your free will and with your blessing?"

Without a word, the earl reached under the neck of his tunic and lifted out the ring she knew he always wore on a chain. She gasped as he tugged on the chain, breaking it and freeing the ring. He did not hesitate in handing it to the king. Richard closed his hand around it and nodded to the herald again.

The herald read out all of the earl's holdings in England, those in his name and in his wife's. When he finished, the king spoke.

"Christian Dumont, Earl of Harbridge, whom do you designate as heir to those lands just named?"

"I name my son, Gaspar Dumont, as my heir, with all rights to those lands and titles."

"Do you swear fealty to me as King of England, before God and this assembly, for the lands and titles confirmed to you this day?"

Richard held out his hands and the earl placed his in the king's grasp. "I am your man, sire."

Before the king released him, the bishop stepped forward and made the sign of the cross above the earl's head, consecrating this oath. Once done, the king released the earl and clapped him on the shoulders, bringing him to his feet. The earl took his place next to the bishop, and Catherine knew it was time for Geoffrey to swear his oath. There could be no prouder day for either of them, and the tears flowed freely now down her cheeks. With a nod, she released his hand so that he might go when called.

This time, the herald called him only by name for, as Eleanor had explained to her earlier, all titles relating to the Langier estates had symbolically been returned to the king by his brother. Geoffrey rose and walked to the place before Richard. Kneeling before the king, he lowered his head in homage as his brother had. The king's deep voice rang out once more, sending shivers through her with each word.

"Geoffrey Dumont, the lands and titles of Langier have been granted to the Dumont family by right of inheritance and in recognition of service to the crown. It is my wish that these lands and titles be conferred upon you this day so that you may serve me by serving them as guardian and steward of their people and their gifts. Do you accept this confirmation of the title of Comte de Langier and all it entails?"

"I do, sire," Geoffrey said. His voice was strong and clear, resonating with power and maturity.

"Geoffrey Dumont, do you swear fealty to me as King of England, Duke of Aquitaine and Normandy and Count of Anjou and Poitou, before God and this assembly, for the lands and titles conferred upon you this day?"

Geoffrey raised his head and met the king's gaze. "I do, sire."

Now the king reached for Geoffrey's hand and slid the ring given by the earl, their father's ring, onto his finger. With his hands between Richard's, Geoffrey lifted his eyes to the king. Before he could say the words, his brother moved to his side and placed a hand on Geoffrey's shoulder. Overwhelmed by this sign of peace between them yet not wanting to intrude or embarrass them, Catherine clutched her napkin to her mouth to cover the sounds of her cries.

"I am your man, sire," Geoff said to the king.

The bishop came forward once more to bless the new count, and then Richard called out his last question.

"Comte de Langier, whom do you designate as your heir?"

"Sire, I name Christian Dumont as my heir until such time as, by God's will, I am blessed with children."

"It is declared that Geoffrey Dumont is, from this day forward, the Comte de Langier, holder of all of the lands and titles conferred upon him as belonging to Langier. Further, it will be known that Christian Dumont will stand as heir of his brother's holdings."

A great cheer went through the chamber, almost deafening in its intensity, and Catherine let the sobs she'd held in through the formal procedure out now. Masked by the celebration, she could weep openly for many inspired by such a commanding and impressive ceremony did so. She watched with pride and joy as Geoffrey and his brother first hugged each other and then were greeted and congratulated by many friends and court members.

Although she wanted to be with Geoff, she understood her place was not there, not yet. He needed time to adjust to the demands and expectations of his new position. So she sat at the table and sipped some wine. Soon she realized that she would not want to distract Geoffrey from the celebrations he deserved.

"Your Grace?" she said, leaning closer to the queen. "Would it be inappropriate for me to retire for the evening?"

Eleanor smiled and patted her hand. "Appropriate and wise, my dear. Lady Constance will accompany you back to our suite." Catherine rose and walked with Constance off the dais and out through the corridor leading to the royal apartments.

The sound of running footsteps behind them startled her, and she turned just as Geoffrey caught up to her and swept her off her feet. Spinning her around and around, he laughed, calling out her name. Then, already dizzy from the spinning, he wrapped his arms around her and kissed her hungrily—so ardently that they fell against the wall, to the obvious amusement of Constance, who burst out laughing.

"Where do you go, my lady?"

"Geoffrey…er, my lord," Catherine said, realizing now that he held a much higher rank and could not be called by his familiar name in the presence of anyone but family. "You must attend to the king and to others, and I did not want to intrude on this special time for you. Go now." She pushed at his shoulders, but he would not release her. "Please."

He stepped back a tiny bit and then looked down into her eyes. "Were you crying?"

"Aye, my lord. I was."

"Were you impressed?"

"Aye, my lord, you were most impressive," she teased, but meant it nonetheless.

"I will endeavor always to impress you, my lady." He kissed her again and then let her go.

She did want him to know the part of the ceremony that had made the deepest impact on her, so she pulled him close and whispered, "I am most happy that you and your brother are at peace."

"I am as well, Cate."

When it seemed as though he would stay longer, she waved him off. He claimed one more kiss before running back to the hall. Constance laughed and, as they turned back to their path, another sound behind them made Catherine glance back. Christian Dumont stood watching. He nodded to her, then followed his brother.

Only much later, as she drifted off to sleep, did Catherine realize that for the first time in their acquaintance, the earl's eyes had not turned cold and hard when he'd looked at her in the corridor. For once, only troubled concern filled his gaze.

## Chapter Eighteen

Geoffrey observed the meeting with a sense of awe. Although he had some amount of experience in tournaments and a few minor battles, the scope of the engagements being discussed were beyond anything he knew. And to be in the presence of the greatest warriors and military strategists of the age was a humbling experience. The king demonstrated the quick mind and excellence in planning a campaign that had earned him the respect of most of the world. Now, his attention was focused on the intentions of Phillip Augustus of France.

"What say you, Guillaume? Is Rouen safe?"

The man known as le Maréchal answered his king. "Aumale gives some protection to Rouen, and with that intact it is safe. If what we hear is correct, that area will be Phillip's first target."

"Not Gaillard or even Rouen itself?" the king asked.

"Nay, sire," le Maréchal explained as he pointed at a map spread out on the table before them. "Despite his claims otherwise, Gaillard will withstand any siege. And, of course, he must get to it in order to set up a siege.'' He pointed again to the map. ''And we control the lands surrounding Gaillard, up to Gisors itself.''

''Phillip has no liking of that!'' the king called out to everyone present. ''As I have no liking that the Vexin is under French control. Would that I could…'' His words drifted off, but their meaning was clear.

''But sire, we are all ever mindful of the Treaty of Louviers, and only seek to protect what is ours,'' Guillaume le Maréchal placated. ''If Phillip makes the first move—''

Richard jumped to his feet and walked around the table, leaning over to look more closely at the cities of Normandy and France. ''He will, Guillaume. I know him and it goads him to be stopped at Gisors as much as it bothers me that he is there at all. He will move. And he will do it soon.'' Looking at his commander, he asked, ''Are we ready for whatever comes?''

''Mercadier is making arrangements now, sire. He awaits your word and presence to finalize the plans.''

''Then let us join him at Gaillard and prepare a warm welcome for the French king.''

His words signaled the end of the council session, and Geoffrey was not surprised to discover that the move to Gaillard was already underway. He spotted Christian off on one side of the room and made his way there. The final details of moving men and nobles and the king to his war castle on the Seine would take some time to arrange, so Geoffrey guessed that they would not leave for at least two or three days.

Christian did not speak, but nodded at him to follow. His brother kept his own counsel in these situations and Geoff knew he would not speak in the open about his feelings on the king's plans. A few minutes later, they stood outside on the ramparts of Caen Castle, watching the activities in the yard below. Luc and Aymer approached.

"We are to Gaillard then, my lord?" Luc asked Christian.

"Aye, and it is as you suspected, Luc."

"'Tis the way of kings to take and relinquish and take back again."

"How did you know this, Luc? Were you present in the council discussions?"

Christian smiled at him. "Luc can discover the truth of most situations before others suspect. He has…"

"Spies?" Geoff asked. He knew his brother relied on this knight, as castellan of Greystone and more.

"I prefer to call them informants."

"And what have they told you?" he asked. Interestingly, he noticed that Luc waited for his brother's nod of permission before continuing. He hoped that one day Aymer would be his "Luc."

"The provocation that Richard needs is coming. Phillip craves an opening to the sea, and with the limitations placed by Richard's Rock, Aumale is his next target. The mustering of forces is making Phillip nervous enough to do something unwise. Since Aumale is so important to the defenses of Rouen, Richard cannot afford to lose it. And that will be his pretext for taking back Gisors and the Vexin."

The depth of Luc's knowledge impressed Geof-

frey, and he looked to Christian for his opinion. He
and his men were already sworn to Richard's campaign and he wanted to understand all the players in
this game. ''You think the king will go that far?'' he
asked.

''Control of the Vexin is at the heart of this, and
each king picks at old wounds. The one who makes
the first move may regret having done so when it is
finished,'' Christian explained.

''Just so,'' Luc confirmed.

''Our part?'' Geoff asked.

''Why, to be faithful vassals to our king!'' Christian smacked him on the shoulder and laughed.
''That is the easy part.''

''Easy? How so?''

''With Guillaume le Maréchal and Mercadier di-
recting our strategies and Coeur-de-Lion leading us
in battle, we will be unstoppable. I would not want
to be Phillip if he initiates this fight.''

Geoffrey thought on his brother's words. More
than a little nervousness passed through him at the
thought of his first true battles ahead. That was mixed
with a hearty dose of expectation and excitement at
the challenges and experiences to come.

''You see, Luc. Newly raised to his titles and he
is already chaffing to do battle for his king.''

It struck Geoff, then. He would march into battle
in a few days. His heart pounded and his palms grew
sweaty. This was happening. Finally, all that he had
planned for and prepared for over the last three years
was coming to fruition.

''I am ready,'' he answered.

There was much laughing and boasting, but something bothered Geoffrey. His first step taken, he wanted to secure his marriage to Catherine before he left on the king's campaign. If anything happened to him, she would be alone. As much as he wanted to believe that Christian supported him, Geoff did not trust that his benevolence would extend to Catherine now that she—now that they both—had defied him.

He pulled Christian aside to ask a more personal question. "How does Emalie manage the separations? What do you do to prepare for times like this?" He needed to tell Catherine that he was off to fight, but lacked the finesse he thought would be needed to handle it with care.

"Emalie was raised to expect this life. Her father traveled between his estates, just as ours did, and Emalie watched and imitated her mother. With Luc normally in charge of the castle and defenses, she keeps busy with all of the other daily responsibilities that a chatelaine must."

"I know that, Chris. I mean in a personal way. How do you leave her? What words do you say when they may be your last to her?"

A stricken look passed over his brother's face and then pain filled his eyes. "Not the right ones this time, I fear," he said in a whisper. "We had not settled the discord between us and there were no soft words of farewell."

"This was my fault, Chris. I am sorry for having caused these problems for you and Emalie."

"Nay, brother. You were the catalyst, I admit, but the fault of these difficulties between us is mine." Christian walked to the side of the ramparts and looked over the crenellated wall at the courtyard below. "I thought I had dealt with all the demons that plague our marriage. I began to believe that I was worthy of the love she bears me. But old enmities raise themselves and I do not have the right weapons to vanquish them."

He spoke as though he meant a real person, but Geoff was not certain of it.

"Is there aught I can do to help you? I would do anything for you and your wife, who have done so much for me."

Christian began to answer, then stopped. Thinking for a moment, he said, "There is not, for only I can make it right between us."

Uncomfortable with the tone and direction of these comments, Geoff tried to lighten the moment. "Then you must make certain that you return to your wife and repair the breach between you."

"I will try. And I hope you will cover my back in battle to ensure that?"

"Aye, brother."

"I see someone who has bided her time until she could speak with you. Go to her now and speak the words so there are no regrets when you leave."

Geoff looked down and saw Catherine standing below, in conversation with one of Eleanor's ladies. Could his brother's words mean he had accepted their betrothal?

"Do I have your support then?" he asked, holding his breath as he waited to hear the words.

"I cannot give you what you wish for, Geoff."

Shaking his head, he prepared to go. He had thought that Christian's presence here and his participation in the ceremony last evening bespoke a new understanding between them, but he was wrong.

"Geoff, hear me. Please." Chris stopped him with a hand on his arm. "I would ask that you consider your actions before taking them. You acted in haste that day at the convent, and we have not yet sorted it out. Do not repeat your hurriedness and do something that cannot be undone."

"I will marry her." Why could Chris not just let this go? Why must he try to stand in the way of how it would be?

"If you will, wait until we return from the king's campaign. Give yourself and Catherine time to consider what this will mean. The impact and importance of it."

"You mean give you time to find a way to annul it, do you not?"

"I have no power over you now, Geoff. The ceremony last night severed any links that caused one of us to be master over the other. Now we are only two brothers in service to the same king." Christian walked closer to him. "And I say what I mean—take these next days or weeks and know that the feelings just discovered, just recognized and voiced between you, are true. Do not rush into this. If the betrothal process had occurred as we were planning, you and your bride would have had months to accommodate yourselves to the marriage. Take some time now to contemplate this."

"And if I am convinced when we return from Gaillard? Will you still oppose her?"

"I will take the same time to examine my objections. From brother to brother, I urge you—do not act in haste.''

Catherine looked up just then and saw him watching her. Her face lit with a smile and she waved to him. He had not spoken to her since the ceremony last evening, and there was so much now to say to her. Not the least of which was his brother's request to postpone their wedding until his return.

With a nod to Christian, he walked the ramparts to the nearest tower and made his way to the courtyard where Catherine waited. The same young woman who had been with her in the corridor accompanied her now. At his approach, they both curtsied before him, a symbol of his new rank.

''My lord,'' they said in unison.

''My ladies,'' he answered.

''Sir Knight,'' they said, curtsying once more. Startled, he noticed that Aymer was at his side.

''Lady Catherine. Lady Constance.'' His friend bowed to each, and then they stood in a strange silence for a moment or two.

''Shall we walk?'' Geoffrey held out his arm to Catherine and she placed her hand on it, coming to his side. Lady Constance did the same with Aymer and soon they were walking in the large though somewhat crowded expanse of courtyard within Caen Castle. When Aymer and Constance drew back a bit from them, Geoff said the words he had been feeling all day.

''I miss you, Catherine.''

''And I miss you, my lord,'' she answered. Then she reached up and whispered in his ear. ''Geoffrey.''

"I especially miss you in my bed," he whispered back, and he received the reaction he'd hoped for.

A deep blush rose from her neck to her face, and she looked away. The best part was that he knew, could feel, that her response to his words affected her body. When he lowered his gaze, he could see that her nipples pressed against her gown, even as his hardness pressed against his breeches. He guided her to a more secluded alcove along the wall and stopped. Geoffrey drew her closer, kissing her mouth and remembering the taste of her essence when last they'd loved.

When he felt their kisses become too heated for such a public scene, he held her away and took a deep breath. Guiding her to a stone bench, he sat down with her at his side.

"Catherine, there is so much to say."

"When do you leave?"

"How did you know?" Was he the only one in the castle who had no foreknowledge of that which was to come?

"All manner of noblemen and courtiers and messengers come to Eleanor. I simply listen."

"I leave with the king in two or three days' time. Will you stay here with the queen?"

She entwined her fingers in his. "She has invited me to do so. Without you, I have no place to go, so I will accept her offer."

He had not considered her lack of position here among strangers. Until they married, she would have no true place among the court. If anything happened to him, the betrothal agreement provided for her income, but she would be dependent on the kindness of others, as she had been for the last three years.

"Your face is so grave. What worries you?" She touched his cheek with her hand.

"We should marry before I leave."

"That did not sound convincing, my lord. Would you like to try once more?"

"What do you mean?" Was this the rashness that Christian had meant? When would he develop the control needed to think before speaking or acting?

"Your words sounded as though you were attempting to convince yourself of the need to finish what is between us, and not truly asking for it to be."

"I confess to making it less than the enthusiastic request that my heart urges me to, Catherine. There are so many things new in my life and I am adjusting as best I can."

"This is why I stopped you that night. You have doubts about the rightness of this. Doubts that I want resolved before any more vows are spoken."

"Do not doubt my love for you."

"I do not. But I ask for your honesty when discussing our future. Will you give it to me always? Now?"

She knew his fears. She knew his weaknesses. Still she loved him.

"My brother has asked that we postpone our marriage vows until our return with the king."

He searched her face as she thought on his words. Then he saw her gaze go the ramparts across the yard, and knew she'd observed them together. "What think you?"

"In deference to his wisdom and his past kindnesses to me, I would do whatever he asks. Do you think his opposition to me will lessen in that time or strengthen?"

Tempted to soothe her fears of his brother's objections, he did not. There would always be honesty between them, as she had requested. "I know not, Catherine. He battles his own demons from the past. I do sense that he is trying to…understand my reasons."

"Do you ever have the feeling that he knows more and says nothing? That he struggles not to give his true reasons to either of us?"

Christian had said as much to him. Even in revealing her identity, he had withheld something from Geoffrey, something that would explain his reaction to Catherine. What could it be? Why had he done it?

"It is linked to your brother— I know that for certain. I fear there is no way to avoid his connection with the animosity between Christian and you."

"And with my brother being dead, there is no way to seek peace from the past."

"If you agree to wait for my return…" Geoffrey paused and waited for her acceptance. Once given, he continued, "I will try to speak to him and discover what he keeps to himself."

"That would seem a sound plan, my lord."

"Catherine, I need to take you somewhere private and remind you of my name. And I need to hear it on your lips as I touch those places that are only for me."

She shifted on the bench, even as he felt the need to do the same. Her response to his suggestive words inflamed him even more. He longed to spirit her away as he'd said, but with the attention of the queen, it would be impossible. He could only wait until Catherine was his to take.

"Now that we have settled that, we must plan our time carefully, for we have only two days before I leave. Do you think the queen would disapprove if we rode to the river's edge? Mayhap if we take Aymer and Lady Constance, she will not object?"

And Geoffrey decided to make every moment of the next days matter, so that when he left with the king, he did not wear the look of pain and desperation that his brother wore.

# Chapter Nineteen

One good aspect of staying with Eleanor was that news from Château Gaillard arrived several times each day. The first few weeks were uneventful, but when King Phillip threatened the Norman city of Aumale, the battles began. Although not directly involved, Catherine was certain that the queen was apprised of everything Richard did and every plan made to combat the French incursion into Normandy. And as the words she dictated to her clerks demonstrated, Eleanor did not hesitate to give her son advice on conducting the defense of his realm.

Catherine found much to do to occupy her time while awaiting Geoffrey's return. There was no lack of nobles, courtiers, churchmen, troubadors and other courtly visitors who came to present themselves to the king's mother. In spite of their introduction, she and Constance became friends. Her first friend, she realized one day. She was not so dull as to think that Constance's attraction to Sir Aymer did not play a part in it, but there was a genuine affection between them.

Catherine enjoyed the letters that Geoffrey sent to her during his first excursion in the service of his king. Not certain if he had a clerk write them for him or if they were in his own hand, she knew the correspondence reflected his sense of humor and his excitement in his service. And if he were ever in danger or if the battles were overwhelming, he never revealed it to her in his missives.

Finally, when St. Matthew's feast had passed and Michaelmas approached, the queen received the news of Richard's resounding victory that gained him not only a safe boundary, but also regained him control of Gisors and the Vexin. Concern that this might inflame the tensions between the kingdoms lasted only a short time, and Eleanor was ready to celebrate by the time Richard and his commanders and vassals arrived back in Caen.

Crowds lined the streets leading into the city and along the northern approach, but Catherine waited inside with Eleanor and the other nobles. Standing behind the queen's chair in the main hall, she nervously twisted the ring that Geoffrey had placed on her finger at his departure. She'd tried to refuse his action, but he'd insisted that she should wear his father's ring as a sign of their pledges. Because of its size, she tied a piece of ribbon on it and fastened that to her wrist for fear she would lose it.

Finally, when she thought she could endure the anticipation no longer, she saw him. There was a confidence in his step that had not been there before. A sense of comradery exuded from the entire retinue of the king, one born in sharing danger and defeating it together. Now she understood even more clearly the Angevin arrogance that the countess had always described in connection to her husband's bearing and attitude. Geoffrey and his brother strode in, side by side, and she was pleased to see that they seemed in good accord.

Once the king greeted his mother and le Marechal was presented and acclaimed for his role in the Norman victory, the crowd spread out through the hall, and Catherine saw Geoffrey looking for her. She waved to him and watched as he pushed his way through the throng of people on the dais and reached her side.

Tears filled her eyes as she offered up a prayer of thanksgiving for his safe return. He wrapped his arms around her so tightly she feared he might squeeze the very breath from her, but there was no compulsion in the world that would have forced her to make him loosen his hold. All of the worries, all of the womanly concerns that had darkened her thoughts and her dreams during his absence pressed on her now that he was safe.

She loved him and would never permit harm to come to him if she could prevent it. Catherine knew that this was backward, that he would do the protecting, but somehow the thoughts gave her comfort. She cried out in joy, in fear and in love as he held her.

"Catherine, love," he soothed. "I am unharmed. Let me look at you, for I swear I have hungered for even a glimpse of you in these past weeks."

He released her and allowed her to move away only enough so that he could see her face. He lifted her chin and turned her head from side to side, examining everything there. "Your beauty is still as perfect as I remember it to be, my lady." Then he kissed her.

This kiss was not the ravenous one she expected. Instead, with the softest of touches of his lips on hers, he learned her again. Moving his mouth over hers, he breathed in as he kissed her, as though trying to remember her scent. When she could stand his gentleness no longer, she reached up, threaded her fingers in his hair and pulled him closer so she could have her fill.

Since many other such reunions were occurring all through the hall, the castle and even the city, Catherine did not feel the need to curb her enthusiasm for her betrothed. Only the voice of the earl, loud enough to be heard over the din, broke into her kiss.

"So, 'twould seem that she did not lose affection for him while we kept him away."

Geoffrey laughed into her mouth and they parted. Standing back and adjusting her gown and veil, she was surprised by the joviality in Lord Harbridge's greeting. Geoffrey stood next to her, keeping her close with his arm around her waist.

"My lord, you look well," she said, nodding to the earl. "And Sir Luc, 'tis good to see you hale and hearty on your return from battle."

"I had to keep him safe, Catherine," Christian declared, "or else Fatin would use her mysterious Eastern ways and put a curse on my ballocks—" He stopped as she gasped and both Geoffrey and Luc shouted his name.

The whole event took on a strange perspective for her. They were soon seated at table with the knights of both the houses of Langier and Harbridge, and so Catherine was among those she knew. The earl's ease and familiarity since their return added to the incongruity. She tried not to worry, for Geoffrey and his brother were safe.

The feasting and celebration went on long into the night, but Catherine would not miss a moment of it. Many of the knights left, in groups or in the company of willing women, and even Luc and Aymer asked for leave to go. When the queen retired, Catherine knew she must depart as well.

"Wait, I will walk with you," Geoffrey said, standing when she did.

They had had no private moments since Geoffrey's triumphant return, and she craved some with him, to hear of his adventures and his thoughts on how his men had fought. All manner of questions raced through her. She welcomed some time to evaluate the changes in him that could be seen.

He held out his arm to her and, placing her hand on it, she walked at his side out of the hall and toward the queen's apartments. Savoring his nearness, Catherine did not speak. They reached the floor on which the queen stayed, but instead of turning into the corridor to the left, Geoffrey guided her to the right, and stopped before a closed door. He turned the knob and opened it before her. Puzzled, she entered the room with him.

There was a bed in one corner, and several candles lit on a table and in a wall sconce, as well. The only other objects in the room were a basin and a water jug next to the table. She turned, surveying the room, until she faced Geoffrey. His gaze on her was intense, sending shivers down her arms and making the tiny hairs on them stand on end. She saw much in his eyes—confidence, arrogance, self-awareness, desire and fear. As he walked to her, she trembled from the strength of the emotions pouring from him.

"I have seen much death in these last weeks, Cate. More than I expected or could have imagined. And when death was closest to me, all I could think about was coming back to you. All I could see was your face smiling at me. All I could hear was your voice urging me on." He stepped closer and placed his hands on her shoulders. "When we were trapped in a valley well away from the main fighting, and I was not certain that we would make it out alive, all I could think of was my pledge to you to return."

The sobs she fought to contain rose at his words. He did love her.

"My brother and I have spoken and he will not raise an objection to our marriage. If it is still your wish to be my wife, you have only to say the word. If you have doubts, then I will wait for you."

Could they be together? Could two people who loved truly find the happiness they'd never expected to have? She knew she must reveal the one truth that plagued her. Would he still want her if he knew someone else had taken her virginity?

Lifting her eyes to meet his, she swallowed, trying to clear her throat. "This will be difficult to confess, my lord... Geoffrey." She said his name when he frowned. "'Tis something I am not certain I could have told you that night near London."

"Cate, if it distresses you, speak not of it. This

night I would have only happiness between us. I want to—"

She touched her fingers to his mouth and stopped him from saying more. Part of her quaked in terror at revealing what she had remembered that night. She knew there was more just beyond the edge of the shadows in her memory, but fear kept her from pushing past that boundary. She believed the rest was better left in the darkness and not acknowledged.

"I had not thought we would come to this place between us, Geoff. Truly, part of me believed, and still does, that marriage between us will not happen. 'Tis a weak excuse for not telling you immediately, but I do want, nay, I could not stand to see the love in your eyes replaced by disappointment and loathing."

She turned from him, still not willing to see his reaction to the words she must speak. Gathering her courage and knowing that he must hear the truth, she took a deep breath. Before she could say a word, he stood behind her, his body against hers, and whispered in her ear.

"You are not a virgin."

Gasping, she pulled away from him. Then she searched his face for some indication of his feelings about her impure state. Would he repudiate her now or even give her the opportunity to explain what little she did know?

"How did you know this?" Was there some sign that her maidenhead was breached? She knew that blood had marked it the first time, but was it something visible, that he could have seen its absence or presence during their nights together?

"From the few details my brother has told me of your travails before coming to the convent, I suspected that you had been violated. Then on the night we…almost completed the act, I did not notice the barrier when I touched you there…inside. I had not thought on it until my brother and I spoke about—"

"You spoke of this with the earl?" Horrified that such a personal matter had been addressed, she shook her head. "He knows?"

"Cate, we spoke of this in a general way. He wanted to be certain that I understood you had been held at the prince's command in custody, and that you did not remember what had passed there."

"And if I cannot give a full accounting of that time…" Or would not. She was beginning to think that all of it was known to her, but that she was purposely keeping it hidden in her mind.

"I will tell you what I told my brother, and these words seemed to overcome his objections. You have lived a chaste, respectful and modest life for these three years past, learning and recuperating under the guidance of holy sisters. You have become a helpmate to my sister-by-marriage and you have become my friend. I know everything about your nature and you that I need to know in order to love you and want you as my wife."

"But if the danger from the prince is not yet past?"

"For three years, he has thought you dead. Now you are under my protection, and as my wife, you will be safe at our home in lands far away from him. The danger from him is naught or will be once he knows that your memory of that time is gone."

She still had something the prince wanted, even needed, and she doubted that he was willing to give up his quest for it. But if she had not succumbed to his methods three years ago and now did not remember any of it, what recourse would he have? None, now that she was protected by the Dumonts and the sponsorship of Eleanor. It was over.

"And now, what stands between us?" she asked.

"Love and wanting and far too many garments for my liking," he said, smiling at her in the way that made her stomach quiver and her hands itch to touch him. "I confess," he said, coming closer and lifting his hands to the veils and caplet she wore. "I brought you here for reasons of seduction and lust and claiming."

She shivered then at his words and at the tickling feeling as his fingers slid under the restraining wimple that held her hair back. He found the place where it was tied and loosened it, releasing her hair in waves that fell over her shoulders and down her back. The expression on his face changed from wonderment to pure male lust and sinful though it might be, she felt an aching to be touched by him as the throbbing increased in that place near her womanly core.

"The blood of my Viking ancestors was heated by the battles of these last weeks and rises again with your nearness. Blood lust it is called, and all I can think of when the heat invades me is claiming you. In all ways. Marking you with my mouth and my hands and filling you with my seed." Her legs nearly buckled at the force of his words. The need in her grew even as he spoke. "You will be mine, Cate, and regardless of who came before, there will be no part of you that is not mine when this night is done."

He took her mouth, pressing against it, rubbing it with his own until her lips felt swollen and sensitive. She ached for him, wanting the claiming as much as he did. She arched her body to his and he slid his hands down her sides. Even with her gown between them, she felt his touch teasing her. His palm came to rest at the apex of her thighs and he looked at her.

"And no pain, Cate. Only pleasure ahead for both of us."

Her legs did give out then and so he leaned down and swept her into his arms. Placing her on the bed, he peeled off his tunic and loosened his hose and removed the breechcloth under it all. His manhood jutted out from the springy hair on his belly, and she reached out bravely to touch it.

"Ah, no, love," he said, moving back from her. "There is far too much to accomplish between us before it can have its satisfaction. Touch it not now, but later when I ask."

She did as he requested, but that did not stop her from feeling the hardness of the muscles in his arms and chest or from gazing at his tumescence as he began to undress her. Finally, when they were both naked and lay facing each other on the bed, he began the claiming.

He had spoken the truth to her. The blood lust roared within him and all his body wanted to do was thrust into hers. He knew she would moan and make those wondrous noises in her throat as he took her, and he ached for them. But he was not out of control and knew he must take care of her this first time together. With the uncertainty of her past experiences looming between them, Geoff knew that the way he loved her now would determine many things about their life ahead. And so he reined in his lust and put her pleasure before his own.

He knelt beside her and skimmed her body with his hands, barely touching some places and rubbing others more vigorously to find out what pleasured her the most. Knowing that her large, rosy-pink nipples, the underside of her breasts and the delicate skin on the inside of her thighs were highly sensitive, he used his mouth and tongue there, to bring her near to her peak. And when her body tightened and arched and she moved restlessly beneath his touch, he stopped and soothed her with deep kisses, wanting to draw out and prolong the taking.

Geoff knew he could not withhold his desire much longer and so he knelt between her thighs and pulled her toward him until her hips rested on his legs. In this position, her own legs fell open and he could see the moistened folds there. Using his fingers, he spread the flesh apart and found the hidden bud that would give her the most intense pleasure. Geoff dipped inside her, using the wetness there to make the path of his fingers slippery. First, back and forth, then in widening and narrowing circles, he touched and rubbed and teased and pleasured her aroused flesh until he could feel the spasms begin within her core.

She arched off the bed as passion filled her, keening with pleasure as her body found its release under his hands. He pressed his thumb on the bud, slid several fingers inside her womanly passage and let her come against them. When he felt the contractions lessening, he knew it was time. Moving from where he knelt, he lifted her hips and placed himself there. Leaning forward, he covered her with his body and waited for her passion-filled gaze to focus on him.

"Now," he whispered to her. "Now, the rest of it." Never breaking from her gaze, he thrust inside of her, filling her and stretching her until they were together like a hand in a fitted glove. He pushed his hardness in until he pressed against her womb. She accommodated him perfectly.

Catherine ran her hands over his shoulders and back and urged him deeper. Her legs encircled his hips, holding him there. He moved within her, pressing deeply, then easing back, again and again. The tension grew as their breathing became labored and heat poured off them from their exertions. The muscles deep inside her tightened around his shaft and he felt himself thicken and harden more, as his own completion neared.

She threw her head back as her body clenched beneath him, and he knew her scream would begin even as the urge to yell out his satisfaction seized him. Geoff covered her mouth and drank in the noises of her passion even as he thrust for the final time. Holding her close, he emptied his seed into her as he brought her to the peak of her own pleasure.

Relaxing on her and then rolling slowly onto his side so that his weight did not crush her, Geoff waited for the ability to speak and breathe to return. Several quiet minutes passed and finally she opened her eyes to look into his.

"Are you well? Did I hurt you? How do you

feel?'' The questions tumbled from him, and although she was not a virgin, he worried that in his lust he may have been too rough for her.

"I feel…" she began, and then she arched against him, stretching like a cat in the sun. "I feel claimed."

He smiled, for her words and movements told him of her satisfaction. "Glad I am to know that I was successful in my efforts."

She moved against him once more and, unbelievably, his body reacted. "Will you claim me again, my lord?"

"Every night of our lives together, until we are too old and feeble to move our bodies this way." She laughed at his words. "And in the bright light of day as well," he promised.

"During the day? This is possible?"

His betrothed was an innocent in the ways of the flesh, no matter what had happened to her before they met.

"When we return to Greystone, I will show you. The stables there are empty during the day, and I will take you to the loft and lay you on the soft hay and have my way with you even as the sun shines in through the slats of the roof." He kissed her and then teased her with one more thing. "We could even mate there as the stallions do with the mares. It can be a pleasurable way of claiming."

"Must we try it in the stables? Would a bed not work?" Her uninhibited reaction pleased him and promised that they would have no difficulties in the marital duties of their relationship.

"A bed will work for most things, Cate."

In the next several hours, he demonstrated to her how many ways of loving could be accomplished on a comfortable bed.

Christian had followed Geoff to the room where his brother had led Catherine. He stood in the hall, knowing that if his brother claimed her in that room this night, there would be no turning back for them. Consummated, the betrothal became a marriage. For even though the church now insisted on adding its own blessing, it was not required that anything more than consent and consummation occur.

Twice he had stopped dogging their path, but he had followed them to this chamber, to this place and time of decision. And twice more, on hearing sounds within, he found his hand on the door, ready to intervene, but both times he came back to his senses in time.

Part of him admired Geoffrey for claiming the woman he loved in spite of the opposition Christian had him shown. Part of him was jealous of his younger brother's decision to marry for love and not for the usual reasons between noble families. Only the extraordinary arrangements between the Dumonts and the king and Geoffrey's own courage had allowed him and Catherine to get this far.

But what worried Christian was the part deep inside that knew something bad, something very bad, was about to happen. He did not consider himself one who worried or was vexed by the future. Indeed, his concerns were drawn from the past, a past that came back to threaten the Dumonts again and again. Unfortunately, the threat was Catherine's brother.

Unfortunately, he was dead.

However, the specter of this dead brother still haunted everyone who'd known him while he was in league with the prince. And the prince was still very much alive and very able to continue to wreak havoc where and on whom he chose to. In claiming Catherine, Geoffrey held fast to the past, one he knew little about, one they could only imagine and dread. All Christian could do was be at his brother's side when the true battle came. And God help them all.

He heard the steps in the corridor outside their chamber now, and did not even bother to feign sleep when Geoffrey pushed open the door to enter. Christian did not doubt that Luc was awake as well, and able to hear anything spoken.

Geoff pulled off his tunic, hose and boots and lay down on the pallet he claimed. The room settled back to darkness, but the quiet did not bely the fact that no one would sleep until they knew.

"Catherine?" Christian asked.

"She is back in her chambers."

"And?" He needed to know the status of things in order to be ready.

"She is mine."

Geoff's simple words of possession told him everything he must know. His brother would never disavow or repudiate Catherine. No matter the reason or the risk to himself, they were joined now.

Christian tried to ignore the gnawing worry in his gut that plagued him through the night. But Luc's words to him on entering the Exchequer's Hall the next morn chilled his blood and foretold of anguish and suffering.

''The last of the eaglets has returned. to the nest.''

John Lackland, the last of the Plantagenet princes, was there at Caen Castle.

## Chapter Twenty

Geoff had met Prince John before, but only a very few times and not in meetings with any substance. John kept to England much as Richard stayed abroad, and so the opportunity for them to have dealings with each other was limited. But Geoff did recognize him. So he waited and he watched as prince greeted king.

"Do nothing that will bring attention to yourself, Geoff," Christian urged under his breath. "There is mayhem afoot and this is the beginning of it now."

In silence, he watched the warm, albeit completely false exchange of affection as John congratulated Richard on his recent victories and the reclaiming of the Vexin. Luc positioned himself closer to Christian and Aymer as the conversation continued.

The prince then announced that he was off to see their mother, and Richard directed him to the donjon to find her holding her own court there. As John passed their group, he and Christian exchanged glances, and the prince looked wonderfully pleased as he walked by.

Geoff turned to follow him, but Christian stopped

him, grabbing his wrist before he could move. "Stay here." At his brother's nod, Luc trailed the entourage as it made its way to the old keep and the queen. When the king had gone off on his own business and most everyone had left, Geoffrey turned to his brother.

"He saw you?"

"Aye. And he is planning something that will help no one and harm many. 'Tis his way."

"I should go to Catherine. She will be frightened by his appearance here."

"No, Geoff. He is hunting right now, not even certain if she truly lives and if she is here. He is hoping that we'll make the move to reveal her whereabouts."

"She is there with the queen," he argued. "She should not be alone when he discovers her."

"Eleanor will not let harm come to her. Geoff, you must do nothing right now. If he does not see what he wants, he will lose interest."

"Your words say that, but I can tell by the look you wear that you believe it not. Come. I will be by her side if the prince is a danger to her."

He left the Exchequer's Hall and strode to the donjon. Going to the second story, he found his way to Eleanor's presence chamber and entered. Glancing around the room, he did not see Catherine or Constance among the women attending the queen. Luc met him and explained.

"The queen has given Catherine leave this morn, since she said she did not sleep well," he said, with a hint of sarcasm, knowing fully why she might be tired today. "The lady remains in her chamber with Constance as her companion."

So that the prince did not see them gathering, Christian led them outside into the back courtyard. Geoff was anxious to guarantee Catherine's safety.

"I want to take her away from here now. Before John learns of her presence," Geoff stated.

"If he is here, he is following her trail, my lord," Luc explained. "The prince wastes neither his time nor his efforts on something that will not return his investment plus more. I would suggest—" he looked to Christian and then back to Geoff "—that we discover what the lady may know about his reasons. With that knowledge we may better prepare our strategy."

Geoffrey agreed that they needed to speak with Catherine. Mayhap she could remember some detail, even a small and seemingly inconsequential one, that might help them understand the prince's intentions.

"We should gather before the noon meal and talk," he stated. "I could have Aymer escort her and Lady Constance to the chapel."

"Christian, 'tis time for him to hear the whole of it from you," Luc declared. "He has faced death with you. Surely he can face the truths you must tell him."

Geoff whirled at this unexpected exchange between his brother and his man. He did not remember Luc ever being so intense. Even in the thick of battle, he retained a certain irreverent attitude. But this tone revealed a matter of importance that could not be joked about. And what did Luc and Christian know that had not been shared with him?

Without waiting for an answer, Luc left them, and Geoff faced his brother, looking for an explanation.

"Come, hear the whole sordid story and mayhap we can find a way out of this predicament together." They walked away from the men training in the courtyards and climbed one of the towers to the ramparts. When they found an area far enough away from the guards for privacy, Christian began.

"When Richard offered his bargain that would save our lives, he did not trust the Dumonts not to betray him again. Part of the agreement—which I signed without reading, due to our desperate situation—was to split the lands that I gained from marriage to Emalie from the lands that I was to inherit from Father." Christian smiled grimly at him. "Richard wanted us beholden to him for everything we had.

"None of that mattered so long as I kept us alive and so long as Dumont lands and the Langier title remained with one of us. I went to England at Eleanor's call and married Emalie a day later."

"She is not such a difficult price to pay, is she?" Geoff asked in jest, but his brother's expression darkened.

"John had run rampant over the English kingdom while Richard was imprisoned, and was trying to tighten his grasp on the choicest of lands and heiresses before Richard could notice. Emalie was one of those heiresses whose fiefs were targeted by John. Since he could not grab them outright, he pressured one of his cronies, his champion actually, to take possession of Emalie and the Harbridge title and Montgomerie lands."

"William de Severin." Catherine's brother.

"But Emalie's plea to her godmother brought the help she needed, and Eleanor decided that I would be the one to foil their plans. The prince was not happy about his mother's interference and pushed de Severin into claiming a prior betrothal by Emalie's father before his death."

"That was the cause of the court hearings with the bishop in Lincoln. Why did you never tell me this?"

Christian faced him. "You were young and still on the mend from our prison ordeal. You idolized her from the beginning and I could not spoil that for you."

"How could he claim anything? She carried your child...." His words drifted off as the truth struck him. 'Twas not Christian's child.

His brother nodded, acknowledging without words that Geoffrey finally understood.

"I never knew." He thought on his brother's treatment of their first child and could not remember anything that hinted that she was not his. From her birth and even through the birth of his son, Christian had done nothing to give away the true parentage. "She carried de Severin's bastard."

"Not bastard by their proof, for John produced the betrothal agreement and even Gaspar Montgomerie's will. William had, as John explained, anticipated their wedding and consummated their betrothal. As an honorable man, William desired to claim his betrothed wife and child, as was his right. And with the control John had over the bishop and other clerics in Lincoln, a decision in his favor was inevitable."

"Until you challenged him to trial by combat?

You took a risk fighting one of the best in the realm.''

''The field of battle was the one place where I was even with him and where the prince could not interfere. At least those were my thoughts.'' Chris turned and leaned against the stone wall. Pushing his hair back from his face, he rubbed his hands over his eyes. ''But John had a weapon that Luc was finally able to discover.''

At the bleak look he received, Geoff found his own stomach churning.

''Catherine,'' he said, already knowing the answer.

''William was not as enthusiastic a follower as he had been, so John took his sister as surety for his behavior. So long as William continued at his master's beck and call, John promised her safety.''

''He lied.'' After last night, he knew there was no question that John had not kept her safe.

''As he does best. However, one of John's gifts is that he always wraps his lies around enough of the truth that even reasonable people cannot discern them easily. So, you confirm that she was not a virgin when she came to you last evening?''

''Is it an issue?'' 'Twas personal and he did not want Catherine embarrassed by too many knowing her condition.

''I assure you that if John finds her and wants her for whatever his perverted reasons are, he will make it an issue.''

Geoff still hesitated in naming her dishonor. She would carry the stigma despite his belief that she'd done nothing to deserve the name that would be attached to her if this became known.

"The reverend mother suspected that she had been violated, as I told you, but there was no way to prove it. Catherine was like a wild animal when my men took her, and they had to knock her unconscious to get her out of Evesham's vassal's keep. For days, she screamed on and on about blood, but there was no mark on her. We did not know if she had been injured or if she had witnessed something so horrible that her mind fled. She collapsed and then, upon awakening, had no memory of those days."

Geoff felt sick, the bile rolling in his gut until it forced its way up. Bending over, he vomited on the ground. That something so vile had touched her and caused her such illness was more than he could take. Wiping his mouth on the sleeve of his tunic, he looked at his brother.

"Why did you not tell me this before?" he asked with some bitterness. If he had known, he could have…he would have… He did not know what he might have done differently, but he should have been told.

"Until last month, I was sure that there was nothing between you but an inappropriate friendship of sorts that would end when you married another. I ignored Emalie's warnings that there was more, and did not believe you would defy me by pursuing her. Why ruin her repute to you? Why tell you when it would have no bearing on anything?"

"That was sound then, but what about when I came to you and told you of my feelings?"

"Again, Geoff, after a day, you agreed to a betrothal to another woman and seemed to finally accept my counsel on the matter of a wife. Catherine assured me of her desire to enter the convent. There was no reason to besmirch her in your eyes.''

When he would have argued, Christian halted him. ''And I told you that she had been held by the prince. You have traveled the realm, seen and heard enough to know of his sordid reputation when it comes to women and his desires. You may argue this, but somewhere inside you knew, or at least suspected, that she came to you without her virtue.''

Geoffrey could not refute that. Sometime between the night she had stopped him and last night, when she'd tried to tell him, he had come to that conclusion.

''Do you still want her? Do you still think to take her as wife?''

''How can you ask that?'' He glared at his brother.

''It is necessary for you to think on it before anything happens. For if you wish to honor this betrothal, when the prince makes his move to distract and disarm you, you must be ready to face him. Or face complete destruction.''

The words chilled his soul in their stark explanation of the threat that faced him. That his brother spoke from experience was even more unnerving.

''I want her.'' Geoffrey stated it plainly.

''And Catherine? Will she stand by her pledge?''

''Yes,'' he said without hesitation.

Chris looked out at the river running its course, and cursed under his breath. ''You will not like this, but I think the most strategic thing we can do is leave. Get Catherine as far away from the Plantagenets and make her your wife. Then I will escort you to Château d'Azure and see you settled before returning home to Greystone.''

"Leave? Now?"

It made sense. John would not make trouble in Aquitaine or Poitou, where his brother ruled and where his mother's base of power was at its strongest. And with the constant threat of Arthur of Brittany's better claim, John did not want to take any chance of angering or alienating his royal friend Phillip. Taking Catherine to their home, to his home now, was the best plan. ''Can you make the arrangements? I suppose we will seek Richard's permission to leave.''

''I doubt that will be a problem, since you came at your king's summons and fought well for his interests. Many are leaving each day now to get back to their lands for the harvest season,'' Christian said. ''We will seek out an audience after we speak with Catherine, and leave in the morn.''

''Let us go gently with her,'' he cautioned. ''She has told me that she remembers nothing of the time before the convent, and I would not humiliate her with what you have told me. Allow her some semblance of honor.''

''She has nothing to fear from me, Geoff. Her enemy will not quibble over honor or respect. He will get what he seeks or wants by any means necessary, and destroy any who stand in his way.''

''Just so, step carefully when we question her. And, although I value Luc's assistance, I prefer that he not be present.''

''As you wish,'' his brother answered, nodding to

him. "Come, let us make our arrangements. We will speak to Richard's man to ask if the king will see us later today."

"Then I must find Catherine. She needs to know that the prince is here."

She knew the prince was here.

After resting in her chamber this morn, fearing that one and all would see the night of pleasure somehow in her eyes or in the smile she could not keep from her face, she had decided that a walk would do her much good. 'Twas as she left the queen's apartments that word came, by way of the servants, of course, that Eleanor's youngest son had arrived in Caen.

Afraid of what he might do, Catherine had sought out Geoffrey. And she had found him, with his brother, walking the ramparts on the south wall. They were deep in conversation and did not hear her calls or see her waving from below. So she walked to the tower nearest them and climbed it, intent on informing them of the news. Instead, their words shocked her into silence, and from her hiding place on the tower stairs she listened to the sordid tale of her brother's infamy and the scandal that had nearly destroyed the Dumonts.

Worse yet was that their words forced her to remember all that had been done to her during her year in John's custody. They mentioned only the barest details of the story, but once she was confronted with those, the wall she had carefully constructed fell, and she was faced with the full extent of her dishonor. The requests that had turned into threats that gave way to tortures were all there in her mind. And she was filled once more with the terrible anger that had given her the strength to fight once before.

But the last time she'd had only herself to protect. She had given up on being saved by her brother; his evil had brought her into this. Nay, she thought, shaking her head. He was not evil. He had loved her, and Catherine believed with everything in her soul that William could not know, had not known, the deprivations and abuses being heaped on her by his master. Only when she was weak had she begun to believe the lies she knew John told about William.

Now there were others involved. And she could no more let John take action against them for their part in saving her than she could deny her love for Geoffrey. But how? How would she meet this challenge and explain away any questions raised? She smiled grimly as she pulled out the linen cloth tucked in her sleeve and wiped the perspiration from her brow and face.

Catherine decided that she would simply not remember any of it. Her answer to all questions would be the same— *I have no memory of that time.* With the head injury that the earl had disclosed, it would be easy and believable enough to blame it on that. The reverend mother had told her of many people who suffered blows to the head and whose memory was foggy and incomplete after that.

And to keep his love, Catherine knew that Geoffrey must never learn of the depths of depravity to which she'd been exposed. He was uncommonly kind in accepting her lack of virtue, but if he were faced with the real knowledge of her sins, his love for her would die a quick death.

With a promise to herself that she would never bring dishonor to his name or to his family, she also promised that she would be a good wife to him. She would be the reserved and respectful and cooperative woman he had come to know, and he would never see the darkness within her. He would never know.

# Chapter Twenty-One

How she had managed to get through the discussion with Geoffrey and the earl, she would never know. Geoffrey looked on her with such love and offered her such support as they explained to her about the prince's appearance here and the link it might have to her. And to each question, she answered with the same words: *I have no memory of that time.*

She swore to the Almighty that she would spend the rest of her life praying and doing penance for the lies she told directly, and for those of omission, as well. And Geoffrey believed her. He promised his love and he believed that she did not remember.

She was shaking uncontrollably by the time they'd asked all the questions they must, and Geoffrey praised her for holding herself together so well in this difficult situation. The shame tore through her at each word or sign of his love, but she was doing this to protect him as much as to protect herself. If she had survived those horrors, it must be because there was a plan for her. If she could offer him her love and give him even a small measure of the joy he had given her, then any guilt she must suffer was worth the pain it would cost her to keep this from him.

Geoffrey told her that the king would see them prior to the evening meal, and they would ask leave to go to their castle in Poitou. Now that the major battles were done and Richard firmly in control of the area, the king planned to return to Gaillard for the next several months with his commanders. Eleanor had already spoken of traveling to her favorite retreat at Fontrevault, so Caen would go back to being the administrative capital of the Norman holdings.

This was, as Geoffrey explained, the perfect time to leave.

And so the Count of Langier, the Earl of Harbridge and their companies of knights stood before the king and queen awaiting his permission to be on their way.

"This has been quite the adventure for you, has it not, Langier? You and the knights under your banner acquitted yourselves with honor and bravery in the service of your king."

"My thanks for your kind words, sire." Geoffrey bowed to Richard. "I stand ready, as is my duty to my liege."

He said the correct words with the correct tone, and Catherine could tell Richard was pleased. He listened to something Eleanor whispered to him and nodded at her words.

"Harbridge? If you have no objection, I would approve the betrothal before me. As her guardian, you are being most generous in dowering her with the only Dumont lands still in your possession."

"They were my mother's holdings, sire, and adjoin my brother's southern borders. They will complement what he holds and protects."

After the weeks and weeks of hostility and protests against Geoffrey's decision, this surprised Catherine as well. The earl had promised her a small amount of gold, but never had he included anything else. Now, even being one of the few who knew of her dishonor, he gifted her before the king.

Richard looked to his clerk to record the approval, but a voice broke into the silence.

"Brother," the prince called out. "Be not hasty in this approval." She felt Geoffrey tense beside her and saw the earl's stance grow rigid.

"John, what place have you in this? Neither the count nor the earl are your vassals."

The prince ignored the king's question and as Catherine held her breath, he walked directly to where she stood. Staring at her face, he spoke to her with words so false she nearly cried out.

"Catherine? God in Heaven be praised! It is you, Catherine." He took her hand and, despite her efforts to pull free, held it to his mouth and kissed it. "I have prayed daily for your safe return, and now, it seems, the Almighty has answered my prayers."

"John? Explain yourself," his mother called out.

"Mother, this is Catherine de Severin, the sister of William, who was killed—pardon, who died in a matter of honor—nearly three years ago." His eyes were cold as he looked from her to the earl and then to Geoffrey. Still he held her hand in his.

"She disappeared on the same day that William fought the earl, and I have been trying to find her since that time. To ascertain what had happened to her and who was responsible for taking her from my care and custody.''

The earl was correct. The prince mixed lies, innuendos and half truths, all in a tone of voice that sounded sincere. If she were not the one being discussed and if she had no knowledge of the events that day, he would have convinced her of his concern.

"Harbridge, is this so?" the king asked. Although his expression suggested he did not believe his brother, Richard must give him the benefit of seeming to accept his words in public. Catherine knew that it was up to the earl now.

"Sire, she is indeed Catherine de Severin, sister of the late William. When she was discovered by the sisters at the convent near Lincoln, they summoned me, as one of their sponsors, to determine what should become of her. As is my duty as lord of those lands, I accepted responsibility for her and, when no one came forward, I took her as my ward, with the reverend mother standing as her guardian.''

"And now she is betrothed and about to marry the Count of Langier. Your charity has no bounds, Harbridge.''

"I do not hold de Severin's sister responsible for his crimes against me any more than you hold me responsible for the crimes of my father, sire. I have tried to learn by your good example.''

His words swayed the king, for she saw his wide smile as he savored the words that praised him for setting the example. Eleanor also nodded in approval.

Catherine let some hope trickle that this would work into her soul.

"But, brother, I hold her guardianship, and no betrothal can be approved except by me. It matters not where she was found, for her brother begged me to see to her if anything happened to him. I even had his last testament and his will." John paused and pointed to one of his servants. "Etienne will bring the documents to the hall so that this may be resolved."

As onlookers commented on the proceedings and the issue became murkier, she saw Richard's disdain for carrying this on before so many. Instead of a simple pro forma approval, there was now contention and disagreement. The king stopped everything with a wave of his hand.

"John, present the documents to my clerk for their examination. Harbridge, you endow her because she is your ward. If she proves not to be?"

The earl did not answer, but the result of such a decision was she would be the penniless sister of a dead man.

"John, why do you put out so much effort to regain her wardship when she will be without wealth? I know how you like your gold…." the king said.

Gazing back at her, he answered, "Some things, brother, are more important than coin. Catherine has…great value to me, for the honor debt I owe her brother."

*Catherine has something I want.*

Had anyone else heard the words she knew he meant?

"Just so," Richard said. "We will deal with this

on the morrow, after there has been an examination of the documents you say you have, John. Mother…'' The king nodded at Eleanor and left the hall, followed by his entourage.

Their chance for resolution and escape had been stolen from them. Catherine closed her eyes and shook her head. But Geoffrey clasped her hand and whispered words of encouragement. ''Worry not, Cate. We will prevail in this.''

She wanted to believe him, but if John proved his claim, she would belong to him, to be disposed of in any manner that pleased him. Catherine did not want to think on what that meant.

''This is the distraction I warned of, Geoff,'' the earl said. ''Look for him to take the next step before the morrow.''

He had already taken that step. The Dumonts simply did not recognize it. *Catherine has…*

He still sought what she had managed to keep from him throughout her imprisonment. The thing that she had hidden from him at the behest of her brother, even through the worst John and his cronies could do to her. William had sent it to her, urging her to keep it safe at all costs until he could claim it from her. He never had.

''Catherine.''

She turned at the queen's voice and went to the dais.

''Attend me after the meal,'' Eleanor ordered. ''In my chambers.''

She nodded and returned to Geoffrey's side. He entwined his fingers with hers and pulled her close, even as he talked with his brother and the other men.

Catherine decided to savor these moments, for she knew the end was coming.

"Move the knights outside the castle, Aymer, and then report to me. We may need to act quickly, and I do not want you to be trapped within the walls."

"Aye, my lord," Aymer said, and with a look and a nod, he ordered the Langier knights from the hall.

"Luc." It was all the earl had to say for his men to do the same.

"Is that wise?" she asked. "Leaving will defy the king."

"Fear not, Cate. Our intention is not to disobey the king, but to be ready for whatever comes."

"A good plan." Not that they would see the prince's machinations coming at them in time to re-act, but they were trying.

"Christian, if you would excuse us?" Geoffrey looked at her and then continued, "I think Catherine needs to walk a bit before she goes to the queen."

The earl nodded to them both and left them. Geoff held out his arm to her and then escorted her from the Exchequer's Hall toward the church where they'd met earlier. Once inside, he guided her to one of the stone benches along the wall and sat with her.

"You appeared to need some quiet, and this seemed to provide it." He smiled at her. "Unless you wish to join in the meal?"

Her stomach rebelled at the thought. "Nay, this is a good place to be. I am glad you thought to bring me here."

"I also brought you here so that I could hold you in my arms and tell you of my love for you."

He pulled her into his embrace and she leaned

against him, accepting the comfort he offered. How would he react to what she was sure John would say? Geoffrey did love her—she felt it in every part of her being—but what man could listen to what he would be told, and still love her afterward?

She said nothing, but simply relished in his embrace. A few minutes passed and he spoke again.

"Now that it is just the two of us, can you tell me anything you might remember that you did not wish to speak of before my brother? Is there something that could give us a hint of why John seeks you?"

Had she shown the truth to him somehow? Had she, by a glance or word, betrayed herself? He must not suspect that she remembered it all. Not yet. Not ever.

"I have tried, Geoffrey," she said, laying her head on his chest. "I have no memory of those days."

"But you knew you were not a..." He did not finish.

"I cannot explain that, either. 'Twas something I just knew. Mayhap I heard the nuns speak of it during my time of recovery?"

"Mayhap," he replied. "Cate, you do know that you can tell me anything, anything at all, and it will not affect my love for you or my desire to have you as my wife?"

The tears so clogged her throat that she could not have responded even if she'd wanted to. She nodded against his chest. Catherine knew she must try to hold out, for there was nothing she wanted more than to be with Geoffrey.

They sat without speaking for a long time, and when the noises outside told them that the meal was done, she knew she must go to the queen. He stood when she did, and kissed her softly.

"Come to me with anything you remember, Cate."

They parted as they entered the donjon, Catherine going to Eleanor and he to find his brother and Aymer and Luc. She climbed the steps and had just entered the corridor when a rough grasp pulled her into a small storage chamber there. The voice that greeted her sent icy fingers of terror along her spine.

"My dear Catherine, so good to see you again."

She pulled as far away from John as she could and tried to regain her control. He was far too smart and far too insightful for her to fool without having all of her wits about her.

"Your Grace," she said, curtsying to him.

"I thought you dead these last three years. I am glad to see you are not."

She did not meet his eyes. She knew they would be cold and lifeless.

"The last time I saw you...let me think on this...was just days before your brother's death."

"I remember not, Your Grace. My memories of that time are gone."

"Gone?" he said as he lifted her face to his. "I think not." He stepped closer, bringing his body to hers and trapping her between himself and the door in the tiny room. "I think you remember much of our special time together. It is because I am sure of that that I come to you now seeking that which I am also certain you still possess."

Steeling herself against the physical reaction his nearness and even his voice caused within her, she

repeated her words. "My memories of the time before the convent are gone, Your Grace. The nuns said
the head injury I sustained…"

"Lying bitches, every one of them. And you, too,
Catherine. You see, I know that William stole the
papers from me and I know that he sent them to you.
He told me so when I presented him with a token of
your blood to wear into his battle with the earl. He
said that since you had already given yourself to me,
you might as well stay my whore. He died that day
knowing you'd betrayed him."

She could not stop the tremors that pulsed through
her. She must be calm. She must not give away anything to him or he would use it to break her. This
time, at least, she knew his methods.

"I know not of what you speak, Your Grace. I
have nothing of yours. My memories—"

"Of that time are gone. You continue to say that
but I know it is false." He lifted his hand to her face
and rubbed the back of his finger over her cheek. "I
must say I would feel very insulted if you did not
remember my touch…." His hand moved lower, to
her mouth now. "My kisses…"

His mouth was so close to hers that if she spoke,
their lips would touch. She pressed harder against the
door, trying to gain space between them. He slid his
hand boldly over her breasts and stomach, holding at
the top of her thighs. He drew circles over the area,
sometimes touching and sometimes not, until finally,
as she expected, he thrust his hand roughly between
her legs.

"You must remember the day you offered me your
virtue, Catherine. The day you begged me to take

you? The day I marked you as mine with the blood of your maidenhead? Surely you remember it?''

She had repeated the words over and over in her thoughts as he taunted her and tried to weaken her resolve against him. Some of the ability she'd developed to block out his words and deeds reasserted itself, and she was able to stay detached as he groped her. Finally, she met his cold eyes.

''I fear my memories of that time are gone.''

Before he could retaliate, she heard her name being called in the corridor. It was Constance. Before John could stop her, she called out in answer. He stepped away, allowing her to open the door, but before she could move from his grasp, he whispered to her.

''I know you have it. I want it back. Give it to me and I swear on my soul that this ends now. You can marry Langier and continue with your story of not remembering our time together.'' He circled his fingers around her upper arm and squeezed so painfully that she gasped. ''If you do not give it to me, I will get you back in my custody. Then I will turn you over to someone who will make you beg me to punish you for this disobedience. His methods of pain will make you plead for me to take back what you stole. And when I have it back, he will make you ask for death ten times over before I grant it to you.''

Her legs buckled under her and she fell against the door. He pulled her back up and opened the door himself. She could hear Constance coming closer, still calling for her. Before Prince John thrust her out in the corridor, he used his final threat, the one she knew he must.

''The Dumonts must also pay for their involvement in trying to keep you from me. I will not forget their part in this.''

He shoved her and she stumbled into the hallway.

# Chapter Twenty-Two

Constance found her as she regained her feet.

"Catherine, what happened?"

She shook out her gown and hid her trembling hands by rearranging her veils and caplet. "I heard something in that storage closet and looked in to see what it was. When I heard you calling, I turned and my gown caught on the door. I nearly landed on the floor." She laughed nervously.

"You should take more care. You could have been hurt," her friend. "Now come, for the queen is waiting for you."

Catherine followed Constance to the queen's chamber. All she truly wanted to do was find her bed, climb in it and cry the hurt out. Mayhap she was wrong about all of this? Mayhap John would honor his word if she gave him back the papers he wanted so badly? She needed to be resolved in her plan.

They entered the queen's chamber and Catherine dropped into a curtsy before her. Eleanor did not give her permission to rise, and so she stayed as she was. From the sounds of footsteps around her, she could tell that the queen had ordered her chamber cleared. Finally, her name was spoken and she rose.

"You do not look well, Catherine. Pray, be seated here and have something to drink."

Catherine sat down where the queen directed and accepted the cup of wine offered by the queen's lady-in-waiting, who then left the room, as well. Sipping it, Catherine closed her eyes and tried to calm herself after the encounter with the prince.

"Do you wish to tell me how the outline of a hand became imprinted on your gown? Should I call the guards?"

Horrified, Catherine looked down and saw what Eleanor was referring to. The pale-colored gown could not hide the handprint on the front of it, or on the sleeve where John had taken hold of her. "'Tis of no consequence, Your Grace." She swallowed more wine, hoping to calm her rattled nerves.

"So, you are from Anjou, then? The de Severin family has a proud history going back many generations. You are the last?"

"Aye, Your Grace."

"Your marriage to Geoffrey now of Langier is an advantageous one for you. How did you accomplish it?"

"You have heard the story of it, Your Grace."

"Along with many lies, I suspect," Eleanor said bluntly. "This is your opportunity to give me the truth. Once John begins, there is no telling where this will lead."

"'Tis as I told you on our first meeting. I have lived at the convent these last three years and fell in love with my lord Geoffrey on visits to his brother's estates.''

"You are not related to the countess, then?"

Catherine shook her head. "Nay, Your Grace. They gave out that explanation, since it is an acceptable one. No one asked questions about the destitute female relation who lived on the earl's mercy. The earl and countess always knew who I was.''

"Why were you not betrothed or married?''

"I thought that was why my brother summoned me to England. I was ten-and-five and of marriageable age. I believed he would arrange it, as was his due.''

"That is not what happened? How came you to my son?''

How much should she reveal to his mother? Did Eleanor really want to know of his depravity and baseness? Unsure of where Eleanor's loyalties would lie, Catherine continued with her excuse.

"My memories of that time are gone, Your Grace. I find only darkness when I search my mind for them." She drank from the cup again.

"But surely, Catherine, you must remember something? There is an entire year missing from your life—does not a speck of it remain within you? Can you not remember feasts or traveling or spending time with your brother?''

The entire year from anticipated beginning to horrific end raced through her mind in a mere moment, despite her efforts to reconstruct the wall of protection around it. She flinched at the onslaught and then realized that Eleanor was watching her closely.

"Nothing, Your Grace."

''Did you not retain anything, any possessions from that time? Did you come to the convent empty-handed?''

''Only a box with some clothing.'' *Which I burned before they could stop me.*

''Most perplexing, Catherine. What do you think of John's claim to your wardship?''

''I know nothing of it, Your Grace. The earl took me under his protection and I knew only that my brother was dead. The nuns made certain that I learned of the earl's generous behavior, and I thank God each day for it.''

''Generous, yes, but I find it difficult to believe that the earl supported this marriage. Considering his history with your brother and your lack of property and title, it is unlikely.''

Catherine knew she must speak the truth on this. She stood and walked to the table where wine and other beverages sat. Pouring another cup for herself, she offered Eleanor one as well, but the queen declined. Catherine sat back in the chair and put herself and her love for Geoffrey before the queen.

''Geoffrey and I did not expect a marriage between us. Although there was love, there was also the understanding and acceptance that he would marry as appropriate to his status on accession of his title.'' She paused for a moment. ''And I would marry elsewhere. The earl set up a small dowry of gold so that I was not precluded from that honored state. As I discovered quickly, I wanted to marry no other and preferred the convent to being wife to someone else.''

''But you are not in the convent, are you?''

Catherine permitted a smile to break through as she remembered Geoffrey arriving at the convent and taking her out of the path of danger. Now, of course, she understood the danger and she knew it—*he*—had followed them across the Channel.

"No, Your Grace. Although I did return there intent on taking my vows. Geoffrey—my lord Geoffrey—came the next day and announced his intention to marry me. His first obstacle was the reverend mother, though. Once convinced of his honorable aims, and presented with his orders from the king, she approved the betrothal contract and stood as witness for me."

"Approved it? Not the earl?" Eleanor seemed confused over this aspect of the arrangements.

"She has papers that name her and the earl as my guardians, and so she stood in stead for the earl and signed the contracts."

If that had seemed strange before, Catherine had not dwelled on it. The queen's interest in the topic brought a frown to her regal face, but after a moment's hesitation Eleanor looked at her and smiled. Catherine sipped from her cup again as she waited for the questioning to continue. There were some important queries that had not been asked yet.

Eleanor pointed to the table and Catherine poured some wine for her. After handing it to her, she walked around the chamber while waiting on the queen.

"The earl supports the marriage now, even going so far as to add to your dowry. Why did he change his opinion on it?"

"I have not asked the earl his reasons. I understood his opposition—he was justified in seeking a better match for his brother. But with words or actions, my lord Geoffrey has been able to convince him of the rightness of this.''

''Why does my son want you? He does not bestir himself from England or into his brother's presence unless there is some pressing need. That he is here, speaking to Richard to gain your custody and risking the anger of the nobles of Poitou and Aquitaine by interfering in matters of one of their own, says much about your importance to him.''

Could she reveal the truth to the queen? Would Eleanor protect her against John's wishes? Could Eleanor stand against her son for someone not of Plantagenet blood? The facts included in the letters pointed the finger of guilt at many nobles and even some in the royal family. Should she hold on to that proof or relinquish it to the queen and hope for the best?

Catherine met Eleanor's gaze and shook her head. ''Your Grace, I know not why the prince seeks my custody.''

Eleanor closed her eyes for a brief second and then shook her head in turn. ''You can trust me, my dear.''

''I trusted my brother and you see how that turned out.''

She could have bitten her tongue as the words escaped. She'd let her bitterness seep in, and had lashed out without thinking. Would Eleanor recognize the gaffe?

''I suggest that you keep yourself in these apartments for the remainder of this day. I will send my maid to you with a sleeping draught, for I can see that you need to rest. Richard will decide this in the morning.''

''Aye, Your Grace,'' Catherine said, lowering herself into a curtsy. As she reached the door, the queen spoke again.

''I knew not that William had a sister.''

Something in the queen's tone made her feel as though an apology had just been offered to her.

''Eleanor has confined her to her chamber.''

''I know you do not want to hear this, but 'tis safer for her that way, brother.''

They sat not at the high table but together with Luc and Aymer on the main floor of the great hall. Although Geoff would rather have missed this meal completely, Christian had convinced him of the wisdom of being seen there by the king. Geoff simply wanted to be with Catherine.

The meal continued, but each course served tasted bland and indistinguishable to his palate. Geoff knew it was him and not the food. Before the last dish was brought out, he become aware of Lady Constance trying to get the attention of Aymer. Geoff nudged him into noticing, and the knight followed the lady's gestures into the corridor. After a short time, he returned, his face grim.

''What is it?'' Geoff asked.

''The prince has approached Catherine, my lord.''

Fury built inside him as he thought of the damage John could do to her. Without memories to guide her, she would be vulnerable to any lies the prince told her.

"When? Where?" he demanded through clenched teeth.

"Near the queen's rooms. Earlier today. Constance was sent looking for her and found her staggering in the corridor."

"If he has harmed her…" Geoff began.

"Brother, calm yourself or you will give him another weapon." Geoff accepted Christian's words of warning.

"What else did the lady say?" Had she witnessed the exchange? he wondered.

"She escorted Catherine to the queen and observed John leaving the room near where she'd found Catherine."

Geoff pounded his fist on the table, so hard that their cups shook. "He is too bold!"

"He is a prince," Christian said. "Do not forget that. And he comes this way."

John stepped down from the dais and came directly to their table. Geoffrey tried to think of his brother's earlier warnings as the prince spoke to them.

"Stay, friends, do not let me interrupt your meal," he said. "I come to bring you some friendly advice for your use on the morrow."

"And what would that be, Your Grace?" Geoffrey asked, preparing himself for the worst.

"Do not believe her words, for she lies like the rest of the de Severins."

"I have never found her deceitful, Your Grace. In these last three years, she has been kind and modest and all things that are hoped for in a woman and wife." He tried to play the game, tempering his rebuttal with a respectful tone, but his head pounded from the fury building in his blood.

"No matter what her assurances are to the contrary, my lords, she knows exactly what we did in our time together. She whored in my bed even while her brother whored on the battlefields for me. Still, 'tis my fervent wish that she has demonstrated some of her more charming skills for you before she returns to my custody."

Geoff could not help himself. In that next instant he shoved away from the table and stood, moving to confront John directly. "You will not insult my betrothed wife in this way."

"I am trying to save you and your family from more scandals involving your choices of wives. There is time to dissolve this and leave her to me."

Geoff felt Christian come to his side now. "There is no reason for your concern or for your involvement," his brother stated.

"I have never met men who are so willing to take another man's leavings before. Tell me, does a royal plowing make the path smoother for those who follow? I suppose that the lack of a maidenhead does make for a better fuck, does it not, my lord?" John laughed and continued in a lower tone, unaware of how close to death he was. "Does she still scream in that throaty voice when she reaches her peak?"

Geoff's hand was on his sword and he felt it sliding from the scabbard before he even thought about it. He would kill John for heaping such insults not only on Catherine but on Emalie, as well. The sound of metal scraping on metal brought every gaze to where they stood. His only regret was that this death would be too quick to make the prince suffer, as he surely deserved.

"Do not draw your sword on the prince, my lord." Aymer held his hand fast so that his blade could not escape the scabbard. "'Tis treason to do so."

With the blood seething in his veins, it was difficult for Geoff to hear or see anything. Everything in him wanted to strike out at this whoreson who claimed such lies about Catherine and her past.

"My lord," Aymer insisted. "Do not break the peace of the king's hall. Do not draw on the prince."

John stood before him with his arms at his sides and a knowing smirk on his face, which Geoff longed to remove. But Aymer's warnings forced him to diffuse the situation. He stepped back, slid the sword completely into its scabbard and lifted his hand from its hilt.

He realized that Luc was holding his brother back as well, and Geoff knew they needed to leave the hall before his control was overwhelmed. As he turned his back on the prince, an insult in itself to one of royal blood, he heard John's final words.

"What better way for her to seek revenge for her brother's death than to marry his killer's brother and end their line with her barren womb? Think on that as well, my lords."

Aymer grabbed Geoff and pulled him away before he could act on the slurs just voiced. Geoff heard the king call out to John, but 'twas too late. So many insults had been issued against Catherine that he did not know how to keep some of them from sinking in. Despite his efforts not to hear the words, John had been successful in planting doubts.

Once outside, Geoff let out the rage that had built inside of him with a roar. "I will kill him!"

His cry pierced the quiet of the night and he shook with the fury of it. He dropped to his knees and tried to pull air into his lungs. When he came back to his senses, Christian looked no better than he felt, and even Luc and Aymer looked shaken and grim.

"I will," he repeated, even though he knew he could do no such thing. Pushing back his hair, he stood and faced his friends. "I am sorry for letting him goad me into losing control. You warned me of his method and yet still I failed."

"He has had years of training in his craft, my lord," Luc said. "Others more learned and more experienced than you have fallen into his traps."

"I have failed Catherine in this, for now his words about her will spread through the entire castle and she will be held in disrepute because of them."

"Do you believe them?" Christian asked.

Geoff could not answer, for some of the accusations rang true. She was not a virgin. And John's comment about the noises Catherine made…

"Do you believe him?" Chris asked insistently.

"I am trying to sort through his words and recognize them for the lies they are."

"Come, walk with me," his brother said, and gaining his feet, Geoff walked beside him. When they were separated from Luc and Aymer by some distance, Chris faced him.

"Now you know the claims he will make on the morrow, before the king and his court. If you believe his words, if you will not stand by her, tell me now and I will go to the king on your behalf."

''Go to the king? And say what?'' How could John know such personal details about Catherine if he had not...if she had not... The worst part was that Geoff thought John was right about Catherine remembering her past. There was something in her eyes whenever she disavowed knowledge or said her memories of that time were gone that made him think she did remember it. And that she remembered it all and would not admit it to him.

''I will say whatever is necessary to break the betrothal. I will ask the king to exert his influence on the bishop to issue an annulment and have her put away in a convent.''

''There can be no annulment of this, Chris. You know we have consummated our pledge.''

What could he do now? If he did not fight for her before the king, his honor was lost, for he had pledged himself to her. If he did, he was certain that John would sully her reputation even more. How could Geoff keep her as wife if he was not sure of her part in this? Was this about revenge? Was John's claim about her being barren another lie? How would he know? Geoff shook his head, not even wanting to contemplate the extent of the prince's knowledge.

''Tell me what to do,'' he begged.

''I fear that I cannot. I struggle even now with the knowledge that there has been one before me in Emalie's bed. Even in spite of knowing who it was and knowing that she has been faithful to me from the time we took our vows before the priest. It picks at me still. If what John says is true, will you know how many came before you? Does it matter?''

He paused and gazed at Geoffrey with bleak eyes,

a look he'd seen before when he spoke of his discord with Emalie. "For months I learned the truth, I suspected every man at Greystone and watched Emalie for sôme sign of her sins. It nearly killed me. So I am not the man to tell you how to deal with whatever the truth is with Catherine."

There it was. The fear that existed beneath all the layers about honor and pledges and truth and lies. The ugly fear that was so base he did not want to acknowledge it even to himself. How could he trust her in the future if she lied about her past?

"I must think about the best way to handle this," Geoffrey mumbled the only comment he could make.

"I know you love her, Geoff. Think about what public consideration of these accusations, lies and half truths will do to her if this is brought before the king on the morrow. No matter that there may something in his words, everyone who hears the gossip will believe it all and she will be damned as women who lose their virtue are. Is that what you want for her?"

"I know not…" He choked on the doubting words.

"Speak to her. Hear her words. Gain her explanation before this goes to the king."

Christian nodded to him and walked away, leaving Geoff alone to contemplate all he had heard and all he knew. His love for Catherine had never been tested before. It had existed between them without planning or forethought, and he knew she returned his feelings. But now, doubt and fear had crept into his soul. How could he face her if he did not trust her word?

He was not ready for sleep, so there was no use in going back to his chambers. Although he would like to get drunk enough to forget the words spoken tonight, he also realized that the morning would be even more difficult to face than it already promised to be. So he climbed to the ramparts and walked and thought about the depth of his love for Catherine and the best path to take in this.

When dawn came hours later, he was still walking.

## Chapter Twenty-Three

'Twas about an hour past terce when she was summoned to the Exchequer's Hall to answer to the prince's petition for her custody. Unusual though it was for the woman involved to be present, apparently the king and bishop had given leave for her to be there. When she saw Eleanor next to the king, she knew why.

Since they were still busy with some other question or petition, Catherine stayed in the back of the hall. That was where Geoffrey found her.

He looked wonderful. He looked terrible. Although he was dressed in his finest garments, with his gold chain around his neck, nothing could hide the circles under his eyes from lack of sleep. She supposed they were matched in that, for she had not closed her eyes once during the night. When he did not kiss her or even touch her hand, she knew the worst had happened.

Constance had already revealed to her the scene caused by the prince in the hall last evening, and although she would not repeat all the words said, her look of pity spoke clearly. Now, reading the doubt in Geoff's eyes, Catherine could not let this go on. She loved him too much to subject him to the humiliation that the prince planned for opposing him.

"My lord," she said as he stepped nearer. "We must talk."

"Aye, Catherine," he agreed.

"I have discovered that the queen is retiring to Fontrevault. With your consent, I would accompany her there."

"You may visit the queen anytime you'd like. Fontrevault is not far at all from Château d'Azure."

"I mean not to visit, my lord. I mean to stay there."

He flinched at her words as he realized what she was asking. She must conclude this quickly before she lost her nerve. "We are betrothed, Cate."

"I find I am not suited for marriage, after all, my lord. I would ask for release from our betrothal."

He flinched again and this time, he shook his head. "You love me. We consummated our pledge. You cannot disavow this now."

"But that was before you learned the truth." She was giving him a way out, but he would not make this easy.

"What truth did I learn, Catherine? Do you remember what happened to you during that year? Tell me so I may know the truth."

"The prince has made it clear to everyone last evening what I did, what I am…. Surely you believe him?"

"Because you give me nothing else!" He stepped

closer and examined her face. "He said you remember everything. Do you? Do you remember?"

She could not say so, for if she acknowledged it even to him, it would be a weapon in the prince's hands. Once she let down her guard, the rest of her would fall.

But Geoff must have read the truth in her eyes, for he backed away. "Tell me. Tell me what he did to you." He did touch her now, taking her by the shoulders and pulling her close. "I need to hear it from you."

"My lord… Geoffrey…do you not see what has happened? Even if I tell you or if I deny his words, you will always wonder if I ever spoke the truth. You have lost faith in me and I do not think you will ever regain it."

"Just tell me, Catherine. Please."

A part of her wanted to say it all. She wanted to scream out her rage and her hatred and her pain. It had taken three years of praying and living a quiet life to recover her self-control, and she would not relinquish it now and let the prince win.

"Do you love me?" she asked.

"I do, Cate, with all my heart."

"Will you honor this betrothal even if I do not answer your question? If you hear not the words from my mouth about my past, to confirm or deny the prince's accusations, will you take me as wife?"

"I will honor my pledge." The words were gruffly spoken.

"Why? Why would you want me as your wife when you believe I was the prince's whore?"

"I do not believe all that he said," he began.

When he realized how badly that sounded, he went on. "I gave you my word, when you accompanied me here. I promised to wed you."

"So, for your honor's sake, you will take me as wife?"

She saw the pain in his eyes as he admitted it to himself before he admitted it to her. This was no longer about love, this was about obligation and, most hurtfully, this was about pity. The love they shared would die a strangled death if she accepted this agreement, and she could not do that to either of them. A marriage of respect and property and titles was preferable to a marriage of lost hopes and dreams.

She loved him too much to subject him to less than what they had dreamed and planned for. But until the matter with John was settled, she could not risk giving up the only protection she had from the prince. Admitting her past would give him power over her. Remembering the past was remembering the packet of letters her brother had sent to her with instructions about hiding it from everyone. Remembering the past was answering for those who had been tortured or killed on her behalf. And remembering that would be more painful than she could bear.

Untying the ribbon that held it in place, she slid his father's ring from her finger and handed it to him. Catherine managed to hold back the tears, though how she knew not.

"Would you ask the earl to speak for me to the king?"

At Geoff's nod, she excused herself and ran back

to her chamber. Throwing herself on the bed, she cried out at the pain of loss and of betrayal, and she cried for what could have been with Geoffrey.

"The lady has asked for an annulment?"

"Aye, sire. She has asked me to speak on her behalf in the matter."

"An annulment?" The king's tone told of his surprise over this change.

"This is outrageous," John fumed. "But brother, before the issue of the betrothal can be settled, you must decide the custody issue."

"You do not need to remind me of my duties."

Geoffrey watched as the royal siblings fell into their pattern of nipping at each other's heels.

He could not concentrate on their words. Nothing made sense at all. After believing for the last month that his dream of marrying Catherine would be realized, he could not fathom how to go on from here.

The woman he loved had given him the painful gift of bringing an end to their betrothal. She had recognized the humiliation and scandal and dishonor that the accusations made by the prince would bring to his name. Allegations that she was unable to answer. Or unwilling to answer?

That was the problem at the heart of this. He knew that she was lying about her memory. Her eyes disclosed that truth to him. She lied to him. She professed her love and lied in the same breath.

Geoff wanted to be any place but here. He wanted to witness anything but this. He wanted to be able to tell her that nothing mattered. But he could not.

Despite loving her, despite knowing that nothing

that had happened to her was her fault, he could not trust her now.

''If you will use your influence with the bishop to nullify this betrothal, the lady Catherine wishes to enter the convent.''

''That would be appropriate in light of what is being said about her past behavior. Time to contemplate her sins and pray for forgiveness, sire. I would not be opposed to this.'' Charles, bishop of Caen, added his esteemed opinion on the matter.

Her sins? Forgiveness? Did they even know of what or whom they spoke? She was one of the gentlest, kindest, most decent people he knew. She did not need to be forgiven.

Or did she? What had happened between her and the prince? Had he been the one to take her virtue? Had he been the only one or had there been others?

Geoff shook his head at the absurdity of it. He knew her, he loved her. Why then had he let the sordid words affect him? What fault was in him that caused him to hesitate instead of trusting her?

She'd lied to him. He had lost his faith in her words.

''My lord Langier? What say you on this matter?''

The king's query brought him back to this sorry scene. What could he say? She had offered him a way out without his honor being offended. He would have completed the marriage—his word to her would have been carried out and he would take her back to his lands and try to forget all of the ugliness. The images of her and John that flooded his thoughts. The scenes of debauchery that John's words had caused in his mind. The sound of her throaty cries as she reached her release that echoed in his memory. His stomach turned as he suspected that John's words contained some of the truth.

What could he say?

"Sire, I would not think of coming between Catherine and her desire to pledge her life to God. If she has asked for a release from our agreement, I would not oppose it."

Richard appeared confused and leaned to confer with the queen and the bishop. Geoff stood, stunned into silence over his words with Catherine, and watched as they continued for several minutes. All he knew was that Christian was beside him, that the prince paced angrily on the dais behind the king and that Catherine was gone. Finally, the bishop spoke aloud for them all to hear.

"Although annulling a betrothal is a grievous matter and a regrettable action for all involved, I find that there was a lack of consent on the part of the *desponsata* on entering into the betrothal, and will support the king's decision to declare it to be void. The count is free to enter into lawful marriage to another."

Geoffrey nearly laughed at that, but realized it would be inappropriate to do so. The only woman he wanted to marry was gone now, and he could not conceive of how to go back and live without her.

If only he could have given her the answer she needed instead of the one he had. If only he could have offered her the trust that she had given him each step of their journey. Love was not, as Christian warned him, enough. Trust and faith had to be present as well.

The rest of the proceedings went by in a blur. Geoff thought that Christian had offered to John an amount matching the original dowry he had held for Catherine. Once the king awarded her wardship to Eleanor, Geoffrey could not bring his attention to any more of it, for Catherine was no longer his. Aymer finally shook him from his dazed state and pulled him from the hall.

The grand adventure of rescuing the woman he loved from danger and bringing her to safety and a happy marriage had turned into a horrible tragedy. And he was not certain how he could bear the pain of knowing that, if he had not acted in the name of love and in such great haste, it might have ended very differently for all of them. Yet, once again, Catherine would bear the heaviest punishment for the sins of others.

# Chapter Twenty-Four

With the help of an abundance of ale and wine, the days moved one to the next for him. Soon, with the king's permission, both he and his brother prepared to take their leave of Caen. On the day they planned to depart for his lands, Aymer found him, bringing Lady Constance in an agitated condition.

"I know that the betrothal is ended, but you were the only one I could think of coming to about this," she said, clutching Aymer's willing arm for support.

"How can I be of service to you, my lady?"

"The last time this happened, I know that she was hurt."

Geoffrey looked at Aymer over her head, but the knight shrugged. "Calm yourself and tell me how I might help."

"'Tis Catherine. She leaves for Fontrevault in the morn, but she seeks out the prince for an audience."

"The prince?" Geoff asked. "John?" He could not imagine why she would seek out the person who had done her the most harm.

"I tried to stop her. She would not listen."

"What did she say?"

"That she heard about John's threats against the Dumonts and that she would settle it before she leaves. I reminded her of the last time she met with him and came out with hand marks all over her gown and bruises on her arm."

Geoff blinked and tried to understand what was happening. Even though he had not spoken to Catherine since that morning when their betrothal was ended, he could not stand by and let harm come to her.

"Where does she meet him?"

"In the chapel, my lord. She thought to meet him elsewhere, but I suggested the church for her safety, for surely the prince would not desecrate..."

The lady's words drifted off, sounding less confident at the end than at the beginning. Other men, honorable men, would never dream of violating the sanctity of a church, but the prince was not other men. Catherine was not safe with him in any place. Geoff was already considering his course of action as he turned to leave.

"My lord, remember he is the prince. Tread carefully."

"I will."

"Let me escort Lady Constance to her chambers and I will accompany you," Aymer said, looking from Geoffrey to the distressed lady clinging to his arm.

"Nay, Aymer. See to this lady's safety and I will see to Catherine's."

Even if Aymer wanted to follow him, he could not, for Lady Constance threw herself into the knight's

arms and would not be moved. 'Twas better, for
Geoff did not want another witness to the exchange
between Catherine and John. The fewer witnesses the
better.... He left them and went the quickest way to
the chapel. Entering a side door, he waited for his
eyes to adjust to the darkness inside the stone church.
He saw no one.

Then he heard the voices behind him and looked
up to find Catherine confronting the prince in the loft
at the back of the church. With as much stealth as
possible, Geoffrey moved slowly so as to not alert
them to his presence. He climbed the stairs at one
side, but stayed in the stairwell, ready to intervene if
Catherine was threatened. The words he heard chilled
his soul.

"No one has won in this," she said.

"I have, for the Dumonts are humiliated and Langier has given you up for the whore you are," John
taunted. "I hope he enjoyed your beauty while he
had you and I hope he chokes on his loss."

"I know the truth. I do not fear your lies because
I remember that year. I remember every day of fear
and loathing and pain."

"You remember now, do you? Fear? Oh, yes.
Loathing? I hope so, since I strived mightily for it.
Pain? Was it worth it, Catherine, when it could have
been so different for you? Was it worth the lives of
the others who paid for your willfulness?"

She gasped and Geoffrey could hear her struggling
to get out the words. He nearly left his place in the
shadows to go to her.

"I will pay for their suffering and their lives and

their souls with my own, but no one else will suffer because of me. I swear this.''

"So, you think that if you come to me and confess, I will let you go? I think that you must pay for the trouble you have caused me these last three years. Just think of the hours and days I spent worrying that you had revealed my secret to someone after you disappeared. I waited to discover if you were telling me the truth or if you indeed had the papers.'' Geoffrey heard the scraping of soft boots on the stone floor. John was moving closer to her.

"I did not come here to confess, Your Grace. I came to warn you.'' Her voice trembled, but she did not falter. "Leave them be.''

John clapped his hands, the sound jarring in the silence of the chapel. "A wonderful show of bravado, my dear. But why should I fear you? A woman alone? A woman scorned by the man who claimed to love her? A whore who I marked as my own?''

"That is not true,'' she replied. Geoff knew from the shakiness of her voice that she was crying. "I am no whore.''

"Catherine, you are still so naive. I thought that our experiences together would have shown you how untrustworthy men can be. Your brother betrayed you. That knight who promised you aid deserted your cause for my gold. Your Dumont believed my words, and it took so little to make him doubt you. Did you tell him how it was that I took your virginity? No? You see, you trust him as little as he trusts you.''

"You poisoned him with your lies,'' she cried.

"But will he believe your denials now? How will he separate my words from yours? Ah, but if he loved you, what little faith he showed, eh?'' John laughed and the evil within it made Geoffrey's skin crawl. '''Twas his so-called love of you that led me to you. I would never have known you lived if his attentions your way had not pointed the finger in your direction.''

He had caused this. If he had listened to Christian and not pursued Catherine she would still be safe. Geoff's heart pounded as the gravity of his mistake struck him.

''I have tired of this game and end it now. I want the papers.''

''You will not hurt them.''

''If you give me what I seek, I will consider your plea.''

''It is not a plea. You will not hurt them.''

''You have changed, my dear. I do not remember this temper in you. Does the blush of anger on your face cover those lovely breasts, too? Do you remember how you would scream for me?''

John's tactic of distracting her with taunts infuriated Geoffrey. He was already up two more of the steps when his brother's grip stopped him. Christian touched his finger to his mouth to keep him silent.

''Do not interfere in this, Geoff,'' he whispered quietly. ''The least we can do is stand quiet and let her regain her dignity, even if ours suffers for it.''

Then her voice, her very resolved voice, reached him and stopped his progress. ''You will not hurt them or me again.'' Geoff heard something thrown on the ground and waited as it was picked up.

''You did have my letter, you bitch. All that worrying and you had it all this time?''

"There were three copies of it and, lest you forget, your ring. The ring given you by your father. The one he gave to each of his sons, the Plantagenet eaglets, as they were called," she said defiantly. "You may have that to remind you of your treacherous plot to assassinate your nephew Arthur. The names of the other conspirators who signed along with you are known throughout the kingdom. They will suffer your fate as well if you do not leave the Dumonts in peace."

An assassination plot to kill Arthur of Brittany? Many here on the Continent believed Arthur's claim to the Angevin empire was stronger than the prince's. If John was actively trying to kill the boy, most of the provinces would outright oppose the prince as heir to Richard. The empire would be divided and Richard would have to fight his own vassals if he supported John. God in heaven!

"I want the rest of them. I want them now."

"I have learned from our time together, Your Grace. I will not be threatened by you again. My copy of the letter will protect me if you seek me out or send your minions to harm me. I have given the last copy and your ring to someone who will not hesitate to make them known to your brother and to the nobles here."

"I want that ring!" John screamed into the empty church, his words echoing through the alcoves and recesses of the stone building.

There were no sounds then and Geoffrey stared at Christian and waited. Catherine had managed to best the most deceitful of the royals. How would he take this defeat? For it was indeed one.

"You have not won," John whispered dangerously. "Do not think it." Then Geoffrey heard the prince's footsteps going down the other stairs.

"You are correct, Your Grace," she said in a soft, defeated voice, as though the prince was still there. "I have lost all."

When Geoffrey would have gone to her, Christian kept hold of him.

"She has lost much on our behalf, brother. Let her be."

"I will not harm her," he assured Chris. "I would—"

"You cannot do anything but hurt her. She has paid much for our safety. Do not diminish her sacrifices or undo her work by going to her now."

Although he disagreed, Geoff knew that he should not ignore his brother's advice. Too many times he was correct—too many times to ignore him now. Nodding, he followed his brother down the stairs and out of the church. He would send Lady Constance to her to assure her safe return to Eleanor's apartments.

When they reached their own chambers to finish the preparations for their journey south, Luc handed him a package and a sealed letter. Geoff recognized the neat handwriting immediately as Catherine's and did not wait for privacy to open it.

I cannot ask your forgiveness for my lies to you, but I do ask forgiveness for my lack of trust in you. I did not possess the courage to share my secrets with you, but I will share the prince's secrets.

Use these as you see fit to protect those you love.

Catherine

She did not have courage? If he had not witnessed the scene just now, he might have believed it. But one without courage did not face down a prince.

Geoff tore open the package to discover an old prayer book inside, elaborately illustrated and engraved with her family name. He leafed through it for some sign of its importance. The false binding revealed a small space, and he reached into it and pulled out a folded parchment and a small ring.

John's ring, engraved with an eagle.

He handed it to Christian and then examined the paper. As Catherine had said, the letter documented John's plan to kill his nephew to prevent him from being considered as heir to Richard. Other names were scrawled at the bottom, attesting to their participation in the plot.

*Use these as you see fit to protect those you love.*

His eyes burned as he handed the paper and book to his brother. He would honor her actions as she requested. After doing so much damage himself, 'twas the least he could do for her.

For two weeks, she tortured him in his sleep, in his waking hours—indeed every hour, for he could not get the visions of her out of his head. Contrary to what he thought would happen, the images that plagued him most were not lascivious ones or ones in which he imagined her with other men. Nay, the ones that troubled him the most were set in the church, where he could almost see her face as she challenged the prince.

The most terrible ones were when he saw the look in her eyes as she lied to him about knowing her past, and as she realized he believed the worst about her. The best were ones of her laughing on the ship, with her hair loosened from its cap and flowing out behind her. Or of her in those moments just before she would wake in the morning in his arms and gift him with a smile.

They'd arrived in Poitou and then at the château, and he knew his men and Christian's were thanking the Almighty for finally finishing their journey. *Sullen* was too kind a word for Geoffrey's mood. Albert's questioning gaze when they entered through the gates simply added to his already foul temper.

Although Christian seemed pleased to be there, Geoffrey knew he wanted to return to Emalie. Luc's grumbling was not subtle at all, and everyone at the château knew he missed his wife. Geoff's brother finally announced that he would take his leave in two days, and the earl and his knights from the Harbridge lands prepared to travel home. That last night, he walked the battlements of the castle with his brother.

"Does Emalie know of your return?"

"Aye, I sent her word as soon as we decided."

Geoffrey watched as his brother closed his eyes and turned his face into the warm winds that chased along the castle walls. The Loire River lay before them, its picturesque valley, rolling hills and lush farmlands all as inviting and enticing as ever. Harbridge lands were fruitful, just not as blessed by the warmer rays of the sun as here. And now it was all Geoff's.

"Will you two settle the discord between you?" he asked. He was the cause of most of the problems the Dumonts had faced in the last two months, and hoped that Christian's marriage would not suffer because of his actions.

"We will." His brother sounded certain.

"How can you be sure?"

Chris turned and smiled at him. "Because beneath all of our disagreements and our conflicts, in spite of our fears and occasional mistrust, there lies love. I love her more than anyone else in this world and I know here—" he placed his fist on his chest "—that her love for me is the same. That love will heal the breach between us."

"But you are the pragmatic one. You were the one always urging me to think not with my heart, but with my head. How can you now admit the power of love in your life?"

Christian laughed aloud at his indignant words and, reaching out, smacked him on the back.

"At times I am the fool that Emalie accuses me of being. I try to see only the practical sides of everything. Our marriage was an arrangement, a joining of lands and titles and wealth. We did not have love before we married, but I thank the Almighty that we found it afterward. I do not claim to understand how it works between us, I only know that it does and it strengthens me and completes all that I am."

Geoff had no doubt that his brother loved Emalie. "Does she know that you feel this way?" he asked.

"I believe so. It frustrates her when I forget what

we've learned in our lives together, and it forces her to take actions that infuriate me into realizing the truth of it.''

"And her past? Can you forget it?"

"I will never forget it, brother. But when I begin to have my doubts, I only have to look into her eyes to find the truth of her love there." Chris spied Luc over on one of the adjacent towers and nodded. "Or Luc gives me a good swift kick in the arse to remind me not to be stupid."

They laughed together and it felt very right to Geoffrey. At least one thing was settled. Christian would return to his wife and they would mend their relationship because they had such a love.

The sun was setting and its light cast shadows between the hills and past the castle. Autumn was here, the harvest was underway and preparations for the chill of winter were begun. Their winters were milder than the ones in England, but food must be preserved and stored and the castle and village made ready. With their conversation at an end, Geoff turned to go back down into the keep, but Christian's hand stayed him.

"I was furious when Emalie delayed telling me the news that you had gone to the convent and taken Catherine. Angry that she'd disobeyed my commands. Frustrated that she did not know her place. Hurt that both you and she did not trust me enough with the truth until it was too late." Chris's eyes revealed that not all of those feelings were resolved yet. "I would not have you experience the same thing, since I know the pain of it." '

"What do you mean?" he asked.

"Catherine is not at Fontrevault."

"What? How do you know this? Where is she?" She was safe with Eleanor at Fontrevault. The queen's favorite retreat, the abbey at Fontrevault housed many repudiated women who had no other place to live. Like Catherine.

"The queen sent me word that Catherine chose to seek sanctuary at a place more distant from Château d'Azure."

"More distant? In Brittany? Normandy? Where?"

"Lincoln. Catherine told Eleanor 'twas the only place where she could feel at peace."

"Lincoln?"

"Just so," Christian said, and, with a nod, he left Geoffrey alone on the battlements to consider all of his words.

# Chapter Twenty-Five

He'd forgotten what a grueling taskmaster his brother could be, but faced with it now, he would rather not remember. With each mile closer to Greystone Castle, Christian pushed his men relentlessly to travel faster, sleep little, dawdle less. Two days out from home, they had argued, and Geoffrey had told him to go on alone. They still traveled together, but Chris had not lessened in his intense desire to return home as quickly as possible.

Finally, when Greystone lay just two miles from them, Christian galloped off toward the castle...and his wife. Luc did not wait, either, for no sooner had his lord made his intentions known then the knight mumbled something about protecting him and rode off in a mad dash. The other knights traveling with them cheered as they rode away, for they knew the true reasons behind it and they were finally free of the overanxious husbands. By the time Geoffrey arrived at the keep and was greeted by Walter and some others, Christian had already disappeared.

Sir Walter reported that the last time Chris and

Emalie had been separated for as long as this, they had not emerged from their chambers for nigh on three days. Knowing he had plenty of time and that he had his brother's support in his plan this time, Geoffrey accepted a chamber and a hot bath to remove the smells and filth of the road from his body. He also allowed himself a night of sleep before leaving once more. Stepping into his brother's role, he listened to the reports of the steward as well as Sir Walter and several others, issued orders in Christian's name and then enjoyed a night of ease earned by so many on the road.

He delayed his visit to Lincoln, trying to gather his courage, for before he could face Catherine, he must face the reverend mother. Geoff was certain he had broken every vow to the woman of God—he had not married Catherine, he had added to her hurt and pain and he had used her like so many before him. He would fight a battle even to gain permission to speak to Catherine. And then what would he say?

On the second day after his arrival, when Christian and Emalie still gave no sign of leaving their chambers, he decided 'twas time to go. With a small escort of knights assigned by Walter, he traveled to the convent on the outskirts of Lincoln and soon found himself in the private offices of the reverend mother.

An hour later, he waited alone in that same room, still shocked over the words spoken by a woman who was pledged to the service of God. Most men would not have the courage to say the things to him that she had. But he only had to remember that she defended Catherine and he could hold no anger against her for her fierce determination to stop him and his plans. Now he faced the bigger challenge. The footsteps in the hall warned him of Catherine's approach, and he could not find the words to say to her as the door opened and she entered the room.

"Mother? Sister Marie said I should come to..." Her voice drifted off as she saw him instead of the nun she sought there.

His heart pounded and his hands grew damp with sweat at the sight of her. Dressed as she usually did at Greystone, in a plain gown of a serviceable nature, with her head covered, she looked more like a servant than a noblewoman. He drank in her beauty and hesitated to ruin the sublime moment by speaking. Their gazes met and he could see the confusion there.

"Forgive me, my lord," she said as she dipped into a curtsy before him. "I pray you are well?"

What should he say? What words could explain his mistakes? What promises did you make to someone when you had already broken all those given before? Where did he begin?

"I am not well, Catherine."

She startled at his words. Rising, she clasped her hands at her waist and frowned. "You look well, my lord. What brings you here?"

It must have taken an extraordinary will to live with the terrible reality of her past and not let it affect her true innocence. Another woman...another man would have been destroyed or tainted by the existence she'd been forced to live for more than a year. But not Catherine. Goodness still shone within her, even now, even after the sins the prince had committed against her. And the self-control that probably had kept her alive long enough to be rescued by Geoff's brother was still there.

She should be screaming at Geoffrey now, clawing at his face or hitting him for the things he'd done, for his lack of faith, for his inability to keep his promises. Instead, she stood very composed before him, as though they were discussing the wheat crops or the noon meal.

"I find I am still in need of your help," he said, hoping that his plea would be successful.

"My help? My lord, I do not know what assistance I could give you. How did you even know where I was?" Her voice shook a bit and he hoped that meant she was affected by his presence.

"It turns out that fainting is not the lady Melissande's only fault. She cannot ride."

"I do not understand. Lady Melissande cannot ride?"

"I have also discovered that Lady Marguerite snores. Her maid confided to me that, verily, she can wake the dead with her snoring."

"Lady Marguerite snores? What are you saying?"

"I asked you some months ago to help me choose a bride, and as you know, I still have not married. I thought we could discuss my possible choices and you could advise me."

He watched as the tremors moved through her, and hoped she would realize he was trying to goad her into feeling—and admitting that she still loved him.

"I think not, my lord." She nodded to him. "Good day." Catherine turned to leave. He placed himself between her and the door and waited for her to meet his gaze.

"I find myself in the same dilemma that brough me here once before. I will not marry a woman who I love not, and I love none of those who are being considered."

"Please, my lord, let me go."

"Cate, I was a fool. Please hear me out." He reached for her, but she stepped away. "You were right in what you said in Caen. I would always doub your word. I know that there will always be some doubt cast in my mind by John's hateful words, bu I beg you to give me a chance."

"I cannot, my lord. To look in your eyes and see the question would kill me bit by bit each day. And it would kill the love I bear you as well. And I do not deserve to suffer such a fate." Tears filled he eyes and ran down her cheeks. "Even I do not de serve that much pain."

"Catherine, please let me do the right thing be tween us. Let me treat you the way you deserve and not the way that every man has done since you came to England. Let me love you."

"And when you cannot trust me? When the doub about my faithfulness is raised in your mind? How can we live that way? Please, Geoffrey," she begged "let me go."

He stepped closer and took her hands in his. " fear I cannot. For in this very room, I pledged m love and my protection to you, and I am asking fo your forgiveness for my failures to you." Lifting he chin, he wiped some of the tears from her eyes. "B my wife."

"I cannot." She pulled away from him. "That i

over. The betrothal was annulled and I plan to live a quiet life here.''

''That is not what the reverend mother told me. She spoke of displays of temper and arrogance and even, heaven forbid, annoyance.'' He smiled. ''That is not the Catherine who once lived here.''

''No, 'tis not,'' she said, reaching up to wipe her own tears on her sleeve. ''I find that I am different now. I do not have the same tolerances I once did. I must struggle to keep control and composure when faced with challenge.''

''I would not demand composure if you were my wife. Temper and arrogance would be acceptable to me. So long as you do not snore.'' He tried to make her smile. ''Cate, you could show me all that you are and I would welcome it.''

He watched her expression as she thought on his words. He could see the part of her that wanted to accept his offer, but there was also that part that feared the disgust and reprisals when he learned of her past.

He held out his hand to her. ''Tell me your secrets, Cate. Trust me.''

''I do not want to see the hatred in your eyes when you learn of it. I cannot.'' She shook her head and would not take his hand.

He tried again. ''Tell me how he took your virginity.''

Shaking her head more vigorously, she refused again. ''You will look on me with doubt and loathing.''

''Loathing for him. And if I have doubts, then so be it. Your love must help me past doubting, past distrust. My brother tells me that he fails Emalie more often than not and it is her love for him that makes him try again. Is your love strong enough to do that for me?''

"I do love you, Geoffrey. But the pain of your disbelief…''

"Hurts. It hurts you as much as your lack of trust hurts me." She was surprised by his words, and for the first time in a long time, he thought they might have a chance. "Tell me your secrets, Cate, and let our love put them in the past where they belong. Tell me." His hand shook as he waited for her to take it.

She moved toward him and he pulled her into his arms. The past came tumbling out of her in words and tears, and went on and on in a torrent of emotions. Guilt. Fear. Anger. Betrayal. Acceptance. It was all there. When he heard the terrible description of her treatment by the prince, he wept with her. And when the horrible images filled his mind, he forced them out with the knowledge of his love for her.

Then, after the storm inside her raged and was released, he simply held her. At some point, they must have sat down on the floor, for he found himself leaning against the door with Cate in his embrace. When her breathing became even and slow, he roused her with a squeeze.

"You must leave?" she asked as she sat away from him.

"Nay, but the reverend mother awaits us outside."

"How did you convince her to let you speak to me? Although she tried to hide it from me, she was very angry when I returned here."

"I told her the same things I told you. That I have

failed you and will fail you again, but that your love will make me stronger.''

''And what will your brother say about this course of action? This led us down a dangerous path before.''

''He was the one who told me you were here. I suspect he will be disappointed to have missed our wedding.''

''Wedding? Our betrothal was annulled.''

He stood and helped her to stand. ''Actually, love, we were betrothed two weeks ago with the permission of your guardian.''

''My guardian?''

''Eleanor. I went to see her at Fontrevault and she signed this.'' He walked to the table and lifted one of the large parchments from its surface. ''A betrothal agreement between the Count of Langier and the lady Catherine de Severin of Anjou.'' He held it out to her and she took it with trembling hands. ''You do not have to read all of the details, but do not miss this section in which the king restores the ancient title of your family to you and to our sons in perpetuity.''

''This cannot be...'' Her voice trailed off as she read more of the paper.

''It is only with your consent. I am not permitted to browbeat you to get that approval, either, for the reverend mother has threatened bodily harm if I do so. She did not say, though, that I could not use other forms of persuasion.''

He took Catherine in his arms and kissed her softly. Her lips were warm and, after a moment of indecision, they welcomed his. Although his body reacted to her nearness, he would wait for her consent before proceeding. "Please, Cate. Love me."

"I do love you," she said, accepting another kiss.

He stepped back and released her from his embrace. "If you would like to change your gown, I can wait."

"Change?" she said, frowning.

"The reverend mother and the priest are waiting outside to hear our marriage vows. Mother Heloise swore that I would leave here a married man or a dead one, and she fetched the priest for either occasion."

"You jest, my lord," Catherine said as she pulled open the door. Outside stood Mother Heloise and one of the priests.

"What will it be, my lord?" Mother Heloise asked in a stern voice.

"Married, I think, Mother." He looked to Catherine and she nodded. "Married for certain."

The nun and priest walked into the room and the reverend mother exchanged a knowing glance with him. "Married is much less of a mess than a funeral, my lord. 'Twould appear that you are finally learning."

A short while later, Catherine found herself a married woman. A countess in her own right and by her marriage to Geoffrey. She thought again on how Geoffrey placed the ring on her finger as he spoke the words that would join them in marriage.

"I take you as mine so that you are my wife and I am your husband." He slipped the band of gold over the first three fingers of her right hand, one at a time, and then moved it to her left hand, saying as he did, "With this ring I thee wed, with this gold I thee honor, with this dowry I thee endow."

With shaking hands, she slid the ring onto her finger, signifying her acceptance, and repeated his words, making her vow. "I take you as mine so that you are my husband and I am your wife. With this ring, I thee wed."

It could not be. Catherine stared at the gold circle now on her finger, proclaiming to one and all the vows just made, and now blessed by the priest. Shaking her head, she held her hand out in front of her, still disbelieving that it had happened.

"Pray, tell me you are not refusing now."

"Oh, nay, my lord. I am checking to see that it is real."

Mayhap in a day or a week or a month, she would stop worrying that this was a dream. She would rest easily with the fact of her marriage and not wait on someone to take it from her.

Geoffrey had asked for her trust and, though a difficult step to take after so many broken vows, she had given it to him. She gave him her past in exchange for their future. She gave him her love to give them both the strength to fight for it.

The gold glittered, reflecting the flames in the hearth, as she moved her hand. She had never seen this ring before.

He seemed to know her question. "I thought myself prepared, but found I was not. Mother Heloise was generous enough to lend me the use of her ring."

"Her ring?" Catherine looked at the nun, who was

busy gathering all the documents together from the table.

"Apparently, she was married once, and widowed, before answering the call to God's work."

"Married? I am surprised. I never knew."

"I suspected it as soon as she began calling down curses on my head for what I had done to you. Only someone who has been a wife would know those words and say them with such vehemence. I believe some of them are also Emalie's favorites when she is angry with Christian."

She smiled at him. "Mayhap she should teach me...." She turned toward the nun, but he stopped her.

"No need. I am certain that I will inspire you to your own words in our life together."

He kissed her again and the fire within her burned for him as it had before. Although there were witnesses present, there was no doubt that he claimed her with his kiss.

No doubt at all.

Late in the night at the abbey at Fontrevault, the queen took a few minutes before preparing for sleep, and examined the box left for her by the Count of Langier. She thought she knew what would be inside, but something within her prayed that it was not as she suspected.

Untying the leather cord around it, she pried the box open and stared within. There was a folded parchment and a signet ring. Her old heart pounded as she lifted the ring from the box.

Henry had commissioned the four rings at the

same time he had the fresco at the palace at Winchester completed. 'Twas not a pleasant sight, that, for it showed four eaglets attacking their parent. Although he'd made some reference to one of the biblical prophets, she knew it was a vision of his future. One by one, even to his favorite son, John, they had turned on him until they or he died. She did not excuse her own actions from those days, since she was neither unknowing or uninvolved.

Now, the reminder sat before her. Turning the ring, she held it away and tried to read the name and date inscribed inside of the band. Although worn smooth, she could detect "Jean" and that was all she needed to see. Eleanor placed it back inside and took out the paper.

Unfolding it, she held it up and began to read. After a few lines, she shook her head and crumpled it into a ball. She did not need to read more, recognizing it immediately as a copy of the same letter she'd received some three years ago from her son's champion, William de Severin. She'd understood the significance of it then, but did not know of an innocent girl held as pawn to retrieve it.

Despite the conniving, the backstabbing, the political moves and ever-changing loyalties, she could not stand by and watch her grandson be murdered. Eleanor had informed his guardian of a possible plot, and they had thwarted it, all without her son's name coming into connection with it.

Now, others knew of his plotting. Had the new count understood the power he had turned over to her? He'd said it was to enable him to protect Catherine. He'd used it as leverage with Eleanor, then, honorable man that he was, he'd given it to her as promised once the betrothal was approved.

She leaned her head back against the chair and thought about the way to handle this. John was Richard's heir, and in spite of his many shortcomings, he wanted the kingdom—badly enough to do whatever was necessary to get it. Arthur, even with his strong claim, was still a child, and more beholden to Phillip in his loyalties.

If anything happened to Richard, the provinces would be ripe for the picking, and she would be hard-pressed to hold them together at her age. Nay, John was the one. He would remain as Richard's heir and she would support him.

Not willing to change a lifetime of habit, she decided the fate of the proof before her. She would inform John of its existence and her possession of it, and demand that he cease any actions against her grandson. Holding the proof over his head might make him consider his actions a bit more or keep him from acting without thought at all. Once he knew that she had it, she would destroy the letters and have the ring melted down so that no one could ever use it against her son.

She pushed herself out of the chair and went to the storage chest in the corner. Reaching under many layers of clothing, she drew out a locked box and secured the paper and ring inside it. Going back to her bed, she called out to her maid.

Then Eleanor Plantagenet, Queen of England, by the grace of God, went to sleep, knowing that her kingdom was safe for one more night.

# *Epilogue*

The Countess of Harbridge was finishing her conversation with the brewer when the man passed her. A fleeting memory of a shape and a profile drew her attention, and she lifted her firstborn onto her hip and followed the man. It could not be, of course, but she must satisfy her curiosity about this visitor to Geoff and Catherine's wedding.

"Sir?" she called out from behind him. "Good sir, may I speak with you?"

The man stopped, also drawing to a halt the woman beside him, whom Emalie had not noticed before. From the back all she could see was the man's long hair, black streaked with a more than modest amount of gray, and his well-made cloak. From his hesitation, she did not know if he'd heard her or not. Emalie walked closer, whispering to Isabelle as she did. When she was a few paces behind, she called to him once more.

"Are you here to celebrate the wedding of my lord's brother?"

A deep feeling of dread filled her as the couple

turned as one toward her. The man would not meet
her gaze, but there was no doubt now. She faced a
dead man. A man her husband had killed on the field
of honor three years before.

"We are here but as witnesses, my lady. We wish
for nothing more than that."

William de Severin, brother to Catherine and nat-
ural father to the daughter Émalie carried in her arms,
raised his eyes and met hers now. Her breath caught
in her throat as she realized the truth. Somehow, her
husband had not killed him in the fight, although she
knew his body had been carried from the field of
battle and his burial announced. He yet lived and
breathed.

"My lady, we mean to cause you no distress. We
will leave now," the woman at his side said.

The woman's soft voice drew her attention. A
thick tuft of white hair grew in the middle of the
woman's darker hair, making her appear older than
her years. A scar encircled the woman's face, from
the white hair down her forehead across her left
cheek to her chin. A vicious wound from the looks
of it.

Many thoughts and words came to mind, but
Emalie could make nothing come out. Emalie knew
she must look a fool. Her only excuse was that she
had not met many men who came back from the
grave and spoke to her. When she said nothing, the
couple bowed respectfully and began to leave.

They could not! There were things she needed to
know. Things that must be said. Isabelle sensed her
upset and whimpered, the little one's thumb sliding

into her mouth as it did when she needed comfort or soothing. Emalie began to call out his name.

"Will—"

He faced her faster than she thought possible and corrected her. "Royce, my lady. I am called Royce." His gaze now settled on her daughter, his daughter, whom he had never seen. After a momentary pause he spoke again.

"This is my wife," William said, as he nodded in the direction of the woman. "We have traveled from the north of England to be here this day." His gaze never left the face of the child Emalie held. His child.

Wife? He had a new life now. This was something else to discuss with Christian when she found him. Before she did him bodily harm for never disclosing the true resolution of his battle with William.

Emalie nodded to his wife and considered her next action. William had come to see his sister married, risking much to witness the wedding, and would not have encountered Emalie or his daughter if not for her chance sighting of him. Surely he deserved to know?

"This is my daughter Isabelle. She has nearly three years."

His face blanched and his eyes glistened with tears, but he remained silent. He exchanged a glance with his wife and then looked back at his daughter. Some moments later, the shouting of the crowd near the raised dais drew their attention to the couple there.

"Catherine is well and happy in this marriage," Emalie said, trying to reassure him. "They permitted me the joy of hosting their wedding feast before they

travel back to his lands in Aquitaine in two days'
time. They are, she is, happy at last.''

"So it would appear, my lady. A strange twist, is
it not? Catherine married to your lord's brother?''

"'Twould seem that there have been many strange
twists since we met," Emalie said. "Some I still understand not. But this marriage is one made in love,
Royce.'' Emalie could not fathom why she needed
him to know that, but something within her wanted
him at peace. She surely was now that she knew he
had not died that day. In spite of his actions, she
knew he had been a victim in the prince's machinations as much as she had and had regretted his
death. "May I tell her that you were here?''

"Nay, my lady. For then all of your husband's
efforts to save both her and me would be for naught.
If you would but remind her at some appropriate time
that her brother loved her and tried to protect her in
his own way, it would be a great service for me.''

Emalie could only nod, tears now burned in her
throat and eyes as she realized that this was more
than a request for a service, this was his apology for
all that had happened between them.

He looked once more at the child in her arms. "Is
she accepted?''

Emalie smiled now, considering Christian's actions not only in dealing with William but also in
accepting William's child as his own. Tucking some
loosened strands of hair behind her daughter's ear,
she met his gaze.

"He loves her, Royce. She is as his own.''

"Then I have many things for which to thank your
husband, Emalie.''

Momentarily distracted by his use of her name, she
inked to remove the tears from her eyes. Then she
rned in the direction of someone calling out her
ame. Sir Luc approached, waving to get her atten-
on.

"My lady? My lady?" he called, walking toward
r. "My lord said you are needed to send off the
ide."

Emalie glanced back to warn Royce of the ap-
oach of her husband's retainer, but he and the
oman were gone. She stood taller and searched
rough the crowd for them, to no avail.

"Here, my lady, let me take Bella. I will see her
her nurse."

Emalie passed the child to the knight and watched
her daughter made herself quite comfortable in the
ms of the tall warrior. They walked off, deep in
nversation about a game he had taught her and
malie felt a deep sense of contentment fill her soul.
ove had triumphed over duty, honor, and even over
il, not only in her life, but also in those around
r.

She was blessed with a man of honor as her hus-
nd and at times like this, when she learned of his
od deeds, she felt she did not deserve him. She
o knew that she loved him more with each passing
y. Emalie walked toward the wedding feast intent
making certain he knew of her love before another
oment passed them by.

# *Author Note*

Although I have no proof that a plot was hatched by Prince John and his associates against his nephew, Arthur of Brittany, Arthur was taken prisoner by John four years after the setting of my story and never seen alive again.

Richard Lion-Heart was injured during a battle for Chalus castle in the spring of 1199 and died on April 6. His brother John, the last legitimate son of Henry II with his queen, was crowned King of England on May 27, 1199, and ruled until his death in 1216.

Until her death in 1204 at the extraordinary age of eighty-three, Eleanor of Aquitaine, one of the most powerful women in history, remained a staunch supporter of her son John in holding together the empire wrought by her marriage to Henry II.

\* \* \* \* \*

*If you liked THE COUNTESS BRIDE*
*be sure to look for Terri's novella*
*"Love at First Step"*
*in the new Harlequin Historicals'*
*Christmas*
*collection, coming in November 2004.*
*And look for another novel*
*coming in 2005!*

# FALL IN LOVE WITH THESE HANDSOME HEROES FROM HARLEQUIN HISTORICALS

On sale September 2004

## THE PROPOSITION
### by Kate Bridges

Sergeant Major Travis Reid
Honorable Mountie of the Northwest

## WHIRLWIND WEDDING
### by Debra Cowan

Jericho Blue
Texas Ranger out for outlaws

On sale October 2004

## ONE STARRY CHRISTMAS
### by Carolyn Davidson/Carol Finch/Carolyn Banning

Three heart-stopping heroes
for your Christmas stocking!

## THE ONE MONTH MARRIAGE
### by Judith Stacy

Brandon Sayer
Businessman with a mission

**www.eHarlequin.com**

# HARLEQUIN HISTORICALS®